THE SECRET OF VILLA ALBA

LOUISE DOUGLAS

Boldwood

First published in Great Britain in 2023 by Boldwood Books Ltd.

Cover Design by Alice Moore Design

Cover Imagery: Shutterstock and Alamy

A CIP catalogue record for this book is available from the British Library.

Paperback ISBN 978-1-80048-608-9

Large Print ISBN 978-1-80048-609-6

Hardback ISBN 978-1-78513-360-2

Ebook ISBN 978-1-80048-611-9

Kindle ISBN 978-1-80048-610-2

Audio CD ISBN 978-1-80048-603-4

MP3 CD ISBN 978-1-80048-604-1

Digital audio download ISBN 978-1-80048-605-8

Boldwood Books Ltd
23 Bowerdean Street
London SW6 3TN
www.boldwoodbooks.com

For my family, always, I love you, x

PROLOGUE
IRENE

The Gibellina road. Dusk, 23 May 1968

Enzo gets out of the car, slamming the door behind him.

I sit in the passenger seat, holding up the collar of my coat against the encroaching chill. The sun is sinking quickly now and the shadows of the mountains are creeping across the landscape; I can see the darkness as it swallows up each rock, each tree, and smothers it, like a blanket. How easy it is to make things disappear.

Enzo has lifted the bonnet, secured it on the prop and is looking at the engine, using the flame of his cigarette lighter as a torch. It's a charade. My husband is a tuna-fish salesman, not a mechanic.

I can't see him because of the raised bonnet. I don't know what he's doing but I hear him cry, 'Ouch!', and then there's a clatter; he's burned his fingers and dropped the lighter.

'Can you see what's wrong, Enzo?' I ask.

'Hold on,' he replies.

Without the roar of the Spider's engine, the evening is silent. No cicadas, no birdsong, nothing.

The landscape is desolate. We are alone, Enzo and I, with the hills, the rocks and those sparse old olive trees that survived the quake, their gnarled arms reaching towards the fading light. Behind us Gibellina's ruins are black and spiky like a wound, cut into a blood-red sky.

And the darkness is creeping towards us.

1

MADDALENA BORGATA'S LETTER TO APRIL COBAIN

10 July 2003
  Villa Alba
  Trapani, Sicily

Dearest April,
  This is your old friend, Maddalena, writing to you from Sicily.
  I have a huge favour to ask. I know I don't have the right to ask anything of you, but I am desperate and there is nobody else I can turn to.
  The presenter of a television programme called 'Cold Case!', Milo Conti, is investigating the disappearance of my English stepmother, Irene.
  I'm sure you'll remember our conversations about her − & the séance in our school dormitory!
  Irene disappeared in May 1968 & no trace of her has been seen since, nor anything heard of her. Nobody knows if she is alive, or dead, although we fear the latter. At the time of her disappearance, Papa was suspected of harming her in some way, but there was no evidence to prove him either guilty or innocent. No body was ever found & the case was abandoned.

Conti's researchers have been poking around Papa's affairs for some time now & this week, Conti confirmed that my father is to be the subject of his next investigation.

I was only five years old when Irene came into my life, & ten when she vanished out of it. I clearly recall the devastation caused to my family at the time. I also know & love my father, & you know him well enough – don't you, April? – to know he is incapable of harming anyone, let alone somebody he loved.

Please, my dear friend, come to Sicily, & find out what happened to Irene Borgata before Conti frames my father. It will be trial by television, & there will be no coming back from it. Already the strain is affecting Papa. He is in a strange, dark mood & I am afraid for him.

It feels weird writing to you after all this time, but I think of you often & wonder how you are & if you are happy & what you are doing. Can you believe how many years have passed since we last saw one another?

It wasn't easy to find you! Detective work led me to a friend of yours, Roxanne Graden at the Avon and Somerset Police. She told me on the telephone that you'd left the force, & wouldn't give me your address but promised to make sure you received this letter. She also told me about Cobain. I was truly sorry to find out that he had died, April, & send you my deepest condolences.

Thank you, in anticipation, from the bottom of my heart.

Con un sacco di baci

Your friend, Maddalena xxx

PS: I often think about what happened in Bangkok & to this day, I am deeply ashamed. I'm sorry, April. Really, truly sorry.

'So, what does it say?' asked April's friend, Roxanne.

She'd brought the letter round to April's house after her evening dog walk. She was wearing her filthy trainers, mud-spattered leggings and a jacket with a string of poo bags trailing from the pocket, which also contained a bottle of McGuigan rosé. The dog, Dexter, a Labradoodle, was drinking water messily from the bowl April had made for him at pottery class.

Roxie helped herself to two glasses out of April's kitchen cupboard, took the bottle from her pocket, and opened it.

April put the letter on the counter.

'It says Maddalena-the-Psychopath wants me to go to Sicily and find out what happened to her stepmother who disappeared thirty-five years ago. She's afraid that otherwise her father's going to be framed for murder by some celebrity TV investigator.'

'Sicily? Can I come with you?'

'You're welcome to take my place. I'm not going.'

'April, seriously? Why wouldn't you?'

'I haven't spoken to the psycho in decades. And I'm not a private detective. I don't do commissions.'

'She doesn't want to hire you, she wants you to help her father.'

April shrugged.

Roxanne filled the wine glasses and passed one to April. Then she tore off some kitchen paper, dropped it on the floor, and moved it round with her shoe to clear up Dexter's splashes.

'She sounded perfectly rational to me on the phone,' she said.

'Psychopaths never sound like psychopaths, that's the whole point.'

'True.' Roxanne took a drink. 'But why not at least go to Sicily and find out more? It'll be an adventure. It'll get you out of the house.'

April picked up the unspoken hint that she was in stasis. She turned to gaze out of the window into the thin back garden that stretched behind the house that she and Cobain had shared. It was overgrown. The roses he'd nurtured were turning feral, reverting to their wild origins. She kept meaning to go out and do something about them but she never seemed to get round to it.

'Why do you call her "the Psychopath" anyway?' Roxie asked.

'We had a massive fall-out in Thailand when we were eighteen. We'd hooked up with a couple of boys. She wasn't that keen on hers, but I really liked mine.'

'Cobain?'

'Yes. She asked me to stop seeing him and I said I would, but... well, I didn't. And she found us together in the hostel, and honestly, Roxie, she went mad! Cobain had to drag her out of the room and barricade us in. Even then she was screaming and pounding on the door. The duty manager came in the end and calmed her down before he kicked us all out.'

'Shit.'

'We were lucky not to be arrested. We travelled back to Europe on the same plane, but after that we went our separate ways.'

'Is this the first time you've heard from her since?'

'Not the first time, no. Her father tried to persuade us to talk to one another a few months later. He arranged to bring Maddalena to London so we could go round the National Portrait Gallery and then have supper together. I think he thought it'd be like the good old days.'

'And it wasn't?'

'I cancelled.'

'After they'd come all this way?'

'I couldn't face Maddi. I couldn't forget what she'd done. I had bruises on my neck for ages after, Rox; you could see where her fingers had been. And I couldn't get the violence – *how she was* – out of my head. Normal people don't lose control like that. They don't attack their friends.'

'You were the one who ditched her for a boy.'

'I didn't ditch her! It's true, I had lied to her, but I was only a kid myself; I was trying not to hurt anyone's feelings. Anyway, Cobain and I had decided to move in together by that point, and I didn't think she'd accept that. I meant to write to her at some point, or call, but a year went by and then another and then too many years had gone by and I thought that was it, I wouldn't hear from her again. And now this...' She indicated the letter. 'And she's touched a nerve because I was – *am* – fond of her father, Enzo. I used to spend my summers with him and Maddi at their holiday house on the beach in Sicily. He was always good to me, like a surrogate father. He made up for my real dad not being around.'

'You wouldn't have him down as a perpetrator of domestic abuse?'

'No.' A pause. 'Although, he was haunted. When we were on holiday and people invited him for drinks, or to go sailing, he always declined. He said it was because he wanted to devote himself to Maddi and me, but it wasn't that. You could see it in his eyes.'

'See what?'

'Pain. He was missing her – his wife, Irene. He didn't speak of her often, but when he did, he was different: more animated. He really loved her.'

Roxie was quiet for a moment. Then she said, 'You're a bit like Maddalena's father, aren't you?'

'What do you mean?'

'You can't move forward because you can't see a way around your grief.'

April sighed.

'Obviously, you're right, I can't imagine a life without Cobain. I don't *want* a life without him.'

'But that's what you've got, honey, and there's not one single thing you, or anyone else, can do to change it.'

Roxie stood beside April at the window, put an arm over her shoulder and pulled her close.

'At some point, April Cobain, you're going to have to take a deep breath and dive into your life again,' said Roxie. 'This might be the push you need.'

A stiff breeze was blowing through the back garden, shaking the rose blooms, scattering petals: yellow, cream, pink. And the wild-growing stems were climbing into the trees, April knew that they would never have any direction, and would be too weak to flower, unless she put on her gloves and went out to tend to them.

3

APRIL'S EMAIL TO MADDALENA

Hi Maddalena,

Thank you for your letter which I received a few days ago. I was sorry to hear about the trouble your family is facing.

I don't know if it will be possible to establish the truth after all this time, but I will come to Sicily and I'll do my best to help you find out what happened to your stepmother. My phone number is below. If you call me as soon as you receive this message, we can sort out the travel details etc.

In the meantime, would you contact your local police and ask if there's someone we can work with as a point of contact going forward? If they would be willing to let us see the documents from the original investigation that would be ideal. I assume the other members of your family will be happy to talk to me?

I'll see you in a short while.

In the meantime, please give my best wishes to your father.

April

4

TUESDAY 12 AUGUST 2003

Four days until Conti's TV exposé

Maddalena was waiting for April outside the arrivals gate at Palermo airport. April recognised her old friend immediately; she was still slight and slim with the same dark, curly hair she'd had as a teenager, the same wide smile. She was wearing a short dress and flat leather sandals and, although she took them off when she saw April, a pair of Lennon sunglasses, like the ones she favoured when they were travelling.

The anxiety that had followed April from England, concern about how she would feel when she was reunited with Maddalena, and that things would be strained between them, was alleviated when they embraced. April found herself oddly moved to be in the arms of her oldest friend; to feel the softness of her hair against her cheek; to smell the same scent of lemons, sunshine and warm skin.

It was a strange sensation to look into the face of someone she had known so well, and to see that face aged, but still, somehow, exactly the same.

They began to walk across the concourse, in a bubble that contained just the two of them, amongst the throng of strangers.

'Tell me about your father. How is Enzo?' April asked.

'Not good, I'm afraid. He's in hospital. He's had a heart attack.'

'Oh, Maddi! When did this happen?'

'A couple of days ago. It was Milo Conti's fault. He turned up at our villa with a cameraman saying he wanted to give Papa the chance to put his side of the story. So Papa, because he's so polite, you know, invited them in. He thought if he answered Conti's questions honestly and straightforwardly, that Conti would leave him alone. Papa explained what had happened with Irene, and Conti seemed to be listening, he was polite and "charming". But the very next day when Papa turned on the TV news there was Conti, claiming to have won an exclusive interview with Enzo Borgata, taking everything Papa had said out of context, calling him "arrogant" and "smug" and reiterating that he is the prime, indeed the *only* suspect in the case of the presumed murder of Irene Borgata.'

'That's awful.'

'I know. And that same evening some of the local people came to the villa, and they were angry. Our housekeeper, Giuseppa, went to talk to them and they said they didn't feel safe with a murderer in their midst.'

'Why would they turn on your father after all this time?'

'Because they think there's no smoke without fire. And, lately, Papa has become reclusive. He rarely leaves the villa and when he does, well, he's let himself go. People are often suspicious of those they see as "different", aren't they?'

'That's true.'

Maddalena continued: 'Giuseppa managed to persuade the protestors to go away, but a little later Papa complained of pain in his chest. We called an ambulance and the paramedics confirmed it was a heart attack.'

'I'm so sorry.'

'Something had to give. It was all becoming too much for Papa. He's never come to terms with losing Irene in the way he did. He has suffered all this time, and to be accused of killing her now that he's an old man is unbearable for him.'

'I understand.'

April put her arm through Maddelena's and gently steered her towards the sliding doors at the exit to the terminal.

'Have the doctors given a prognosis for your father?' she asked. 'Is he going to recover?'

'They don't know. They won't say. But he's not going to get better while Conti is tormenting him. The stress he's under is immense. His heart isn't strong enough.'

'Have you asked Conti to leave him alone?'

'My aunt, Papa's sister, Daria, contacted the production company and they said if Papa has nothing to hide then he has nothing to worry about and his health isn't their responsibility anyway. She's worried they might spin her attempted intervention into a story of the Borgatas trying to block the truth.'

'I suppose it could be interpreted that way,' said April. She was beginning to understand that the family was in an impossible situation.

'For weeks,' Maddalena said, 'I've had this feeling, April, a feeling of absolute dread. When Papa was having his heart attack, I thought: *This is it! This is what I've been dreading!* but since then the feeling has got stronger. Conti's not going to stop until he's found a way to convince the world that Papa is 100 per cent guilty of Irene's murder. He's not going to stop until he's humiliated and destroyed him. That's what he does. That's why people watch him: he inspires this bloodlust. I know that sounds dramatic, but it's true.'

'It's going to be all right.'

'No, it's *not* going to be all right. It can't be because Conti is playing a game that he always wins. He doesn't care about what he's doing to our family! He doesn't care about the truth, or Irene, or justice, or anything... so long as he gets to tell the story he wants to tell, and make the facts fit that narrative, so that he comes out as the hero.'

Beyond the exit, April could see a bright expanse of blue. It was a long time since she'd been outdoors beneath that kind of sky. She longed to stretch out in the sunshine and let it soothe her grieving body; relax her tired bones.

'Are we going straight to the villa?' she asked, imagining an hour or so of doing nothing; trying to keep the hope out of her voice.

'Not directly,' said Maddalena. 'First, I've arranged a meeting with our family lawyer and a representative from the police.'

5

The firm of lawyers who had looked after the Borgata family's interests for generations was based in a grand old building close to the Piazza della Memoria, and Palermo's Court of Justice.

'What's the piazza in memory of?' April asked.

'The lives of eleven magistrates killed by the Mafia.'

'But the Mafia is finished now, isn't it?'

'I'm afraid not,' said Maddalena. 'It's like a disease, in Sicily. You think it's all been rooted out and our beautiful island is recovering, and then a new infection springs up somewhere.'

As they walked through the square, a group of tourists was assembling for a 'No Mafia' walking tour through the city, to meet the owners of businesses who were resisting the protection rackets. April felt a strong affinity for people brave enough to stand up to corruption. She would have enjoyed being part of that group.

Inside the law firm, Maddalena was greeted with the deference April assumed was reserved for 'old money' clients, and the two women were invited to follow a shiny-shoed clerk up the grand marble staircase and into a large office on the first floor.

Maddalena introduced April to a smart, bald, middle-aged man, Avvocato Dimarco, who said he would do anything he could to help establish the truth about what had happened to Irene Borgata.

Furthermore, he said, from a legal point of view, it would be useful to draw a line under the marriage of Enzo Borgata and Irene Weatherbury. He had been recommending to Enzo that he apply to have Irene declared officially dead for at least two decades. Enzo had been reluctant to do so, for reasons he had chosen not to share.

'What about Milo Conti?' Maddalena asked. 'Is there anything we can do to stop him harassing my father and our family?'

'Unfortunately, Signor Conti is an expert in treading as close as he can to the line of the law, without actually crossing it,' replied the lawyer. 'The general public loves him and he has friends in high places. I would advise against attempting to gag him, unless we can be absolutely certain of success.'

There was a knock at the door and the lawyer's assistant announced the arrival of Inspector Luca Mazzotta of the Palermo police.

Inspector Mazzotta was in his late forties. He was wearing dark glasses, had a five o'clock shadow and looked exactly like April would have expected a Sicilian police officer to look. He exuded confidence and had the air of a busy man who had more important things to attend to.

April stood up and held out a hand.

'I'm April Cobain, formerly a DI with the Avon and Somerset police in England,' she said. 'I'm going to be looking into the Irene Borgata case on behalf of the family. Avvocato Dimarco has assured me I can expect the utmost co-operation from the Palermo police.'

Avvocato Dimarco had done no such thing, but she held her nerve.

The inspector shook her hand.

'You speak Italian!' he said.

'I do. I understand Avvocato Dimarco has submitted a request for access to the documents pertaining to the police investigation carried out at the time of Irene Borgata's disappearance. I assume Signor Conti has made a similar request, and I'm sure you and your colleagues will treat both with the same courtesy.'

She waited a beat and then asked: 'Could you confirm that copies of the original case notes will be made available to us at the earliest opportunity?'

The man shrugged. 'Within the next week, maybe.'

'Within the next twenty-four hours, please.'

Now he squared his shoulders and stood taller.

'The Palermo police force is one of the busiest in Italy,' he said. 'We're combatting the criminal elements found in all major European cities, and organised crime on a massive scale. Historic cases are not a priority.'

'I understand,' said April. 'I'll come to the station tomorrow to collect the file. I'll be there at what? Two o'clock? Avvocato Dimarco will give me directions.'

6

'I knew they'd do that,' Maddalena said as they drove back through the empty countryside of Sicily's north-westerly interior. 'I knew they'd allocate some arrogant, uninterested officer to our case.'

'We don't need to deal with Inspector Mazzotta, we just need him to give us the case notes so that we know what Conti knows, and are starting from a level footing.'

'Do you think he'll have the file ready for you tomorrow?'

'If he doesn't, I'm quite prepared to make a nuisance of myself.'

'Thank you.'

'Pleasure.'

Maddalena sighed. 'Conti *has* got a contact with the Palermo police already. It's the commissario, no less. The commissario is relatively new to the job and loves being in the limelight. It won't do his career any harm to be associated with Conti if he "proves" that Papa killed Irene.'

'He doesn't know yet that he's got to contend with us.'

They went around a corner and suddenly, in front of them, were the remains of a town on the summit of the rocky hill they'd been climbing. It was a strange, lonely sight. The town was derelict. All that was left were the shells of buildings, some almost intact, others reduced to piles of rubble. Walls stood with gaps where the windows should have been.

Weeds had taken hold of little balconies with nothing behind them. Cobbled alleyways led between fallen stones. The location was dramatic, blue mountains stretching away into the distance beyond a green-grey valley. The town must once have been picturesque, clinging to the top of the hill, the streets running down. Now it looked as if it had been repeat-edly bombed. The sun beat down on the abandoned town, through its empty windows. Inside its fallen walls, nothing moved.

'What on earth happened there?' asked April.

'Earthquake,' said Maddalena as they drove past. 'It was in January 1968, a few months before Irene vanished.'

'But that was, what? Thirty-five years ago. Has nobody thought of rebuilding it?'

'Everyone who used to live here lives somewhere else now. They didn't have the heart to bulldoze the buildings, I guess.'

'Can we stop and have a look round?'

Maddi frowned. 'There's nothing to see.'

'I'd still like to explore.'

'Not now, we don't have time. The road that leads down to the villa isn't in great condition. We need to get back before dark and first, I want to show you where it was that Irene disappeared.'

7

Fifteen minutes later, Maddalena stopped her jeep at the side of the road and said: 'This is it. This is the spot where my father's car broke down. My stepmother disappeared from right here.'

They climbed out of the car. April looked around. They were in a vast, parched landscape in the island's mountainous interior. The occasional field of neatly lined vines was patchworked onto the slopes of the mountains, but mostly they were flanked by scrubby, uncultivated grassland. The heat was relentless. Despite the lateness of the afternoon, the sun was still powerful and there was hardly any shade.

Maddalena had been right about the poor condition of the road. It had started off well, but the further they'd progressed into the countryside, the more it had deteriorated until it was little more than a dusty track.

To the left of the jeep, the land fell away sharply. The remains of a vandalised and heavily graffitied industrial building stood desolate a little way below; higher up, a wind turbine turned gently. A line of tough little trees followed the land downwards. Behind the jeep was a great concreted area.

'What is that?' April asked. It gave her the creeps, the concrete lying over the landscape like a shroud.

'It's the Cretto di Burri, an artwork-cum-memorial to the town of Gibellina, destroyed in the earthquake. It's a map of the town. You can walk through it and see where things used to be.'

Someone had smashed a bottle to one side of the road, and there was a tyre, abandoned. They hadn't passed any sign of human habitation since a small olive oil processing plant a few miles back where two men in dirty overalls had been smoking next to drums of oil while a huge dog snoozed in the shade.

'There's nothing here,' April said quietly, because the desolation of the landscape seemed to command a low voice.

'There's the shrine Papa made for Irene.'

Maddalena indicated a small stone monument at the roadside; a plaster Madonna behind a glass window, a molten pile of wax where successive candles had melted over the decades, and a bundle of withered roses.

'Who brings the flowers?'

'Papa. He comes most days.'

Maddi pushed her sunglasses up onto her forehead, holding back her hair. Her eyes were the same as they always had been: clear, brown, clever; but also wary, as if she was constantly expecting something to be taken from her.

April picked up her camera, walked a little way and took in the landscape.

It was beautiful in a sparse, remote way: green and brown, wind and sun swept; olive groves, prickly pear cacti, bare ground and, more distantly, mountains, blue and bruise coloured, textured by the summer light, losing some of their harsh rockiness now that evening was coming in. The air had a dusty herbal smell that April was already come to associate with the interior of this spiritual, old island.

She raised the Canon to her eyes and took a few images for reference, turning a circle to make a panorama.

The Cretto – or 'crack' – was an enormous incongruity, something man-made and even more bleak than the natural landscape around it.

'When did they do this?' April asked Maddalena.

'They started pouring the concrete during the 1980s.'

'So it wouldn't have looked like this in May 1968?'

'No. It would have been a derelict town, like the one we passed earlier.'

A single gust of wind slid through the stillness and the temperature dropped a few degrees.

The two old friends were silent, looking about them.

'Do you feel it?' Maddalena asked.

'What?'

'*Lo abbandono*. The loneliness. This spot is famous for it.'

April felt it.

'When I was a teenager,' Maddalena said, 'if I was upset about something, or in a mood, I used to climb up here and sit at the foot of that tree, next to the shrine, and wait for Irene's spirit to come to me from out of the loneliness.'

'Did it come?'

'No.'

'But you waited for it anyway. Did you like Irene?'

'Not straight away. For the first six months or so, I was hideously jealous of her, coming along and taking my father's affection.'

'You were a child. You were entitled to feel insecure.'

'I was a bit of a brat,' said Maddalena. 'I was used to having Papa's undivided attention. Irene tried to win me over and I wouldn't be won. When she realised I wasn't going to give in, she stopped trying. Her attitude to me was... oh, I don't know, kind of ambivalent and that drove me mad because being ignored was worse than being patronised. After that, there was a truce. We became friends.' Her eyes suddenly filled with tears. 'More than friends. She never tried to be my mother, but she was the closest thing I had to one. I'm pretty sure that she loved me.'

'Oh Maddi! It must have been hard for you, when she disappeared.'

'I missed her terribly. And I was frightened that whoever, or whatever had taken her away might come for me next.'

'*Whatever*? What do you mean?'

'I used to hear the adults talking in low voices, when they didn't think I was listening. I knew they thought something terrible had happened to Irene. I assumed something evil had taken her. I was at that age when my imagination was running riot. It's this place. It's sinister. It's the kind of place that makes you believe monsters might exist.'

Maddalena pulled the arms of the sweater that was looped around her neck to tighten the knot. She was thinner than before, and the skin was looser on her face, but she still had great bones and was unselfconsciously lovely in that Sicilian way of hers. Standing here, the fading sunlight painting one side of her face golden, she looked like a woman from a legend.

'What did the family really think had happened to Irene?' April asked.

'I don't know. My grandmother, who still rules the roost, didn't approve of speculation. It was all "least said, soonest mended" as far as she was concerned.'

'And your father?'

'Papa? He couldn't bear to hear her name.'

8

The sun was lowering and the hills and trees were casting long shadows. Birds flew up into the sky and the wind danced around the scrubland, rattling dried seedheads and sending up whirlwinds of dust. A distant gunshot echoed around the valley. April felt uneasy; as if the shot might provoke something ancient and unpredictable; as if disturbing the peace was disrespectful of the silence that had always been here.

Don't be ridiculous, she told herself, *there are no monsters apart from the human ones. Only those we bring to life in our own minds.*

'Does your father know I'm in Sicily?' she asked Maddalena.

'I told him you were coming, yes.'

'Will he mind me digging into his past, like I'm about to?'

'He has nothing to hide, why should he mind?'

Oh, Maddalena, thought April, *everyone has something to hide.*

'All the family thinks you should start your investigation at once,' said Maddi, 'to catch up with Conti. Obviously, he's only following one line, that Papa killed Irene, but he still has a good head's start.'

'We do have a massive advantage over Conti,' April said. 'I can talk to the immediate family, the closest witnesses. He can't.'

'Except he already has talked to one of us.'

'Oh?'

'My uncle, Samuele, Sam; Papa's younger brother. Conti met him, apparently by chance, in the casino.'

'It wouldn't have been by chance.'

'That's what I thought. Anyway, they got drunk together, or more likely Conti got Sam drunk. Sam can't remember – or *won't* remember – exactly what he told Conti, but no doubt it was more than he should have.' She wrapped her arms about herself. 'Papa doesn't know. He'd be horrified. The whole set-up is so tacky. The casino. The drinking. The being maudlin over Irene. Uncle Sam does that a lot, gets maudlin over women, I mean. He's had lots of girlfriends but none of them stays around for long.'

'Okay. Let's not worry about that for now. Tell me again, Maddalena, now that I'm here, and I can see it with my own eyes, what, as far as you know, happened in this place?'

Maddalena took a deep breath and began to recount the same story that she'd already told April in the car.

'It was 23 May 1968. A Thursday. In the morning, Papa drove Irene to the hospital in Palermo in his Alfa Romeo Spider. It was a cabriolet. It was a struggle to get her fold-up wheelchair in the back—'

'Irene used a wheelchair?'

'She'd lost a leg in the earthquake. That was why she had to go back to the hospital. She'd been recuperating in the villa after the amputation, and she was nervous, because she'd never ventured out with one leg before. She very much wanted to travel in the Alfa Romeo, as they normally would, so Papa made sure to get the wheelchair in for her. He made it work.'

Maddalena paused a moment, then continued, 'My father would do anything for Irene. Sometimes I'd ask Papa for something and he'd refuse, and then Irene would ask him for the same thing and he'd say, "Of course, my love," and then, behind his back, Irene would lift up her sunglasses and give me a triumphant look. A look that said, "See! He loves me more than he loves you!"' She laughed. 'It wasn't malicious, it was funny! And she always gave me whatever it was she'd requested. She was... I don't know... Fun!'

'Fun,' April repeated.

'You know my father. He's lovely but he's quiet. Passive. Irene was the opposite. Full of life! Mischievous. Irreverent. Like a whirlwind.'

April nodded, wondering how the vivacious Irene felt when her husband first brought her to this remote place.

'Anyway,' Maddi said, 'that day, Papa and Irene reached Palermo in good time. Irene spent an hour in the amputation clinic with her consultant. Papa waited in a bar outside, catching up on some business paperwork.'

'What kind of business?'

'Tuna,' Maddalena answered. 'He was managing director of the family's tuna-processing and export business. He'd taken over from my grandmother. That's the only job he ever had.' She frowned. 'I guess we never talked about it during our summers together.'

April remembered that she and Maddalena hadn't been remotely interested in what Maddi's father did for a living, nor the paperwork he pored over in the evenings while they were out with their friends building bonfires on the beach.

Maddi continued: 'After Papa had collected Irene from the hospital, they had a nice, long lunch and shared a bottle of wine. Irene asked him to buy her some cigarettes; she was in an odd mood, he said, anxious, but that was only to be expected. She was self-conscious in the wheelchair. He bought her a long dress that she could wear once she got her prosthetic. "Nobody will even notice," he said to her, and she was upset by this, which I can understand. It was as if he was saying there was shame attached to her injury.'

'Your father told you all this?'

'Yeah. Once, when I was thirteen or fourteen and I'd made a big deal of him never telling me what happened that day. I made an effort to remember every detail because I knew he'd never tell me again.'

'Okay.'

'So, they were driving back at about this time of day – just before sunset – when the car broke down, right here. This place, as you can see, is deserted. If they'd broken down before the earthquake, they could have walked back to Gibellina for help, or gone to a farmhouse, but everywhere had been abandoned. People had been warned to stay away from the ruins. They were afraid that those buildings still standing would collapse, or that there'd be another earthquake. Armed vigilantes patrolled to deter looters. The Mafia was keeping an eye on things. Even if you didn't believe in monsters, it wasn't a nice place to be stuck.'

'No.'

Maddalena drew a deep breath. 'The Villa Alba, the Borgata family home, is about ten kilometres from here. My father decided he'd walk back alone and return for Irene in a different vehicle.'

'Why didn't they go back to the villa together?'

'The road was in such bad condition it would have been difficult to push the wheelchair all that way, and dangerous too. It would be quicker for Papa to go alone and come back for Irene. He didn't want to leave her, but he thought the quicker he set off, the quicker he could get back. He reassured her that he would hurry.

'So, Papa walked back to the villa, and enlisted the help of his sister, Daria, and when they returned in Daria's Cinquecento, the Alfa Romeo was here, but Irene was gone. Her headscarf was still in the car and her sunglasses and her wheelchair, even the dress he'd bought her, still in its bag. Everything was where it should be, except for Irene. It was as if she had vanished into thin air.'

9

The wind blew, and the shadows lengthened. The ancient olive tree stood guarding the spot, and though it must have borne witness to whatever happened to Irene Borgata on that evening, all those years earlier, it wasn't giving up its secrets.

April turned 360 degrees. The road curled around the side of the hill, before looping back on itself. Irene Borgata, left behind in her husband's car, would have been able to watch him walk a fair distance before he disappeared from her view.

How lonely she must have felt as he left her with the light fading.

How vulnerable.

'What do you think happened, Maddalena?' April asked.

Her old friend shrugged.

'I've had many years to think about this. There are only three possibilities as far as I can see. The first is that Irene climbed out of the car by herself, had some kind of accident and fell into the ravine. The second is that she was kidnapped by outlaws. If some opportunist criminal happened across her alone in the car, it's possible they would have taken her.'

'But no ransom was ever demanded?'

'Not that I know of, no.'

'What's the third possibility?'

'That my papa killed Irene. It's what people have always believed – I've even heard his siblings talking about it sometimes, when they didn't realise I was listening. They'd say that my father stopped the car, somewhere between Palermo and here, murdered Irene and buried her body in some remote spot where he knew it would never be found. Or he killed her here. Right here. And buried her under the rubble at Gibellina, in which case she must still be there, somewhere, under all that concrete. They say it's possible that he built the shrine out of guilt; not to mark the way for her return, but to commemorate her departure. It's all rubbish, of course.'

April felt the temperature falling as the sun slipped lower and the shadows lengthened. She could see for miles, but the vista was desolate, not a single person or dwelling.

'Why would anyone think your father might kill his young wife?'

'Because he was jealous.' Maddalena paused and gazed towards the horizon. A breath of air lifted her hair and then let it fall again. 'Jealousy is the curse of the Borgatas,' she continued. 'A family trait. We all have this propensity towards it; we can't help ourselves. When the red mist collides with the green-eyed monster, things tend to get vicious. You've seen it yourself, April.'

'Did your father have reason to be worried about Irene straying?'

'I don't know. I was ten years old. How would I know something like that?'

'I didn't mean to offend you.'

'I'm not offended.'

Maddalena looked back to the point in the sky where a golden glow indicated the departure of the sun.

'I've thought about it a lot, as an adult. Irene can't have had much opportunity to be unfaithful. Most of her life was lived within the confines of the villa, surrounded by her in-laws. Although, of course, if she *was* having an affair, I'd have been shielded from it.'

'Of course.'

'Jealousy isn't a rational emotion. It tends to run hand in hand with its stablemate, paranoia.'

'You're saying Irene might have been suspected of infidelity, even if she'd never even considered it?'

'I'm not saying anything. I'm simply pointing out a possibility.'

'Okay. Thank you.'

Maddalena sighed. 'We'd better get going,' she said. 'Giuseppa will be worried if we're not back at the villa soon. Even after all this time, she doesn't like anyone being out on this road after dark.'

10

They got back into the jeep. Maddalena put her jacket on and April put her camera in the footwell.

'Will we be following the same route as your father took back in 1968?'

'Exactly the same. There is only one way down to Salgareale. The villa is just above the town, on the other side of the ravine.'

'And neither the town nor the villa was affected by the earthquake?'

'Part of the stables collapsed at the villa. That's how Irene was injured. But apart from that, no.'

Maddalena started the engine and glanced at April.

'I didn't think you'd come, you know,' she said as the car pulled away.

'Of course, I came.'

'But you might not have,' Maddalena insisted. 'You might have been too busy. Or you might not have been able to bear the thought of spending time with me and made an excuse. I wouldn't have blamed you.'

April didn't want a heart-to-heart with Maddalena, not this soon into their reunion. When she didn't respond, Maddalena glanced at her anxiously, and then changed the subject.

'Tell me about your career. What happened to you after I last saw you?'

'It all went to plan. After I came home from our travels, I went to university and then I joined the police as a graduate, and worked my up through the ranks.'

'You joined the Criminal Investigation Department?'

'Yes. But I quit to look after Cobain when he became ill.'

'And you're not tempted to go back?'

'No.'

'Did you work on any big cases?'

'Yes.'

'That must have been exciting?'

'It was interesting.'

'Don't you miss the work?'

'Sometimes.'

'It was all you ever wanted to do, wasn't it, be a detective? Whereas I—' a small laugh '—I never knew *what* I wanted. Papa said there'd always be a role for me at the tuna company, but I never saw myself working in the family business and I don't think he did either. We both knew I wouldn't have been an asset.'

'So what did you do?'

'I've had lots of little careers. I started an apprenticeship with a jewellery maker, but then I decided I'd rather work with fabrics so I did some costume designing. And then I worked in an art gallery, and as secretary to a publisher of horticultural books. I was an au pair, I did a bit of teacher training, I was the receptionist for a cosmetic surgeon – *that* was fun, I had as much free Botox as I could handle, and lip filler...' She turned again to April, to show off her pout.

'Keep your eyes on the road, Maddi.'

'Sorry! And office jobs that invariably got boring after a few weeks... I've always envied you, knowing exactly what you wanted to do. It must've made life so much more straightforward.'

'I suppose it did.'

'And Cobain too.'

'Yes.'

April had known how fortunate she had been to find Cobain, who had wanted the same things from life that she had. Their personalities and backgrounds had been very different, but at the core she and he had

been the same; like one person. How rare it was to find one's true soul-
mate. How lucky for her. How raw she felt without him.

She tore herself back to Sicily.

'And you're back living at home, Maddi?'

'If by "home", you mean at the villa, yes, but only temporarily while
this is going on. I wanted to be there to support the family – I wouldn't
have been much use to them from my apartment on the mainland.'

They drove in silence for a while, then Maddalena said, 'We used to
be psychic. Do you remember?'

'We weren't psychic!'

'We were! When we were teenagers, we used to be so close that we
always knew what the other was thinking. We used to say the same thing
at the same time. We'd dream the same dreams. I literally used to know
how it felt to be you.'

Maddalena was trying to rebuild the bridges she'd burned and establish a warm connection with April. And it wasn't that April meant to
reject her old friend, but Maddalena's neediness was anathema to her.
Once, they had been as close as sisters, but Maddalena's outburst in the
Bangkok hostel had destroyed that intimacy and they couldn't simply pick
it up and resume where they had left off. It was naïve of Maddi to think
that they could.

April leaned down to pick up her camera. She switched it on and
looked at the screen on the back, flicking through the pictures she'd taken
of the spot from which Irene Borgata had allegedly vanished. She hadn't
had the exposure setting right; there was glare in almost all the frames,
particularly the ones looking back towards the Cretto. It appeared as if a
crowd of bone-thin people, dressed in white shrouds, had gathered
between the camera lens and the monument to the destroyed town. She
rubbed her temples. Her eyes were tired. She should have set the camera
controls to automatic. Now she'd have to come back and retake the
photos.

She held the camera on her lap and, with one elbow resting on the
base of the open window, she watched as the parched land, darkening
now, the fields and trees passed by as they descended. They slowed for a
farmer driving a three-wheeled Piaggio Ape truck loaded down with

crates of tomatoes, the headlight flying up and down as the vehicle bumped over the ruts and potholes, but that was all the traffic there was.

'Doesn't anybody live here any more?' April asked.

'All the old settlements are gone. Everyone moved into the new towns they built after the earthquake or else they emigrated to Australia or the States.'

'That's a shame.'

'It's a tragedy.'

They had dropped down into the valley now. April thought of Irene, travelling this track for the first time when Enzo brought her to Sicily. Although the sun's dying rays were painting the tops of the hills above them a glorious shade of rose-gold, the trees and fields around them were disappearing into the shadows, and the temperature had fallen too. It felt as if they were a long way from anywhere.

11

IRENE

Early March 1963 – Five years before the earthquake

Here I am, my love, in Sicily. We arrived late yesterday evening, Enzo and I, and spent the night in a hotel in Palermo, so that he could show me the sights today.

It is hot here. Dry. And bright. It's like a place from a storybook. I cannot quite believe that I'm here!

Enzo has been attentive, as always; looking after me; pointing out places of interest, explaining their significance and history. He's very proud of his home-land, and rightly so. It is all wondrous.

Enzo is a good guide, and I'm doing my best to be receptive and interested. I say: 'Ooh!' and 'Ahh!' and I ask questions about Sicilian culture and history which he enjoys answering. You would smile to see him puff out his chest when I pay his homeland a compliment. He is kind and generous and good-humoured. He is a truly excellent husband, but he's not you. That is his only fault.

What else can I tell you? Well, for one thing, they drink tiny cups of bitter coffee here; you can't get a decent pot of tea anywhere. There's no toast for break-fast and they eat pasta instead of potatoes. There are tables outside the restau-

rants on the actual pavements! Can you imagine? I haven't seen a pub or a chippie. I don't understand a word that anyone is saying.

I am doing a good job of pretending that I am absolutely fine, but the truth is, I am completely out of my depth. This morning, Enzo took me to a market – so much fruit! Stacks of crates of olives and tomatoes and many other things I don't recognise. I was distracted by the colours and the smells and the noise! Oh my goodness, it was so noisy! I lost sight of Enzo and I panicked. It was as if I was standing still and the world was spinning round me and I couldn't make it stop. We were only apart a few minutes, but by the time Enzo came back to me, I felt helpless as a lamb.

'Are you alright?' he asked. 'Did something happen?'

And I had to reassure him that I was fine. 'It was just that I didn't know what I would do if you didn't come back,' I told him.

'Of course, I came back,' he said. 'I will always be there for you, Irene; always.'

The roads are an education. There are no rules as far as I can tell. In Palermo, it was a right free-for-all; I thought London was bad but here, it's every driver for themselves, cars pushing in, nobody giving way, everyone using their horns all the time. Even Enzo, polite, humble Enzo was having a go at the other drivers. The cars have all been through the wars: dents and scrapes and barely an intact wing mirror in sight. Nobody bothers to get them repaired. My dad would be horrified.

That was Palermo.

Now, we're on our way to the Borgata villa, driving through the countryside and we have left the traffic behind. Out here, it's nothing but the occasional ancient fairy-tale town built on the crown of a hill, and donkey carts.

We've been driving through these bleak mountains for what feels like hours. Bumping over pot holes and swerving to avoid rockfalls and once even a bull that was standing in the middle of the road. Enzo had to get out of the car to shoo it away.

'Go on!' he was shouting, 'Move on!' and flapping his hands at the animal.

You'd have laughed, my love! Even as I was watching Enzo and calling: 'Be careful!', I was thinking of you. I keep you close. You know that, don't you? I never let you out of my heart.

I thought the change of scenery would make me miss you less. It hasn't.

It's hot in Sicily. So hot for this early in the year, and not the damp heat, like exhaled breath, that I'm used to in England, but a dry, dusty heat that burns the bare skin on my arms and face. I like the light here. I'm not sure about the heat. It picks me up and knocks me down in equal measures.

We drive down a track, a long track that winds down the side of the mountain. I hold tightly onto the side of the car door, terrified by the steep drop. I wonder if Enzo would be offended if I asked him to let me out, so I could walk, but even as I'm thinking this, he stops the car.

'Here we are,' he says. 'This is it!'

We're looking down over the crowns of very green trees and terracotta roofs. The view reminds me of one of the cards we used to be given at Sunday School, the one about Jesus being an oasis. Because that's what this is, an oasis of gardens and flowers in a wild landscape. From somewhere in amongst those gardens comes the sound of a child, singing.

'This is your house?' I ask my husband.

'Our house,' Enzo replies. 'Our villa. Villa Alba. Our home.' And he takes hold of my hand. His expression is a mixture of pride and pleading. It's important to him that I love this place as much as he does.

'It looks grand,' I say quietly.

'But?'

Oh, Lord, there are so many 'buts'. I reach for the nearest. 'What if your family doesn't like me?'

'Of course, they'll like you!' he says. 'Oh, my darling, how could they not adore you?'

He lifts my hand to his lips and kisses the back of it. 'They'll love you, Irene. They'll love you as I do; just you wait and see.'

12

The jeep rounded a bend and in front of it the roof and chimneys of an old building came into view, mostly hidden by the branches of trees.

'Here we are,' said Maddalena. 'Welcome to Villa Alba.'

Lights had been turned on in the villa, and in the gardens, glowing amongst the deep darkness. They pulled up at the gates at the end of the drive.

'Oh no!' Maddalena exclaimed. 'Not again!'

A huge piece of cardboard had been tied clumsily to the gates. On it was one single word, painted in thick red paint. *Assassino.* Murderer.

April and Maddalena got out and approached the gates.

'We've been dealing with this kind of crap for the last few weeks,' Maddalena said, tugging at one side of the card. April helped her. 'It's all because of Conti. He goes on television and asks questions. "Why would a loving husband, somebody who cared about his young wife's welfare, wait until so late in the day to drive her across a remote part of the country-side?", he says, and people put two and two together and come up with their own answers. It's all Conti has to do. He doesn't need actual physical evidence, he just needs people to believe his insinuations and his work is done.'

She clawed at the card.

'This is why Giuseppa won't go grocery shopping on her own! This is why my poor niece, Elissabeta, is too scared to walk into Salgareale! People think they have the right to play judge and juror, to find my papa guilty even when they don't know anything about him! Most of these amateur vigilantes weren't even born when Irene disappeared! Picking on Papa just makes them feel superior! Jesus!'

Now, she was almost swinging from the card, trying to tear it from the plastic string that had been used to secure it. With April's help, she managed to pull it down, then she folded it in half, and then quarters, and then stamped on it as if she were trying to kill it.

'Idiots!' she muttered. 'Bloody idiots.'

'Don't let them get to you, Maddalena. Don't cry.'

'I'm not crying!' Maddalena said, climbing back into the jeep. 'I'm just so fucking angry. Sanctimonious fucking bastards.'

She slammed the door. April retook her seat on the passenger side and glanced at her friend.

Maddalena sat panting. She put her hands over her face, already streaked with paint, and murmured, 'Bastards, bastards, bastards.'

Then she shivered and blew out her breath. She looked how April imagined a banshee might look: bright-eyed, hectic and wild.

Maddalena picked up a remote control, pressed it and the gates opened.

'Sorry,' she said. 'Sorry to swear, April, but I'm so worried about Papa and I'm so angry about what Conti is doing, and how he's poisoning our neighbours against us.'

She drove the jeep through the gates, which closed automatically behind them. The villa came into view, lit by the moon above and by its own lights further down below. It was a wide building, with roof tiles the same buff colour as the stone in the walls.

It had seen better days.

There were archways and statues and flourishes of the Sicilian baroque architecture for which the island was famous, although some of the render had crumbled away in places and tiles were missing, or had slipped and were sitting at odd angles on the roof.

Weeds were growing in cracks in the plasterwork and from the bases of the chimneys. Around the bottom of the walls, huge planters contained palms and their lips tumbled with waterfalls of flowers, pink, red and white. The trees had become too big for the pots, and the thick terracotta was cracked, pale roots fingering their way out.

The great age of the building was revealed by the wear and tear of the plasterwork, the hand-hewn stones, the drystone walls and the wooden shutters, which had weathered to silver. April had never seen a house more perfectly suited to its location. It might have grown out of the rock beneath it; it seemed more organic than made by human hands. It was grand and shabby, and welcoming at the same time, a villa that invited you in; a villa that had existed for hundreds of years and would still exist long after its current inhabitants were gone.

'Wow!' she said to Maddalena. 'It's beautiful.'

'It would be better if it wasn't falling down around us. Neither Papa nor Uncle Sam is any good with DIY, Daria wouldn't know one end of a hammer from the other and Nonna Donatella, who holds the purse strings, doesn't like getting outsiders in to do repairs because she doesn't trust strangers. Giuseppa does what she can. Only the other week, we had to yell at her to come down because she was up a ladder on her own trying to repair the grouting in the chimney stack. She's pushing seventy.'

Maddalena pulled the jeep up beneath a wooden canopy, from which bougainvillea trailed bunches of pink, tissue-paper flowers that seemed to glow in the reflected light. To one corner, a statue of a Roman goddess stood, one chipped shoulder bare in the moonlight, holding the hem of her robe over her breasts. Lights set into the paving stones led the way around the corner towards the villa. Half of the bulbs weren't working.

A yellow dog came trotting out of the villa, wagging his tail joyously, to greet them. As he came close, he dropped onto the ground and commando-crawled towards them.

'This is Troy and that's his party piece,' said Maddalena affectionately. 'Silly dog!'

She heaved April's case from the back of the jeep and April took it and extended the handle. She wondered how the young bride, Irene Borgata, felt when she was brought here for the first time.

How beautiful, she must have thought, gazing up at the villa. How perfectly, exquisitely beautiful. But also, how remote. How far from home.

How lonely.

13

IRENE

Enzo pulls the car up outside the villa and turns off the engine. He turns to look at me.

'So,' he says.

'So,' I echo.

'Here we are.'

'Yes.'

'Are you ready to meet the family, Signora Borgata?' he asks.

'As ready as I'll ever be!'

We get out of the car. I dust off my skirt. Around the side of the building a little girl comes running. She's only five years old; a wild-haired, dark-eyed poppet in a pinafore dress. I recognise her of course, Maddalena. Enzo has shown me the photograph he keeps in his wallet.

'Papa!' she cries, and Enzo is out of the car in an instant, catching the child as she leaps into his arms and wraps her skinny legs around his waist and her arms around his neck. He spins her round.

'Maddalena!' he cries. 'Mia topolina!'

Behind, approaching more cautiously, is a plain, long-faced girl, a little younger than me. She is holding a child's tricycle by the handlebars. She looks at me shyly from behind a long fringe. Enzo introduces her as his sister, Daria.

They talk in Italian for a few minutes while the child peeps at me over her papa's shoulder. I get the impression that not everyone is happy about Enzo bringing home a new, English bride. I hear Daria say the word 'Mamma' often, each time accompanied by a frown and a stream of words that makes me suspect Mamma has a monk on. I try not to dwell on the possibility that my new mother-in-law is not best pleased that I'm here. The little girl, Maddalena, lifts her head and sticks out her tongue at me. I pull a stupid face back. She hides her face.

Enzo speaks to his sister in a tone of voice that I suspect means he said something along the lines of: 'Mother will just have to deal with it,' then he turns to me.

'Didn't you bring a present for Maddalena, Irene?'

'Oh yes! I forgot!'

I go to the car, lean in, take a box out of the bag on the back seat and pass it to Maddalena.

'For you,' I say. 'From me. I hope we will be friends.'

She takes it reluctantly, and Enzo sets her down so she can unwrap it. Daria crouches beside her and makes encouraging noises. The child tears off the paper. Inside is a box containing a doll wearing an air hostess's uniform. She's holding a flag that reads: 'Jet BOAC to Swinging London'. It's the kind of thing I'd have killed for when I was her age.

'Do you like it, Maddalena?' I ask her.

She stares at the doll for a moment before raising her arm and throwing the box onto the ground.

Daria gasps. Enzo laughs, embarrassed. Maddalena glares at me, as if to say: Your move.

Enzo takes my hand. 'Come on,' he says, 'I'll show you around your new home.'

'See you later, alligator!' I say to Maddalena.

'In a while, crocodile,' she replies, in English. Little minx! She does know a few words!

My heart lifts. Perhaps this will work out. Perhaps I will be happy here after all. Perhaps I might even do some good.

Oh, Lord, it's beautiful: the flowers, the fountains, the birds, the afternoon light that's brighter and clearer than any I ever saw back home. I wish you could see it, Jack. I wish this incredible sun weren't shining only for me.

14

April followed Maddalena around one corner of the villa and beneath an archway trailing with jasmine whose tiny white trumpet-flowers perfumed the night air. On the other side of the wall was an enclosed courtyard. More enormous clay pots were grouped around the edges, these planted with lemon trees and honeysuckle and smaller plants.

They went through an open door on the far side of the courtyard, and now they were in an inner space, a square, with the four sides covered by a tiled roof and a small circular pool in the centre that was open to the sky with a fountain that was spitting, rather than splashing. This pool was illuminated; goldfish were swimming in water that was clogged with plant life. Lilies jostled for space on its surface. A tiny woman, in late middle age, wearing a spotlessly clean but threadbare maid's outfit, appeared in front of them.

'Good evening,' the woman said. She had a strong Sicilian accent. Her greying hair was parted in the middle and pulled back into a tight bun. She had fierce eyebrows and warts dotted about her cheeks and neck. She leaned forward to peer at Maddalena's face. *'Ti sei fatto male?'* she asked. *Have you hurt yourself?*

'It's paint,' said April, 'from the cardboard on the gate.'

Maddalena explained. The older woman let off a stream of invective.

When she had calmed down, Maddalena hugged her and she dabbed at her eyes with the hem of her apron, still muttering.

'*Imbecilli!*' she said. '*Vandali!*'

Maddalena turned to April. 'This is Giuseppa,' she said, 'upon whom the entire Borgata family relies and without whom nothing would ever get done.'

April held out a hand. 'I'm pleased to meet you, Giuseppa.'

Giuseppa ignored April's hand, and instead took hold of the handle of her suitcase.

'It's heavy,' said April. 'I'll take it.'

'Let Giuseppa take it,' said Maddalena. 'She'll be offended if you won't. She'll show you to your room. I'll go and clean myself up, and I'll see you shortly for dinner. My grandmother likes us to dress up for the meal. She's a stickler for tradition.'

April followed Giuseppa through a hallway, up a stone staircase, along a landing and into a bedroom: huge old wooden boards on the floor, cotton rugs, an enormous bed, age-spotted mirrors; dusty artworks and dustier bookshelves and gauze drapes at the window, billowing in the slightest of draughts.

Giuseppa heaved the case onto a stand by the wall.

'The bathroom is through there,' she said. 'Make yourself at home. The family meets for an aperitif on the terrace at nine o'clock. Come down the stairs and turn left, you'll hear the voices.'

As the sound of her footsteps faded, April crossed to the window. Stars were revealing themselves in a deep velvet-black sky, and the moon was rising in the east making silhouettes of the mountains. Light spilled from the windows on this side of the villa, but beyond that was darkness as far as it was possible to see. Only the song of the cicadas interrupted the silence.

But then April heard a crunch of gravel, and she smelled something she recognised from her years in the police force: cannabis smoke.

She stepped to one side to hide herself from the gaze of whoever was on the path below and looked out. A man stepped into the lozenge of light cast from the window. April observed the top of his head; dark hair so curly it appeared to be ringleted and a pair of sturdy shoulders in a T-shirt. He had passed beneath the window and was some distance away when she heard a 'woof' and the dog, Troy, came wagging out of the darkness to greet him. The man stopped to play with the dog, ruffling the fur on his shoulders, holding the joint between his lips while the dog weaved between his legs, until they were interrupted by the trill of an incoming phone call. The man stood up straight, patted his pockets, located the phone and held it to his ear. He listened for a moment, then he said:

'*Sì, sì È arrivata. La donna inglese è qui.*'

She's arrived, he'd said. *The Englishwoman is here,* and then he continued on his way, talking to whoever was at the other end of the line.

April was slightly disconcerted by this but decided not to overthink it. She went into the bathroom. It contained a suite that looked as if it had been installed in the 1970s.

On the floor were two ceramic planters each the size and shape of a human head, one male, one female, each crowned and garlanded with fruits and flowers. Both pots contained a spiky aloe vera plant. The planters appeared old, but April had noticed similar ones stacked outside the multitude of souvenir shops she and Maddalena had passed on the outskirts of Palermo. The glazed faces were smiling, but there was something sinister in the lips and especially in the wolfish expression of the bearded male character, with his red-tipped ears and bushy eyebrows.

April took off her shirt and draped it over the male planter's face.

'Problem solved,' she said quietly, and she took off the rest of her clothes and stepped into the shower.

15

When she was showered, and dressed in a slate-grey slip dress and sandals, with her damp hair piled onto her head, and wearing the long silver earrings that Cobain had given her years ago to apologise for something – she could no longer remember what the transgression had been – April left her room and, following Giuseppa's instructions, made her way down through the villa. She tried to put herself in Irene's shoes; imagining how it must have felt for the young Englishwoman to come down for dinner on her first night at the villa. Did Enzo hold her hand? Did he reassure her? Even if he did, she must have been anxious; wondering what kind of reception she would receive.

April didn't know what Irene's background was, but 'Irene' wasn't the kind of name she associated with the British upper classes in the sixties. Coming here, to this grand villa deep in the heartland of Sicily, would almost certainly have been an enormous cultural leap for the young woman. She must have had some backbone to agree to marry Enzo in the first place. Did she know what to expect? Did she have any idea what she was letting herself in for? Did she realise how isolated she would be in the villa? Had things, perhaps, started to go wrong for Irene Borgata almost from the moment she arrived?

No, no! April reined her imagination in. She mustn't start overlaying the few facts she knew about Irene with a story of her own making. Making assumptions and attributing behaviours to people were how investigative errors were made.

April found the terrace easily enough at the back of the villa, over-looking a garden that stepped upwards until it disappeared into the dark-ness. Cypress trees were silhouetted against the mountains and the night sky, with the Milky Way draped around their black spires. The terrace was illuminated by candles, in jam jars, stuck onto old saucers, and balanced directly onto walls made of blocks of hewn lava. Strings of fairy lights were strung through the branches. Music was playing through a hidden sound system, a slow-voiced Italian singer accompanying a single Spanish guitar. April had never been to this part of Sicily before, never – as far as she remembered – heard that singer before, nor the song, but she had a strong sense of déjà vu as she walked slowly towards the people gathered at the far end.

As she approached, the dog thumped his tail in greeting. Maddalena, who had been perched on the edge of a wooden table, stood up and smiled; she too had changed, into white palazzo pants and a wide-sleeved silk top and her black hair was loose and damp from her shower. A stocky, darker-skinned young woman standing at the counter of a small bar turned and her movement prompted the man standing behind the bar to look up. He had a cocktail shaker in his hands and glasses were lined up on the bar beside a small bowl of limes and a jug of ice. The man was wearing a white shirt and jeans. He was slight, with an attractive, care-worn face, dark, heavy eyebrows, and dark eyes, rimmed with black lashes. None of the three looked like either of the others, yet the family resemblance between them was clear.

The fifth person present on the terrace behind the Villa Alba that evening was a tall woman with a long nose and a low brow. She was wearing a skirt, too heavy for the warmth of the evening, and a sleeved blouse. A silver crucifix hung on a chain around her neck. She wore tan tights and flat shoes and her hair was greying and straight.

Maddalena introduced them in turn. 'This—' the man '—is my uncle,

Sam, and this—' the stocky young woman '—is his daughter, my cousin, Elissabeta, and this—' turning to the woman '—is my aunt, Daria.'

So, thought April, three of the four, everyone except Elissabeta, who hadn't been born yet, would have been here on Irene's first night in the villa.

16

IRENE

First evening at the Villa Alba

We are changed into our glad rags. I am dolled up to the nines. I want to look attractive and fashionable; I don't want to look like a slapper. I don't know what's okay and what's not okay here. It will take me a while to learn.

Enzo says I look 'bellissima'. 'Like an angel,' he says, kissing the tips of his fingers because he knows it will make me laugh.

Then he looks at me as if he can't quite believe his luck.

He holds my hand firmly as we walk onto the terrace. Into the lion's den! I think. We glance at one another and he smiles encouragement. He is wearing a bow tie and his hair is slicked down with oil. I can see the pride in his eyes. It makes him happy to have me at his side. And that's the most important thing, isn't it, that he's happy and that I'm trying?

Not trying to forget you, Jack, or pretend you and I never happened. Simply trying to get by; to put one foot in front of the other. To exist in a world without you in it. To make the best of things.

My heels click on the black paving stones and the petticoats rustle about my thighs. The air is warm and smells fragrant and insects are making a right cacophony in the shrubs. Lanterns are casting a glow on the terrace, but all around is dark. Far away, in the distance, I can make out the shapes of the mountains that surround this valley in the moonlight. High on the hill, twinkling, are the lights of the town we passed on the way down, Gibellina.

Enzo's siblings have been waiting for us: the teenage Daria, who I've already met, and a boy, no more than about ten years old.

The boy is closer.

'This is my brother, Sam,' says Enzo. 'Sam, this is my new, English wife, Irene.'

Sam grins up at me. He has the most beautiful brown eyes and a cheeky smile – he reminds me of the neighbour's lads who I used to play with back home.

'Hello, Sam,' I say, holding out my hand, thinking we should have bought him a present too.

'Ciau,' he says. He looks at my hand, glances at Enzo, who gives a small nod, and then shakes it enthusiastically.

Daria looks awkward in a high-necked dress that doesn't suit her.

'Bona sira,' she mutters without looking me in the eye.

'Bona sira,' I reply, the words feeling strange in my born-and-bred Yorkshire mouth.

I'm wearing my cocktail dress, the pale blue taffeta, with the bow over the left shoulder. It's creased from the suitcase but I can't do anything about that. When I was dressing, I asked Enzo if it was suitable attire and he said I looked perfect but he's not the best judge of these things. Now I see how conservatively Daria is dressed, I'm more conscious of my nipped in waist and the sweetheart neckline, of how the corset pushes up my breasts and shows off my figure. I'm aware of how much pale skin is on display. Daria's dress is so modest it wouldn't embarrass a nun.

Enzo has told me, teasingly, that he is a mother's boy, his mamma's favourite child. I suspect this is a subtle way of warning me that she will be suspicious of me and my motives. I don't want her to be watching me, wondering, asking questions. This role I'm acting, the happy young bride, is effective because people want to believe it. People like the idea of newly-weds and the story of Enzo and me is a good one: he the widowed Sicilian obliged by a bout of flu to spend Christmas in London; me the young waitress, struggling to make ends meet in a

less-than-charming businessmen's hotel delivering hot drinks and aspirin to his
bedside. We spent Christmas day together, the two of us, he in his dressing
gown, blowing his nose, me making chicken soup in the hotel's kitchen and
bringing it up to him on a tray. We listened to the Queen's speech on the radio in
the guests' sitting room. We each had a small schooner of sweet sherry.

'Cheers,' I said to Enzo, as we chinked glasses, although I felt no cheer at all.
I was lonely, missing you so badly, that I thought I might die. Enzo was my only
reason to keep going. I held onto him as a drowning woman might cling to a
lifebelt. He was lonely too, missing his family. Without me, he would have been
entirely alone in a cold room with frost on the window, and nothing to keep him
company save the pigeons roosting in the eaves.

In the fictional version of Enzo and me, people picture us walking through
snow-covered streets when he was feeling better, lights twinkling above us, and
sipping drinks in the snug bars of pubs; eating hot chestnuts from the paper with
our be-gloved fingers and we did do those things, yes. It was nice to be with
someone who had plenty of money, I won't deny that. I liked being looked after. I
liked the way Enzo looked at me, as if I was his own, private Christmas miracle
and took me to dinner in the restaurants of upmarket hotels. It wasn't as if he
replaced you, not for a minute, but being with him was a million times better
than being alone, in London, without you.

And now here I am, in Sicily, wearing the blue dress that was your
favourite.

I want to charm Enzo's mother, but the outfit is risky.

You only have one chance to make a good first impression, as my dad always
says. My mother-in-law might look at me in this and think I'm not good enough
for her best son. She might think I seduced him into marrying me. She might
think...

Daria touches the skirt of my dress; feels the slipperiness of the fabric
between her fingers.

'Where did you get this?' she asks in English.

'I made it myself.'

Her eyes widen.

'I could make something similar for you,' I say, thinking this might be a way
to break the ice.

'I don't think it would suit me at all,' Daria says, and then she looks behind *me, over my shoulder, to the French doors, which we left wide open, and I turn to follow her gaze and see an older couple, formally dressed, emerging from inside the villa. The man is smiling, the woman isn't. She, my new mother-in-law, is holding Maddalena's hand. Maddalena is wearing a bow in her hair, a daffodil-yellow satin dress and a scowl. But it's the mother-in-law who commands my attention.*

Her expression is so chilling that the temperature drops and I swear all three Borgata siblings, Enzo, Daria and Sam, shrink into themselves.

I, on the other hand, lift my chin and straighten my shoulders.

'Uh oh,' I hear you whisper from inside my heart. 'You might be up against it here, lass.'

'Let her do her worst,' I murmur.

I've never been one to shrink from a challenge.

17

The youngest of the group assembled on the terrace, Sam's daughter, stepped forward to greet April.

'I'm Elissabeta, but everyone calls me Elissa,' she said. She was wearing a torn T-shirt and a pair of loose velour jogging bottoms that sat low on her hips. Her skin was flecked with acne, and her hair was long and multicoloured. She had her father's eyes, but in every other way she'd tried to make herself not look like him.

'It's nice to meet you,' April said.

'We're pleased to meet you too,' said Sam in a low, heavily accented voice. 'Thank you for coming to help our family in its time of crisis.'

'Crisis caused by you,' murmured Daria.

'I made one mistake,' said Sam. 'I trusted a friend...'

'Milo Conti is not your friend! He's nobody's friend.'

'Here we go,' said Sam.

'You recognised him when he approached you in the casino. didn't you?' said Daria. 'You knew what he was like before you spoke to him, you must have known that a snake like him was never going to be "friends" with someone like you!'

'I didn't know he was fishing for information! I thought he was a nice guy, okay? If you'd been there...'

'I wouldn't have been there though, would I, Sam? I'm not the one with a gambling problem; I'm not the one who gets filthy-drunk and blows all my cash on an addiction!'

'Don't speak to me like that, Daria!'

'If you had a modicum of self-control then I wouldn't need to!'

Elissa stepped between them. 'Papa! Aunt Daria! You promised, no arguing tonight.'

Daria stepped back, shaking her head.

Sam murmured, 'Fuck!' and lit a cigarette. Daria winced at the expletive. For a moment or two there was silence. Then Sam poured the cocktails, albeit bad-temperedly, and handed out the glasses.

'I'm sorry about that,' Maddalena said to April. 'We're all a bit edgy at the moment.'

'Siblings,' said Daria, 'always know exactly which buttons to press to wind one another up.'

'And nobody's better at button-pressing than you,' said Sam.

Daria wafted a hand in front of her face to indicate that she didn't like the smell of smoke on his breath. The superciliousness of her expression was bordering on cruel. April had seen this dynamic in families before; the 'good' child humiliating the 'bad' one. Daria and Sam must both be in their fifties now; too old to be playing out their traditional roles.

All four Borgatas, Maddalena, her uncle and aunt, and her cousin, had haunted expressions. There were dark shadows around their eyes; they seemed exhausted. It must be awful for them, April thought, to have the tragedy of the missing woman resurrected when they had believed it over a long time ago.

Still, it was a beautiful evening. The stones in the walls of the villa, and the flagstones underfoot, and the rocks in the mountains all around were letting go of the heat they had absorbed during the day. Everything was more clearly defined and more energised than it was back home; as if England were painted in watercolour, Sicily in oils.

April Cobain was neither superstitious nor religious; she did not believe in ghosts or spirits or life after death. She was a pragmatic woman; a born police officer, her colleagues, including her husband, used to tell her; organised, logical and diligent.

Yet that evening, she could not keep her imagination under control. She kept thinking of Irene Borgata, standing where she stood now. If she narrowed her eyes, she could almost feel Irene here, as if she had never left.

Elissa came to stand beside April. She was in her early twenties, and wearing heavy make-up.

'Hi,' she said. She perched on the wall beside April and tossed back her hair. 'Whereabouts in England are you from?'

'Bristol. Do you know it?'

Elissa shook her head. She gazed out over the rim of her glass. Close up, April could see that the rim of her ear was studded with gold, and the delicate skin of the inside of her arms was covered with tattoos.

'What do you do, Elissa?' April asked.

'I was working in a coffee shop, in Naples, but I had to give it up to come here with Papa.'

'To support Enzo?'

'Because we were homeless. We'd run out of options.' She sipped her cocktail. 'By "options" I mean "money". It happens every now and then. When my grandmother, Donatella, gets fed up of us being here, she'll give Papa enough cash for the deposit on a new apartment somewhere. It won't take long. Donatella finds him even more annoying than Daria does. She doesn't even bother pretending that she likes him.'

'That must be hard for your father,' said April.

The girl glanced towards Sam to see if he was listening. He wasn't.

'He's used to it,' she said. 'He's always been Donatella's least favourite child.'

April felt a nudge at her thigh. Troy was standing beside her, wagging his tail at half-mast. She reached down and smoothed his warm ears.

He reminded April of what had happened earlier. 'You might be able to put my mind at rest about something, Elissa. I saw a man walk by outside my bedroom window earlier smoking cannabis. Troy recognised him so I wasn't too worried about him being there, but would you know who that was?'

'It was probably Tonio Oliveri. He's from Salgareale. His father grows vegetables and he brings supplies up to Giuseppa.'

'Oh, okay,' said April.

'It's a secret though. Tonio being here. It's not that he's done anything wrong or anything, but my grandmother hates the Oliveris. She doesn't know that the vegetables we eat come from them.'

'Right.'

'It's too much for Giuseppa to have to go into Salgareale every time she needs something, and nobody else will deliver to the villa. Hence the subterfuge. You won't say anything to Donatella, will you?'

'It's none of my business.'

'Perhaps it would be best if you didn't mention the cannabis to anyone either,' Elissa added. She looked at her watch and jumped off the wall.

'It's time for *Serata* everyone!' she called. She turned to April. 'It's the TV programme. They've got a segment from Milo Conti on tonight. We need to watch to see what he's saying about my uncle Enzo.'

18

The television set was ancient. It was situated in a snug next to the villa's main reception room. April, Maddalena, Sam and Elissa sat on two small sofas facing the screen. Daria stood at the doorway, separate from the group.

Sam turned on the television and jiggled his knees while they waited for the picture to come into focus. *Serata* was a 'magazine' style programme. It began with a piece about the Montalbano author, Andrea Camilleri, followed by another about the cost of cosmetic surgery in Italy. Then the presenter clasped her hands together and said: 'Coming next is the segment you've all been waiting for. Here's our very own celebrity detective, Milo Conti, and I understand he's got news of an intriguing development in the case of the wife who vanished and left no trace.'

'Oh, God,' Sam groaned. 'Is that what they're calling Irene now?'

April leaned forward to watch closely.

The smiling face of a man, probably in his early sixties – although it was hard to tell given that he was evidently a patron of the clinics in the previous segment – appeared on the screen. He was silver-haired, the skin stretched tightly over the bones of his skull and jaw. He was standing beside the roadside shrine that Enzo had made for Irene.

'Weasel,' Sam muttered. 'Ghoul.'

'Shh,' said Daria.

Milo Conti took off his hat and stared into the camera lens.

'Good evening, my friends,' he began. 'I'm speaking to you today from the exact spot where Enzo Borgata claims his car broke down on the evening of 23 May 1968, the evening his young wife, Irene, disappeared. She was only twenty-four. She had suffered horrific injuries in the Belice earthquake. She was beautiful, vulnerable, perhaps afraid...'

There was a long pause for effect. Then Conti walked a little way along the track, so that the Cretto was visible behind him. He was rubbing his hands together.

'There were no witnesses that evening. Nobody who could confirm – or deny – that Enzo was telling the truth when he said that he left Irene in the car while he walked the ten kilometres down this very road, to summon help.'

The camera zoomed in on Conti's face. He had white eyebrows and piercing brown eyes. This close, the edges of the foundation on his face were visible.

The camera was now panning in on a red Alfa Romeo Spider, the same or a similar model to the one Enzo had been driving thirty-five years earlier. A caption popped up that read: *Reconstruction*.

Conti's voice spoke again. 'We've been told by a reliable witness that the car in which Enzo and Irene were travelling on that fateful evening still exists, hidden on the Borgata family's estate near the town of Salgareale. We've also been told...' the picture focussed now on the car's passenger seat '...that there are bloodstains on the leather upholstery; stains that it would be impossible to remove; stains that, given the advances in forensic technology, might tell us more about how, and when, Irene Borgata died.'

Conti was back on screen. 'Enzo Borgata, you might have managed to hide the truth for thirty-five years, but you can't hide any longer! Milo Conti is coming to get you!'

He made the shape of a gun with his right hand and pointed it at the camera, which zoomed in on his fingers and then faded to black.

Sam turned the television off. He held his head low.

'Did you tell Milo Conti about the stains on the passenger seat?' Daria asked. 'Did you, Sam?'

'If he did, he didn't mean to,' said Elissa.

'*Did you?*' Daria cried.

Sam stood up and left the room.

'Unbelievable!' cried Daria.

'Is it true that the car's still here?' April asked Maddalena.

'It's in the barn by the old stables.'

'And the seats are stained with Irene's blood?'

'Yes!' said Maddalena. 'But the blood was from her earthquake injuries! It was already in the car weeks before Irene disappeared!'

19

IRENE

We spend ages on the terrace, sipping cocktails, me getting more and more hungry and worrying in case anyone hears my stomach rumbling — I don't think I'll ever get used to the Sicilian way of eating dinner so late. During all this time, Enzo's mother — whose name is Donatella — has not addressed a single word to me, nor even smiled. She has a face, my love, like a slapped arse.

At last, we move into the dining room for dinner.

This villa is like a palace. I have never been anywhere so grand. The dining room is enormous, honest to goodness you could fit the entire bar of the Beal working men's club into it, and it's... oh! It's beautiful. The walls are covered in paintings, murals, which, Enzo tells me, are based on those found on the walls of ancient Greek and Roman homes on the island. They are scenes from mythology of gods and goddesses drinking, dancing and carousing, enjoying their pleasures in an idealised landscape, where birds fly with garlands in their beaks and swans float on flower-rimmed pools. There's an embarrassment of bare bosoms and bottoms; it makes me smile to think what my ma and pa would have to say about that!

Apart from the art, there are chandeliers and mirrors; silverware like I've never seen! And great pieces of furniture that look as if they belong in a museum.

I can feel Enzo's mother's eyes on me the whole time. If she thinks I'm going to crumble under the pressure, she's got another think coming.

I'm not worried about the food, because Enzo took me to several Italian restaurants while we were in London, so I have an idea of what's coming. I watched the well-to-do guests when I worked in the hotel. I understand how to behave at the table. I know what is expected of me. I'm not the savage Donatella thinks I am.

Sod her. On the plus side, her husband, Enzo's father, Patrick, is Irish-American and he is a hoot! He has a right twinkle in his eye and the love of his life is horses so we have something in common. Already he's a little drunk and he's almost, but not quite, flirting with me.

I take my place at the table beside Enzo. Little Maddalena is between her father and her grandmother. Enzo is considerate. He keeps checking on me, to make sure I'm bearing up, and then he turns to Maddalena. 'Are you all right, my sweetheart?' he asks her in English. He has this idea that, with my help, we can raise her to be bilingual. She merely scowls, little miss mardy-bum.

Me? I hear you ask. How am I doing? Well, thank you for your concern, Jack. I am bearing up. I'm doing all right.

Every once in a while I am overwhelmed by loneliness, because you are gone, and I am married to someone who is not you; sitting beside someone who is not you; he is putting his hand on my knee in an avuncular fashion and he's not you. But then I think: No, Jack's not really gone, he's here, in my heart, and I know you'd be proud of me for keeping going and finding a way forward.

Oh dear God, thinking of you brings a lump to my throat. Here I sit, sipping my wine, smiling when the others smile, laughing when they laugh, but understanding nothing. Enzo squeezes my knee. He leans closer and whispers: 'You're doing wonderfully, my angel! You're charming them, as you charmed me!' And he means to be complimentary and kind, but I want to correct him. I didn't set out to charm him, or seduce him, or anything. I never planned to come here as Enzo's wife. All I did was be kind to a sick stranger who was stuck in a chilly hotel over Christmas, far from his family and home. Anyone in my position would have done the same.

I didn't intend for any of this to happen; but when it did, when Enzo asked me to marry him, I thought, 'Why not?' I didn't have any better offers. I didn't want to spend the rest of my life in London skivvying in the hotel and I certainly wasn't going to go crawling back to Yorkshire with my tail between my legs.

When Enzo proposed, when he said he wanted to bring me here, I realised that there might never be a better opportunity to escape from my old life. So I said: 'Yes.'

I did the right thing, didn't I, Jack? It's what you would have wanted me to do, isn't it?

Please tell me I made the right choice. There's a little, nagging voice in my head that's filling my mind with doubt.

20

The Borgata group moved from the snug into a grand dining room.

The walls were covered in murals, but there were large bare patches, like wounds, where the plaster had crumbled. The mirrors that hung between the paintings were enormous, and ornately framed but so old and de-silvered that they barely reflected anything beyond the flickering candlelight; the settees beneath them were covered in rose and gold coloured velvet; worn and water-stained. Braiding dangled in places where mice had burrowed into the upholstery. The vases were intricate and fancy, the flowers must have been fresh but there were aphids on the stems and already the petals were falling.

The inverse claustrophobia April had experienced outside the villa was magnified in this grand dining room. It was so formal; so large; so intimidating, so decayed. No matter how much Irene had loved her new husband, she must have wondered, when she came into this room, what she had let herself in for. What had Conti said – that she was twenty-four when she disappeared? So she must have been only nineteen when she first came here. A teenager. Little more than a child.

The table was long and narrow, six settings laid at one end with large, ceramic plates with a border decorated with a recurring blue wave motif. The cutlery was silver; the glasses cut crystal, the candles were lit in the candelabras and, with all the silver and the mirrors, myriad reflections cast a strange, flickering light all around.

She was here, April thought, catching sight of her face in one of the mirrors, and not recognising herself for a moment. *Irene sat at this table, on one of these chairs. Her first dinner here would have been exactly like this.*

Maddalena invited April to take her place beside Sam.

'We're waiting for my grandmother, Donatella,' she whispered across the table. 'She likes to make an entrance.'

There followed a kind of hiatus during which nobody spoke.

Then, April heard a squeaking noise, at first so quiet as to be barely noticeable. Through the tall double doors at the far end of the room, both thrown open, April saw a shadow approaching painfully slowly. The squeaking grew louder until, at last, an old-fashioned wheelchair came into view. Hunched in the chair was a very small, very old woman. Her tiny head was like a skull, bald and age-spotted with wisps of white hair here and there. Her shoulders were almost at a level with her ears, and she was wearing a fur wrap and a lime-green dress that sparkled with embellishments. Her ankles were thin, and crooked, the feet below them, on the wheelchair's footrests, were squeezed into leather sandals that matched the dress. As she approached, the old woman raised a hand deformed by arthritis, but which still bore magnificent jewellery. The nails were long and painted. She was wearing a full face of make-up. The effect was grotesque, but compelling.

Giuseppa was behind the chair. She pushed it onto a ramp and raised the ramp via an electric lifting mechanism, until the chair was at a level with the table.

Maddalena, Sam, Daria and Elissabeta all murmured, *'Bona sira,* Nonna Donatella.'

'Bona sira,' the old woman answered. Giuseppa secured the wheelchair's brake, rattled the handles a few times to make sure it wasn't going to move, then stepped back.

After this, the Sicilians all bowed their heads and said grace, and then finally those standing pulled back their chairs and sat down.

Giuseppa withdrew. The atmosphere in the room had become dark and heavy. The four younger Borgatas stared at their plates. Donatella moved her cutlery around with one shaky hand. Then she barked a question to Daria. Daria used the corner of a napkin to wipe spittle from the old lady's lips before she answered.

'Donatella is concerned about Enzo,' Sam explained to April, in English, in a low voice. 'Our father died of a weak heart, and she's afraid Enzo might go the same way.'

'I can understand her worry.'

'The priest came today. He told her that all the talk in Salgareale is of Enzo and Irene. Everyone is speculating. Everyone is suddenly an expert on their marriage and what might have happened. She finds it intolerable.'

'Of course she does.'

Giueseppa appeared again, framed in the doors' opening. This time, she was pushing an enormous trolley, from which she carefully removed a tureen, which she placed on the sideboard. She then proceeded, laboriously, to serve a portion of colourful antipasti in a small bowl to each of the diners. Rather a lot of it was spilled.

When it was served, Giuseppa went to Donatella, lifted her right hand and placed it carefully on the table.

She guided the fingers to the cutlery. 'Here is your spoon.'

Donatella trembled as she picked up the spoon, so that it tapped a faint rhythm on the tabletop.

'Ask Enzo to pour the wine,' she said.

'Enzo's not here, Mother,' said Daria. 'Sam will do it instead.'

'Sam will spill it.'

'No, he won't.'

Sam walked around the table, took a bottle of wine from the rack beside the sideboard, removed the cork, and went around the table filling everyone's glasses. After he'd done this, April, the only one facing the sideboard, saw him drink several swallows of wine from the mouth of the bottle before he put it down beside the tureen.

'*Bon appititu!*' he said.

'*Bon appititu,*' the others echoed and everyone picked up their cutlery and began to eat.

21

IRENE

Enzo ties Maddalena's napkin around her neck to make a bib before we start eating, but she still manages to spill tomato sauce on her dress. When her grand-mother scolds her, she upends her bowl on the table. I have to pretend to cough to stop myself laughing at the child's furious face. Enzo shakes Maddalena, not roughly – I'm sure he's only doing it for his mother's benefit. I tell him to leave the child alone and Donatella glares at me and then banishes Maddalena to bed in disgrace.

She says something to the child that I believe roughly translates as: Your mamma would be ashamed of the way you're carrying on! I only hear the word 'mamma' and guess the rest from the tone.

It's not fair, I think, to invoke the child's dead mother every time she misbehaves.

I admire Maddalena's pluck. I can see how hard she is trying not to cry as she leaves the room. I try to go with her, but Enzo has me sit down. 'Please,' he hisses, 'don't go against Donatella's will.' He says the housekeeper, a surly woman called Giuseppa, will put the little girl to bed.

You'd say I was being paranoid, but I have the distinct feeling that Donatella blames me for the whole palaver, because if I weren't here Maddalena wouldn't have played up. She can think what she wants, it's no skin off my nose. But honest to goodness, who lets a child stay up so late, puts her in a yellow satin gown, makes her wait for ages, sits her on a cushion and expects her to eat spaghetti without making a mess?

On a happier note, Patrick, my father-in-law, is going to show me his horses in the morning. He, Patrick, has hardly stopped talking to me. Judging by the dirty looks she keeps shooting at her husband, Donatella is not too happy about that either. Patrick has the strangest accent, half County Kildare, half New York, and he is friendly. I'm lucky that there's someone else here whose first language is English. I have a feeling he and I are going to get along like a house on fire.

As you well know, I've been looking forward to meeting the horses since we left England.

The fact that there are horses here, and that Patrick speaks English, are two enormous bonuses for me. Plus, at last, there is food in my belly.

Things are looking up, Jack.

Things are getting better.

22

After dinner, Giuseppa materialised again from the shadows. Donatella's children and grandchildren wished her a good night's sleep and then Giuseppa reversed the old lady in her wheelchair from the dining room, the pair of them vanishing, slowly, into the bowels of the villa, the wheels squeaking as before.

Daria said she was going back to her cottage in the villa's grounds, close to the old stables. Sam asked Elissa to accompany him on a walk around the garden but Elissa said she was tired and was going straight to bed.

April and Maddalena were left alone.

Sam had been topping up Maddalena's wine glass throughout dinner and now her eyes were glittery and her cheeks were rosy. 'Would you like to come and see the family portraits?' she asked.

'I'd love to.'

Maddalena led April through the doors at the opposite end of the dining room into a grand drawing room. It was magnificent, but in an even worse state of repair. The huge chandelier that hung from a disintegrating ornamental rose in the centre of the ceiling was at a tilt, its individual glass prisms as well as the scrolls, bobeches and chains were flyblown and cobwebbed. Parts of the ceiling were missing, and plaster and lath was visible where the walls had crumbled. The floor in front of the windows was badly water damaged.

Paintings hung around the room showed various members of the Borgata family alone and in groups. April leaned closer to the wall to look at a picture of a family group standing beneath the archway at the entrance to the villa.

Maddalena came to stand beside her.

'That's Nonna Donatella,' she said. 'And that handsome man in the cowboy hat is my grandfather, Patrick. He died a few years ago.'

'Enzo was nice-looking when he was younger.'

'I think so too! He must've been about twenty in that picture, so already he'd have been working for the family tuna business for six years.'

'He was a bit of a workaholic, wasn't he?'

'He enjoyed the commercial side of things, which is more than my grandfather did. All *he* wanted to do was be up at the stables, with his horses. That was Irene's favourite place too.'

'She rode?'

'Oh yes. She was crazy about horses. She and my grandfather were the best of friends on account of their mutual passion.'

'But Enzo didn't ride, did he?'

'He was too busy running the tuna business.'

'Of course. Is that still in operation?'

'Barely. They shut the processing plant a decade ago; even the canning is being done on the mainland now. Papa kept as many people employed for as long as he could, but eventually he had to let most of them go. And of course, they resent that. They say he wasn't managing the business properly.' She looked around her. 'I wish they could see the state of this place. They think we're rolling in money, but our savings are all gone and we've sold everything we can sell. If Papa is accused of murdering Irene, I don't know how we're even going to pay the lawyers' bills.'

'When did it start going wrong?' April asked.

'After Irene disappeared. Rumours were flying around and colleagues who Papa thought were friends turned their backs on him. Rivals fanned the flames of suspicion. There were even questions about what had happened to Papa's first wife, my mother.'

'What do you mean?'

'She died here, in the villa, unexpectedly, after my birth. People started theorising about her death.'

Maddalena dropped down onto the nearest sofa. 'When Irene first came here, her stardust rubbed off on my father! He was this shy, rather awkward man, but he'd bagged an adorable wife and so everyone treated him with a bit more respect. Until she disappeared. Then they turned on him.'

She stretched her arms above her head and lay back.

'They hate us, you know.'

'Who hates you?'

'Everyone. The employees and former employees; the townspeople; our neighbours; the people Papa used to do business with. They resent us, here in our fancy villa. They'd love it if Papa was found guilty of killing Irene. At last, they'd have some valid reason to despise us, to get out their pitchforks and torches and chase the Borgatas away from this part of Sicily, once and for all.'

'I think you're exaggerating,' said April. She looked around. 'Is there a picture of Irene anywhere?'

'There is one,' said Maddalena, 'but it's not on display.'

'No?'

'Family legend has it that it's cursed,' said Maddi. She looked as if she were about to elaborate on this, but then changed her mind. 'It's a faff getting it out from where it's kept. I'll show you another day.'

23

IRENE

Here I am, in my lime-green baby-doll nightdress, sitting on the bed that Enzo used to share with his first wife. Enzo is in the bathroom, taking a shower. They do that here; have showers, not baths.

There's a picture of her, the first wife, Alia, on the chest of drawers. She looks a bit like me, I think. Only more serious; more of a thinker than a doer. She's wearing a cross around her neck and her brows are heavy, but our eyes are almost the same. She's older than I am now, in the photograph. Enzo said she was twenty-eight when she died so I have a few years to go before I catch her up. I can't imagine her wearing a nightdress like this one. She'd have been covered from head to toe in something more grown up: practical but unarousing.

I'm being mean. But Alia, in the picture, stares out and judges me and all of a sudden I feel ashamed. I delve into my suitcase, find a winceyette nightie, pull what I'm wearing over my head and put the more modest one on instead.

'Is that better?' I ask Alia. She looks a fraction more approving.

All I know about her is that she died of complications after giving birth to Maddalena, that everyone loved her and that – until she inconveniently died – she never put a foot wrong with the family. It makes me feel embarrassed, having her picture there, only a few feet away, looking at the bed that Enzo and I are about to get into, but how can I ask for it to be removed?

Enzo has told me that he wants me to have some of Alia's things, certain pieces of jewellery and so on. Such talk makes me uncomfortable. I don't want to step into a dead woman's shoes, so to speak. I certainly don't wish to be compared with the saintly Alia.

Her face, in the photograph, looks at me, sitting on the bed she used to share with Enzo. It's probably just my imagination, but I swear she looks resentful. Well, she would, wouldn't she? Here I am; alive, married to her husband, charmed by her daughter, and there she is dead. Cold in her grave.

A terrible thought comes into my mind. What if Maddalena was born on this actual bed? What if she, Alia died here? For a moment, I see her there, white as a ghost, eyes wide open, lying right next to where I'm sitting now.

I jump off the bed.

I pick up the photograph frame and lay it flat, so that Alia is facing down into the top of the chest of drawers.

In the same moment, Enzo comes out of the bathroom, one towel around his waist, another covering his shoulders. He comes over to me and kisses me on my mouth. His skin is warm and damp, the black hair on his chest and shoulders gone fluffy.

'What's the matter?' he asks.

'I'm tired, that's all.'

'Of course you are,' he says. 'It's been a long day.'

Enzo stands beside the chest of drawers, poking the corner of the towel into his ear.

'What's happened here?' he asks. He lifts Alia's picture and replaces it in its original position.

'It must have slipped,' he says. Alia looks at me again. I swear her expression is triumphant.

I go back to the bed; sit on it.

I hear a voice whisper: 'This isn't your bed, Irene Weatherbury; this isn't your villa; this isn't your husband; Maddalena is not your child, you don't belong here!'

'None of this is yours! Go away! Get out of here! Go home! Go back to where you belong!'

24

April found it hard to sleep, despite the soft mattress, the width of the bed, and the cotton sheets that had been washed and ironed so many times they had assumed a texture that was almost cloudlike.

Her arms, neck and ankles had been attacked by mosquitoes during the course of the evening, and the bites were driving her mad with their itching. Her brain was trying to process all the new information she'd garnered, but she was struggling. She had no mental filing system organised yet – a habit she'd grown into when she worked for the police – so facts were hopping like fleas through her mind.

Conti making such a big deal about the blood in the car was bothering her. She believed what she'd been told – that the blood had come from Irene's leg injury. If there was anything sinister about the staining, why would Enzo have kept the car for thirty-five years? And surely, *surely*, the police would have examined that vehicle during the original investigation into Irene's disappearance and decided that it was not relevant.

But what if they hadn't? What if there was no mention of a blood-stained passenger seat in the case notes, and the first Conti heard of it was when Sam told him during the drunken conversation in the casino? If it really was new evidence, then Conti might well make a big thing of it, and it would be impossible after all this time for the family to prove when the staining had occurred.

April knew she shouldn't overthink the blood, but her mind was circling and it kept returning to the leather upholstery in the Alfa Romeo and the vulpine expression on Milo Conti's face during the reconstruction on the television earlier.

Eventually, she got up and looked in the cabinets in the bathroom, hoping to find some kind of cream that might alleviate the itching of the mosquito bites and perhaps even something to help her sleep, but they contained nothing useful.

She went back to bed, and lay spreadeagled beneath the large fan that creaked as it spun. Now her thoughts drifted to Cobain. She found herself missing him. Was twenty months too long to mourn a husband? Or not long enough? What if he hadn't exactly been a perfect husband, but rather a difficult, stubborn, often ill-tempered man who drank too much and could be – no, *was* – a constant pain in the arse? What then? How long was too long to mourn a man like that?

Cobain had been *her* pain in the arse.

He had loved her. And she had loved him back.

'You shouldn't have left me, you bastard,' she murmured up at the rotating fan.

She put her hands over her eyes, pressed the heels of her hands into the sockets. *Don't cry, don't cry, don't cry!* She didn't cry, but she might have if she hadn't heard a bump from the other side of the wall behind her bed; a bump loud enough to make her jump and jolt her out of her sadness.

The sound was immediately followed by a silence that seemed weighted, as if whoever, or whatever, had caused it had frozen, and was straining their ears to hear any movement on April's side of the wall that might indicate she had been woken.

April lay stock-still, but her eyes were wide open, her senses alert. She had assumed that the room next to hers was empty – she hadn't heard a sound from it until now. After several seconds of holding her breath, she carefully reached for her little travelling clock at the side of the bed and checked the time. It was almost 3 a.m. She listened as hard as she could, but didn't hear anything else.

What was that?

Something might have fallen from a shelf, perhaps? Or an animal might have come into the room?

Shhh, April told herself as her heart pounded. Perhaps the window was open and the breeze had moved the curtain and the curtain had knocked something...

But then she heard another noise, a scraping, as if a hand had reached out and moved something along a surface.

Slowly, April sat up. She put her arms around her knees and listened. She did not know what she should do.

Probably whoever was in the room next to hers had every right to be there. Perhaps, like her, they couldn't sleep and were searching for... a book, or a phone charger. If she were to get out of bed, and turn on the light and go and investigate, it might be awfully embarrassing for her and for them.

On the other hand, what if it was an intruder and she did nothing?

There was a shuffling from directly behind the bed, but on the other side of the wall, and then another bump, and then the same scraping sound she'd heard before. Then silence fell again.

April listened hard, but she heard nothing else. She decided it was nothing to worry about. An intruder would have searched for longer than that. She scratched her arms and found a cool spot on the sheets. After a while, she relaxed, and her mind went into the dreamy state that preceded the onset of sleep. This time they were good memories: Cobain carrying his surfboard down to the sea in Pembrokeshire. The wind was blowing, making the white horses on the waves gallop and fly, and the sea was crashing. April was sitting on the rug, on the beach, with the coffee flask, hugging her knees, wearing Cobain's parka to keep warm and there he was in the knee-length wetsuit; his skinny white calves, the gap in his teeth wide as he grinned at her, giving her the thumbs-up.

'Cobain!' she called. 'I'm over here!' but before he could answer her, she slept.

25

WEDNESDAY 13 AUGUST 2003

Three days until Conti's TV exposé

April was up at dawn the next morning.

She washed quickly, put on the only pair of trousers she'd packed – they were light cotton harem pants, hardly practical, but the best she could do – and a pale blue cotton jumper, trainers and trainer socks, and she drew back the gauze curtain and looked out of the window to orientate herself.

In the wan daylight, she could see what she had not been able to see the previous night, that there was a pathway beneath the windows, where Tonio had walked, and beyond that was a large hedge, overgrown, but once topiarised into a lovely abstract shape that might have been meant to represent clouds, or perhaps waves. The sun hadn't risen high enough yet to paint the tops of the hedge, but it had reached the mountains and was lighting them, turning them pink and golden.

Beyond the hedge were more trees, large, established trees, still part of the garden and then, further up the hill, were a couple of overgrown paddocks and beyond those, on an area terraced to make it flat, were some single-storey stone buildings that, although they had their back to April, she guessed must be the stables.

'So out of the villa, turn left and head uphill,' she told herself.

She picked up her camera, and went quietly from the room.

26

IRENE

Enzo woke bang on six o'clock, as per. He put on his dressing gown and those silly slippers that slap on the floor tiles and went downstairs. Now he is back with tea in a coffee cup. He places it at the side of my bed like a gift and kisses my forehead.

'You didn't sleep well,' he says, a statement, not a question.

'No,' I say, 'I'm not used to eating so late. I came over a bit unnecessary.'

'You'll soon get used to how we do things,' he says.

'Yes.'

There is a long silence. The tea is disgusting. I don't think the water can have boiled and the milk has a heavy, overly sweet taste. I pretend to sip but really I only wet my lips, waiting for Enzo to leave so I can pour it away.

'I have to call into the tuna-processing plant,' he says. 'I've been away so long. Would you like to come with me?'

There is nothing I would less rather do. Back in England, Enzo described the plant to me: the workers in rubber waders ploughing through a soup of blood, entrails and seawater sloshing about on the floor; the huge fish being butchered and their flesh separated, the 'blood meat' going for pet food, the other cooked ready for canning. And music playing on the radio, and the workers with their huge, hand-held hooks, singing.

'Your father said he'd show me the stables,' I say. 'I've been looking forward to meeting the horses so much, ever since you first told me about them.'

'Of course,' says Enzo. 'If that's what you want to do, that's what you must do.'

I see the disappointment in his eyes, although he does his best to hide it. I have chosen his father and the horses over him and his work.

'You don't mind too much, Enzo, do you?' I ask.

'No,' he answers. 'Of course I don't mind. If you're happy, then I'm happy. Simple as that.'

He loves me, Jack. He really loves me.

27

Outside the air was cool, with a hint of a warm day to come. It was so long since April had been to southern Europe that she'd forgotten how such mornings felt and how the glorious light had an uplifting effect on the body. She followed a path of stone slabs around the terrace at the back of the house, and past the swimming-pool area, flanked by a low hedge. After that, the path went between two lines of trees, which would hide her from the view of anyone looking from an upstairs window of the villa.

The formal gardens did not extend far back; after that came the terraced areas, which had, perhaps, once been cultivated, but were now overgrown. April recognised cherry trees in an orchard, but some of the trees were dead, and those that were still in leaf looked dry and exhausted. Beyond that was a garden full of flowering plants that reminded April of home; everything running riot.

The ground sloped steeply upwards beyond. April climbed steps cut into the rock.

To her left, a small stream was trickling, wetting the stone and pooling in a natural lip. There must be a spring; it probably fed into a reservoir somewhere beneath the villa. A mossy stone bridge crossed the stream, and on the other side of that was a gate, and beyond the gate, enclosed by trees, was a small cemetery, dominated by a stone monument with a door set into it which April assumed was the family vault.

It was dark and green beneath the trees, and because the cemetery was at the side of the mountain, tucked into the woods, the sunlight would never reach it. April would have liked to explore, but wanted to get to the stables before anyone else was up.

She continued uphill, climbing steeply until the path forked. She knew roughly where the stables were, so took the right-hand path, suddenly stepping out into sunlight. The paddocks were to her right, and the stables were in front of her with a barn to the left. A stony track passed around the back of the buildings and disappeared. It must connect with a road somewhere, because it was the only way a vehicle could get in or out of this part of the estate.

April paused for a few moments to catch her breath, then she walked around to the front of the stables.

They were clearly very old. The stones were hand-hewn and weather-worn; the wood that comprised the doors and lintels had silvered with age and was split and cracked, held in place with hand-forged nails, worn black.

It had been a long time since any horses had been there, but swallows were still nesting amongst the beams in the roofs and no doubt there were rats and mice in the footings. April stood in the concreted area between the two rows of buildings, one with four separate loose boxes and one with only two. The last two loose boxes had collapsed, and all that remained was a pile of rubble, mostly stone with broken terracotta tiles amongst it. She narrowed her eyes and imagined the stables as they would have been when they were newly built, with horses in each box looking over the lower doors, shaking their heads and whinnying, and hay stored up in the loft, rakes and brushes and buckets in the centre, and people taking care of the animals; the sound of metal horseshoes scraping against the stone; the smell of warm hay.

She flinched at a sudden movement; it was only a feral cat, jumping from the top of a stable door and stretching in the sunlight, miaowing a welcome to April.

'Hi,' she said to the cat. 'Ciau.'

The cat looked at her, and then it sat on the cobbles and cleaned itself, one back leg extended into the air.

April turned her attention to the barn with one enormous door still on its hinges, its partner fractured into planks that were tumbled together. The roof had collapsed on one side, and the walls were slanting and looked precarious.

She walked towards the building. Swallows dived above her, catching their breakfast. Thousands of midges were hovering, holding the sunlight in their wings.

She reached the door and climbed over the fallen planks. Inside was cool and dark and it smelled of diesel and dust. It took a few moments for her eyes to adjust, but soon she made out shapes in the gloom. There was an ancient old tractor, agricultural tools, oil drums and plastic canisters. Up against the wall, on bricks, was an old sports car.

April stepped carefully over the detritus on the stone floor to reach the car. A tarpaulin was bundled up to one side. She could see, even before she was really close, that someone had been to the car before her. There were fresh footprints in the dust on the floor, and a toolbox lay open nearby.

The front passenger seat was missing.

The same seat, upholstered in the finest leather, that had been stained with Irene Borgata's blood.

28

April was back in her room, sitting at the desk with the laptop open in front of her. Sunlight was streaming in through the huge window, warming her back.

There was a knock at her door.

'Good morning!' It was Sam. 'Giuseppa asked me to bring you some coffee.'

'That's wonderful. Come in.'

Sam entered, and placed a cup and saucer on the desk.

'Thank you.'

'My pleasure. I'm on my way to the swimming pool. If you fancy a dip, you're welcome to join me.'

'Okay, thanks, I'd like that.'

Sam peered over her shoulder at the laptop screen.

'What are you doing?'

'Making a timeline for the day Irene disappeared. It's useful to have a clear idea of where everyone was and what they were doing on the day a crime took place.'

'But you don't know there was a crime here.'

'That's true,' said April, thinking of the missing car seat; the noises from the room next to hers in the early hours of the morning; the crude cardboard sign with the word 'Assassino' that had been fastened to the villa gates, even Enzo's illness.

'I don't suppose you have a couple of minutes now, Sam, to answer a few questions?'

'Fire away. I can't promise I can remember everything, but I'll do the best I can.'

'Okay. How old were you in May 1968?'

'Fifteen.'

'And do you remember what you were doing on the day Irene disappeared?'

'I was with a schoolfriend hunting rabbits in the mountains. We met up early in the morning at his uncle's house and we were out until evening.'

'Did you catch any rabbits?'

'Not one. We never did. We were notoriously bad rabbit hunters.'

April smiled.

'These mountains, I'm assuming they're the same ones that surround the town of Gibellina?'

'Yes. But we were nowhere near there.'

'Did you see anything unusual while you were out?'

'A few abandoned camps. Some of the people displaced by the earthquake moved into farmsteads and shepherd's huts, even tents. We met a single, hungry family and gave them the food we'd brought with us.'

'How were you travelling that day?'

'I cycled down to meet my friend and back to the villa later. We went to the mountains on foot.'

'What time did you get back here?'

'About seven o'clock.'

'Do you remember what the other members of the family were doing? Your parents? Daria?'

'Daria was in her room. My parents were in the dining room with the guests.'

'The guests?'

'Representatives of the powerful families from this part of the region.'

'I didn't know anyone else was here that evening.'

'Perhaps you hadn't asked.'

'Not until now. So why were those people here?'

'They'd come to talk about rebuilding the towns destroyed by the earthquake.'

'I don't understand.'

Sam sighed. 'Somebody needed to reconstruct all those ruined homes; to provide the land, the labour, the materials. The money to pay for all this would have to come from somewhere and the people who'd lost everything couldn't contribute. The government was going to have to provide grants and incentives. The men who gathered in our living room that night were discussing the most effective and efficient ways to get hold of that money.'

'But your family owned a tuna-processing company. They couldn't possibly have benefitted from government regeneration grants.'

'No. But they'd been persuaded to host the meeting here so the others could discuss their business freely. The villa was not being watched. It was a safe place for them to assemble.'

April said, 'Are you telling me, Sam, in a roundabout way, that the men who came to the villa that night were Mafiosi?'

'It's distasteful, I know,' said Sam with a shrug, 'but it's a fact of life. No matter what the disaster, there'll always be entrepreneurs, circling like sharks with an eye on the quarry, waiting for the government to start handing out the cash.'

29

IRENE

Oh, my love, I wish you could see what I'm seeing! You would be in your element here in the stables! We're up high, above the villa, me and my father-in-law — 'Don't stand on ceremony with me, Irene, call me Patrick!' — leaning on the fence admiring a mare and her foal. Behind us the stable hand, a surly man by the name of Quintu, is forking hay down from the loft. The set-up here is perfect. It's old, but there's everything we need to take care of the horses — feed and tack rooms, a lunge paddock, a fenced dressage arena, even a hand-pump for the water. And the views! They couldn't be more different from what we had in Yorkshire. I'm not used to the mountains yet, but I think I could grow to enjoy them.

I've been feeling so displaced; so out of my depth, but here, with the horses, I can be myself. Everything is familiar and I know what to do, and how to behave. And Patrick talks English and we've already established that Alia didn't ride so I'm not invading her territory. This is my place. This is where I shall come to think of you. Just knowing that I'll be able to do this makes me feel so much better.

I lean my chin on my arms on the top of the fence.

The foal walks round his mother's back legs, eyeing us curiously.

'He's a beauty,' I say to Patrick, who is chewing a hay stalk.

'Isn't he just? He has the lines of a champion.'

'I don't think I've ever seen anything more handsome.'

Patrick looks proud. *'Want to give me a hand with the little guy?'* he asks. *'Help me bring him along?'*

Do I ever!

The sun's on my shoulders and I'm looking at the animals; the dam is beautiful, a pretty little liver chestnut; her son has a small white star on his forehead and legs like a giraffe. His pelt flinches as his mother's tail flicks against him. He raises his head, blinks – those eyelashes! – and looks at me, as if he can see straight into my soul.

'Hi, you,' I say.

He makes a little whickering noise.

'What's his name, Patrick?'

'He doesn't have one yet. Do you have any ideas?'

'James,' I say, quick as a flash. 'He's definitely a James.'

'Right you are,' says my affable father-in-law.

He puts on his hat, a wide-brimmed affair with sweat stains around the band that makes him look like a cowboy. 'James it is. What do you think of that, Quintu?'

Quintu doesn't speak English. He continues working. He makes me uneasy. He resents me being here. I bet he liked it better when it was just him and Patrick, all boys together. I suppose my presence means he's slid a notch down the pecking order. But he's just going to have to get used to me, because I intend to spend as much time as I can up here, with the horses; with James.

I smile at Patrick. Patrick smiles at me.

'It's good to have you here, Irene,' he says.

'I'm very happy to be here,' I reply.

Quintu hawks and then spits down onto the cobbles. I hate to see men spitting, it disgusts me, but I don't say anything.

He probably doesn't mean to be so creepy. It's probably just the way he is.

30

Good grief, thought April. The fact that a whole collection of organised crime chiefs had been gathered at the villa on the same evening that Irene had disappeared put a whole new slant on things.

Intrigued as she was, she pulled the line of questioning back to the Borgatas.

'Did you get back to the villa before Enzo that night?' she asked Sam.

'Yes.'

'Did you see him when he came in?'

'I was in the kitchen eating supper. He was out of breath and covered in dust and blood.'

'Blood?'

'He'd fallen over, coming down the hill.'

'Can you tell me what happened exactly, when he came in?'

'Giuseppa was worried that he was in such a state. She asked him where Irene was. "Where is she?", she said. "What have you done with her?"'

'And what did Enzo say?'

'That his car had broken down on the outskirts of Gibellina and that he'd left Irene there. He went to find Daria and they set off in Daria's car to bring Irene back to the villa.'

'And what happened after that?'

'They didn't come back. Giuseppa was getting more and more het up. As soon as the visitors were gone, Giuseppa told Papa what had happened. Papa told me to come with him, and the two of us drove up to Gibellina in his car.'

'What did you find?'

'Daria's car was parked close to Enzo's. They were both on foot, searching for Irene. The car headlights were on, they'd manoeuvred the car so that they covered the widest possible area, and Daria had a torch. At that point, we all believed Irene must have got out of the car and fallen. We knew she couldn't have gone far. We thought she might have banged her head and knocked herself out. I was worried about wolves.'

'Are there wolves in Sicily?'

'There used to be grey wolves. They were declared extinct around about the same time all this was going on. I'd never seen one myself but some people said they were still living in the hills.'

The yellow sun was beaming through the window of April's bedroom. It cast warm blocks of light into the room. Beyond the window the sky was blue, pure, unbroken blue stretching between the tops of the trees and the summits of the mountains.

April was imagining the young woman, Irene, in her husband's car, in the cold and the dark, with the ruins of Gibellina town behind her; incapacitated by her injury; alone. The thought that she might hear, however distantly, the howling of wolves was chilling.

'Is it at all possible that Irene *was* attacked by wolves?' she asked.

'I don't think so. There'd have been evidence if she had been. But they were in my mind. They were bothering me.'

'Okay. How long did you carry on searching?'

'All night. We did the best we could but it was slow work, dangerous; there were craters and holes after the earthquake; loose rocks. In the morning, other people came. Our neighbours from Salgareale, and others. Dozens of people. We searched high and low, but we couldn't find any trace of Irene. Not one thing.'

'When did you contact the police?'

'Later that day, or some time the next day. I don't know. Papa and Enzo drove into Palermo at some point.'

'Why not straight away?'

'Because what could the police do? They were stretched to the limit as it was. Back then, it never occurred to any of us that there might have been a crime committed.' Sam hesitated, then he added: 'Probably there never was.'

'What do you think happened to Irene?'

Sam considered for a moment, then said: 'A tragic accident of some kind is the most likely explanation. I don't see what else it could have been.'

31

When Sam had left the bedroom, April drank her espresso and then changed into her swimming costume, put a dress over the top, picked up a towel from the bathroom and made her way down through the villa, out onto the terrace and beyond to the pool. Sam was there already, swimming lengths. The water was greener than it had looked from a distance last night, and someone, Sam presumably – although given that she seemed to do everything around the villa, it might have been Giuseppa – had been scooping the leaves and insects out with the long-handled net that lay to one side. A pile of wet detritus was heaped beside it.

The air was warm and when April took off her sandals the stones beneath her feet were hot. Beyond the gardens, the flowers and leaves; the climbing plants making their way through the branches of lemon trees; the jasmine, the bougainvillea, the frangipani, pelargoniums in every shade of pink and cream and red, the succulents and cacti and birds of paradise blooms, beyond the cypress trees and palm trees and other trees that April could not name, the mountains rose up, blue and mauve and hazy into a perfectly blue sky.

April perched on a sunbed and slipped off her dress, going forward to the pool and climbing down the steps into the water – how delightfully cold it was against her skin! – without interrupting Sam's exercise. When he realised that she was there, he surfaced, shaking his head. He looked better now, less haggard. This must be what he did every morning: wake up hungover and swim it off.

The sunlight made beautiful patterns in the deep turquoise blue of the water, it rippled and refracted and danced. April let her arms float and moved her fingers as if the water were some kind of musical instrument, and she were playing a tune with the light.

'I meant to ask you earlier, Sam,' she said. 'Who is using the bedroom next to mine?'

'Nobody.'

'I heard someone moving about in that room last night.'

'You can't have done. That room is an old dressing room. Irene used to sleep there sometimes, but nobody's used it for decades.'

'Irene slept there?'

'Yes, but it wasn't a real bedroom. She and Enzo had the corner room, further along. There's a bathroom with connecting doors in between.'

'Oh. Okay.'

Troy emerged from beneath the shadow of a tree and loped over to the swimming pool. He leaned over the rim and began to lap at the water.

'Is he allowed to do that?' April asked.

'He's done it all his life.'

Sam pulled his goggles down over his eyes.

'Excuse me, April, but I want to get a few more lengths in.'

He plunged underwater. The dog stopped drinking and watched him, water dribbling from his jowls.

April turned and climbed out of the pool.

32

Giuseppa had laid out breakfast bowls of fruit, cold meats and cheeses beneath muslin nets on a table in the inner courtyard. The parasol shades had been opened to provide some respite from the sun's rays, but with the courtyard being enclosed, and predominantly made of stone, and the sunshades being so threadbare that they'd been patched up with tape, the temperature in that space was already oven-warm. When April arrived, she found Maddalena pouring cold water from a bucket into the pool in the centre of the courtyard to replenish the liquid that had evaporated. She straightened up and put a hand on the small of her back.

'Oof,' she said. 'Taking care of the fish is usually Papa's job!'

April sat at the table and stretched her legs out into the sun. Little brown birds were fluttering down to drink from the rim of the fish pool. Maddalena came to sit beside April.

'The *zanzare* made a meal of me last night,' April said, showing Maddalena her arms.

Maddalena ran her fingers over April's lumps. 'They've eaten you alive! But don't worry, I have a home-made remedy. I'll bring it up after breakfast.'

Breakfast was traditional Sicilian: a choice of granitas and brioches served with honey and berries.

April and Maddalena were drinking coffee by the time first Sam, and then Elissa turned up at the table. The girl looked tired. She was wearing a floppy hat that shadowed most of her face and a tangerine-coloured kimono over a pair of shorts and a T-shirt. Her movements were languid. She dissolved onto a chair in the shade.

Sam was attentive towards his daughter, passing her a glass of water, a small bunch of grapes, encouraging her to taste one: 'So sweet! So delicious!' before filling his own plate. April put on her sunglasses.

'Where's Daria?' she asked.

'She's not a person of leisure, like the rest of us. She works at the pharmacy in Salgareale.'

'Bloody load of wastrels we are,' said Sam. 'Spoiled rich kids.'

'Hardly kids,' said Maddalena.

Sam sat down opposite April. His face was in the sun so he had to squint to look at her.

'How long do you think your investigation will take, April?' he asked. He tore off a piece of brioche dipped it in a pool of honey on his plate, and put it into his mouth. 'We haven't got long.'

'It depends on how co-operative the police are, and whether or not I can talk to Enzo. Theoretically it could all be wrapped up very quickly.'

'In time to stop Conti?'

'That's the plan.'

Maddalena poured some more coffee. The pot was almost empty. Giuseppa took it. 'I'll fetch some more,' she said, and withdrew back into the house.

'One thing I've been wondering is how did the Alfa Romeo get back here after Irene disappeared?' April asked. 'It had broken down, hadn't it?'

'Enzo was going to have it towed back,' said Sam, 'but the problem was easily fixed so he drove it back here himself.'

'What was the problem?'

'A disconnected fuel pipe or something like that.'

'Was there any suggestion the engine might have been tampered with?'

Sam said, 'Yes, that was suggested.'

'So the breakdown might not have been accidental?'

'No.'

There was a long silence, only broken by Elissa slurping tangerine juice from a glass through a straw.

'Did the police do any forensic investigations?' April asked carefully. 'Did they examine the car, for example?'

Maddalena looked to her uncle. 'Did they, Uncle Sam?'

'I can't say for sure,' Sam replied. 'I don't remember them ever coming down to the villa, but it was a chaotic time.'

'No matter what else was going on, the police should still have conducted a thorough investigation into Irene's disappearance,' said April.

Maddalena shrugged. 'Papa told me they didn't believe his story about Irene disappearing. They thought he'd killed her; that it was a straightforward domestic dispute. It was the obvious and most likely explanation for her disappearance and their attitude was: "Why throw our resources at a case, when we pretty much *know* what happened, but can't prove it?" And, as I understand it, if it wasn't Papa, they thought it must have been Cosa Nostra, because when someone got hurt, if it wasn't a domestic, it was always them, back then. They used to kill over the smallest things: arguments over territory, perceived slights, disloyalties. Everyone knew the Borgatas weren't directly involved with the Mafia, but it was quite possible that some maverick had messed up.'

Giuseppa returned with a fresh pot of coffee. April waited until it had been poured before she asked her next question.

'Might the Palermo detectives have been right about the Mafia being responsible for whatever happened to Irene?'

'It is possible,' said Maddalena, 'but I've listened to my grandparents talking about this many times, and it seems improbable. Yes, it could have been a case of mistaken identity, or just a mistake. But... the Borgatas are an established family in this part of Sicily. In those days, when respect was everything, the Borgatas commanded respect. If it had been a Mafiosa accident, both my grandparents were convinced that the responsible party would have been obliged to do the honourable thing and own up to it. There would have been compensation.' She shook her head. 'I don't believe it was a Cosa Nostra killing. None of us do.'

33

IRENE

On the way back from the stables, I walk through the gardens. Outside the villa is a swimming pool, covered over with a tarpaulin. Maddalena is playing on the terrace beyond, supervised by Giuseppa. Sam is on the lawn, kicking a football around by himself. I am tempted to go and join in with him. Instead, I go towards the housekeeper and the child.

'Ciau, Maddalena!' I say cheerfully.

She scowls at me.

'Do you like horses, Maddi?'

She doesn't understand, so I do a little mime, holding pretend reins, clicking my tongue to make clopping hoof sounds. 'Horse!' I say. 'Horse.' She smiles now, despite herself. Giuseppa says something. 'Cavallo.' Cavallo, I guess, means horse.

I say, 'Cavallo' and Maddi, giggling behind her fingers, says:

'Orse.'

'Cavallo!'

'Orse!'

'Cavallo!'

'Orse!'

She sounds so funny that I burst out laughing.

The football comes bouncing over to me. I kick it back to Sam. He cheers. I point to myself. 'Gordon Banks!' I say.

Now Sam laughs. He points to his chest. 'Stanley Matthews!'

'Nice to meet you, Signor Stanley!'

You always said, didn't you, Jack, that football was the only truly international language?

Feeling more upbeat, I go into the villa the back way, through the French doors, hoping to avoid my mother-in-law, but she's there, in the living room, sitting at a desk attending to some papers. She looks as if she's stepped off a page of Vogue, *of course, and there's me, in my shorts and a sweaty shirt, covered in dust and dung, with bits of hay in my hair and my hands all greasy from grooming.*

Pointedly, she peers at me over the top of her glasses. She looks at my feet. I am wearing an old pair of boots that Patrick found for me in the barn. I have walked dust over the immaculate white tiles.

I speak no Italian, she speaks no English, so we don't say a word to one another, but I feel her resentment and something else.

Is she jealous? I wonder.

Is queen bee Donatella Borgata jealous of me because I married her favourite son?

34

When breakfast was finished, April went back upstairs. She tried the handle of the room next door to hers. It was locked. She tried the next door along, the door to the corner room that Sam had said was Enzo and Irene's bedroom. That didn't open either. She crouched down to peer through the keyhole, but the view was obscured.

She returned to her own room, unfastened the gauze curtain from the clips that held it in place, and went onto the tiny balcony on the outside of the window, leaning over, to see if there was any way she could break into the room next door via its neighbouring balcony.

It might have been physically possible, but the window was closed and, if it had the same mechanism as the one in April's room, would be impossible to force from the outside without breaking glass.

She hung her towel, damp from the morning's swim, and her costume, over the balcony rail, knowing they'd be dry as soon as the sun made its way round to that side of the building, then she poured herself a glass of water and went to sit at the desk. She checked her phone. There was a message from Inspector Mazzotta.

Mrs Cobain. Suggest I give you case notes at lunch. Trattoria ò Scinà, Via del Quattro Aprile, Palermo. 12.30 today?

At that moment, Maddalena breezed in, waving a small bottle. 'Mosquito bite remedy.'

'Maddi, you're exactly the person I need to see!'

'Psychic,' said Maddalena. 'I told you.'

'Could I borrow the jeep to go into Palermo to meet Inspector Mazzotta at lunchtime?'

'I'll drive you.'

'We might be some time. He suggested we meet at a restaurant.' She showed the message to Maddalena. 'Do you know where that is?'

'I know it. It's not fancy but it's supposed to be good. I'll go and visit Papa in the hospital while you're with him; that way we'll kill two birds with one stone.'

'Okay, great.'

'We'll need to leave soon. See you downstairs in fifteen minutes?'

'Sure. Maddi, one more thing, do you know who would have a key to the room next to this one?'

'Giuseppa.'

'Only Giuseppa?'

'Yes. Giuseppa is the keeper of the keys. If you want to look in any of the locked rooms, you'll need to speak to her.'

35

IRENE

Enzo drives me into Palermo in his sports car. I feel like Grace Kelly, with my sunglasses and my soft-as-butter sandals, my silk scarf and my painted toenails. I've made an effort to look nice for Enzo, though really I'd rather be in my shorts and boots, up at the stables. He's trying so hard to please me, it's only right that I try to make him happy too.

The other day, he presented me with several pieces of Alia's jewellery: a couple of necklaces, a ruby brooch that was a gift to Alia from Donatella, and a tiara. Everything is old-fashioned. I've seen a photograph of Alia wearing the tiara and with her colouring, and her queenly gaze, she carried it off, but it doesn't suit me. And the brooch is plain ugly. It's so heavy it pulls at the fabric of whatever it's pinned to and... Oh, Jack, I don't like any of it. It doesn't make me feel beautiful, it makes me feel as if I am possessed. As in 'owned by'. The jewellery is like the name tag on the collar of a dog. It's like it's saying: If found, please return this woman to the Borgata family at the Villa Alba.

Enzo noticed, obviously, that I wasn't best keen.

'I know what the problem is,' he said. 'You want me to buy you something of your own; something that's yours.'

And now I wish I'd just managed to look grateful for the original jewellery because no, that's not the problem, and I don't like the thought of Enzo spending money on me, or heaping me with gifts. All I want is to go up to the stables and spend time with James. Or play football in the garden with Sam and Maddalena.

Anyway, the main reason for the expedition to Palermo, is so that we can choose a present for me together, Enzo and I.

I know I should be grateful. I know how lucky I am. I wish I didn't feel so uncomfortable about everything.

Enzo is proud of me. In London, I used to find his attentiveness endearing. I felt so lost after you were gone, so raw and vulnerable. And he was endlessly kind and concerned and affectionate and all of those things were like a balm to my wounds. I didn't mind the constant hand on my waist, the persistent asking if I was all right. Warm enough. Hungry. Tired. Happy.

Perhaps it's because spring is turning into summer, and the air is warm, that I'm starting to find the touching annoying. And the attention. The interminable watching to make sure that I'm okay. Once or twice I've snapped at him. I mustn't. I must be a better wife.

He takes me to a restaurant. It's in a posh part of the city. We pull up outside and a young man in a uniform opens the car door for me. I step out beneath the awning and then the man takes the keys from Enzo and goes off to park the car. Part of me is wishing my mother could see me... Ha! Imagine her face! Most of me is wondering why, right now, none of this is a distraction from the pain of missing you.

Inside, the place is cool and dark and echoey. It smells of cigar smoke and lilies. The furniture is modern, the waiters immaculately turned out and hovering like flies; the cutlery is silver. Enzo and I sit down at a table, opposite one another. I unfold the napkin on my lap. The menus are heavy as bibles, with gold leather covers and black cord and tassels. It's nothing like the Italian restaurant we used to visit in London. I don't know what any of the words on the menu mean, or what the dishes are, or whether or not I would like them.

'What is: "Nasello alla palermitano"?' I ask my husband.

'Hake with garlic and anchovies.'

'What about: "Coniglio in agrodolce"?'

'Rabbit. Shall I order for you?' asks Enzo. 'It'll be quicker than translating the whole menu.'

'I'll never learn if you keep doing that.'

'I just want you to be happy, sweet Irene.'

He's trying to look after me, but he doesn't understand, I don't want to be in this fancy place, all dolled up, eating dishes whose names I can't pronounce and drinking wine that's going to give me a bad head. I don't want the burden of having to be grateful to him for spending money on things I don't desire. I want to be with you, and, as that's not possible, the next best thing is being up in the paddocks with lovely James, lying in the shade with my arms behind my head while he puffs his sweet breath into my face and nibbles at the ends of my hair.

36

Palermo became busier as Maddalena drove deeper into the city. She'd followed the main road in and was now expertly winding her way around a complicated mix of one-way streets and pedestrianised areas.

The city was a microcosm of the paradoxes of Sicily. One minute they were driving through a semi-derelict area with run-down blocks of flats, burned-out cars and mangy dogs sleeping amongst the rubbish overflowing from communal bins; the next they were passing exquisite buildings and elegant shops; roads shut off from the traffic so shoppers and workers could walk and chat and drink coffee in peace. There were markets packed with covered stalls selling fruit and vegetables so colourful and fresh they looked as if they'd been painted. They drove past a flower market, and beyond that were ranks of stalls selling street food and the perfume of flowers was superseded by the aroma of fried meat and cooked cheese and street vendors shouting and a woman selling fish from ice-filled panniers on the back of a Vespa.

In the commercial areas, smart men in brogues and elegant women in heels were walking between buildings with that busy, forward-leaning stride adopted by businesspeople the world over. Almost all were wearing white shirts and suits, and most were holding phones to their ears and talking loudly. Around the next corner, groups of scruffy youths were sitting astride dented mopeds, smoking and laughing. They passed a stall where a whole pig was roasting, and saw a woman selling puppies from a crate.

As they drew close to the restaurant, Maddalena pointed out a stark monolithic monument dedicated to the memory of all the people who had lost their lives in the fight against Cosa Nostra. It did not affect April as strongly as the memorial Maddalena had shown her yesterday, at the side of the road that connected the airport to the city. That one marked the site of the murder of judge Giovanni Falcone in 1992, a man who had spent most of his professional life trying to combat the Mafia's influence. 'He was blown up,' Maddalena had said, impassively, 'right here.'

It seemed impossible to get away from this dark side of Sicily. The Mafia was like something in the wind, something that couldn't be seen or touched, but that tainted everything.

And yet most of the city was beautiful, full of music and traffic and shouting and laughter and life. Vespas zipped amongst the cars. Traffic police in white gloves controlled the competing streams at intersections; lovers held hands; tourists strolled carrying cameras around their necks. Maddalena drove April past the cathedral, with its Arabic-influenced towers and turrets, its beautiful azure dome shining in the sunlight, and April longed to go inside and explore – 'We'll come back another day,' Maddalena promised. There were tiny, narrow streets and wide roads, and parks and gardens, steps and balconies and arches and window boxes. The architecture was stunning and varied and posters on bill-boards and stuck to the sides of buildings were advertising all manner of wonderful-sounding concerts and theatrical events. And wrapping up the whole city, as if cradling it in their arms, were the lovely blue mountains all around.

By the time Maddalena dropped April off outside the Trattoria ò Scinà, April had fallen in love with Palermo. She realised, as she climbed out of the jeep, that for the last forty minutes or so she had entirely forgotten herself; she'd been immersed in the city. Being out of her own head had felt like a holiday.

She straightened her skirt and her top – she'd worn a loose, long-sleeved cotton shirt as Maddalena had advised – and reached into the footwell for her bag.

'Call me when you're done,' Maddalena said. 'I'll come and pick you up.'

April pushed the jeep door shut and turned and went into the restaurant.

* * *

When April told the proprietor at the trattoria that she'd come to meet Inspector Luca Mazzotta, she was welcomed with a warmth that surprised her and taken through a busy eating area out onto a terrace at the back.

The restaurant didn't directly overlook the docks, but April could smell seawater and hear the call of the gulls.

The Sicilian inspector was already sitting at a table in the corner of the terrace. He had an open bottle of wine and a glass in front of him and was reading some papers, lounging in the chair. He was wearing sunglasses.

When he saw April, he put the papers into his briefcase, stood up and held out his hand. She shook it, and sat down in the chair that he indicated. It was a fraction cooler on the terrace in the shade of the striped awning. Pots of herbs and shrubs had been placed on the inside of the railings. Beyond was a view of rooftops: reds and buffs and dusty oranges; chimneys, water tanks, old walls, ceramic tiles and aerials.

'It's good to see you again,' said the inspector.

'You speak English?'

'I spent three years in the UK as part of an EU initiative to share expertise with colleagues working in the fight against organised crime.'

He was laying out his credentials. April maintained her poker face.

'Can I get you a different drink, or are you happy with wine?' he asked.

'Just water for me, please.'

April took off her hat. A young waiter brought a jug of water and a couple of glasses to the table. The next instant, the proprietor was back, all smiles and a little bow, holding a tea towel in his hands, asking them if they were ready for the chef to start cooking the day's special.

'Are you happy to eat fish?' the inspector asked April. 'This restaurant doesn't have a menu, the chef cooks whatever's come in off the boats this morning.'

'I don't eat meat or fish. I'm happy with anything vegetarian though.'

'Omelette?' the proprietor suggested.

'Not eggs either, no, sorry,' said April. 'Pasta with tomato sauce would be perfect.'

The proprietor shook his head and did not attempt to disguise his disappointment as he headed back towards the ribboned curtain that demarcated the kitchen from the terrace, muttering to himself. April could imagine him complaining to the chef.

'You've just confirmed his prejudice that foreigners don't appreciate good food,' said the inspector. 'It's a shame because you won't find any better or fresher anywhere in Sicily.'

April detected criticism. She ignored it and took a drink of water. It was deliciously cold and lemony.

'It's good of you to make time to see me today, Inspector,' she said. 'I got the impression yesterday that my presence in Palermo was an inconvenience to you.'

'Yesterday was a bad day. I'd come straight from an incident. I had other things on my mind.'

'Oh.'

'And I didn't realise who you were. After you told me your name, I made some enquiries and found out that you were Paul Cobain's widow.'

'You knew Cobain?'

'We collaborated on a drugs case a few years back. I liked him. I was truly sorry to hear of his death.'

April watched a fly make its way around the rim of the bread basket.

'Anyway, knowing that you were his wife was enough to make me want to help you in any way I could. For his sake.'

The inspector's statement fell somewhere between sexist and complimentary. April couldn't work out if she should be offended or pleased. There was an awkward silence between them.

'Did you watch the Conti piece on television last night?' she asked, to change the subject.

'I didn't, no.'

'He was claiming to have discovered bloodstained upholstery on the passenger seat of Enzo Borgata's car.'

'Right.'

'It's not evidence. The blood is Irene's but it predates May 1968 so it has no relevance to her disappearance. I assume this is covered in the case notes.'

'No,' said the inspector. 'It isn't.'

'Right. Well, this morning, I went to check on the car, which is being kept in a barn on the Borgata estate, and the passenger seat had been removed. I fully expect to see Conti produce it on television, and if he does, it means somebody trespassed onto private property, they entered the barn without permission, they stole the seat and they're potentially tampering with evidence.'

'And what do you want me to do about that?'

'I'd like you to be ready to make life difficult for Milo Conti and his team.'

The inspector shrugged. 'They'll have covered their arses. And even if they haven't, they've got the commissario batting for their side.'

April narrowed her eyes. 'That's it? That's all you're going to say about it?'

'Hmm,' said the inspector.

'Can't you at least issue a complaint to the production company, or *something*?'

'I could, but Conti will spin it that you're trying to obstruct his enquiry.'

'This is ridiculous. You, the police, are giving that man free rein to behave exactly as he pleases and never mind the consequences!'

'On the contrary, I believe we should only get involved in the battles we can win. Let Conti exhaust his options trying to make the evidence fit his theory. It gives us the time and space to explore the other possibilities.'

'But there is hardly any time.'

'We'd better work fast then.'

37

Luca Mazzotta's telephone rang. He looked at the caller ID on the screen, said, 'Excuse me,' and picked it up. April heard him say, 'Yes. Yes. No, I can't. You said you'd pick her up this afternoon.' He lowered his voice and half turned his back on April. 'You can't keep changing the arrangements like this. Okay. Five o'clock? Well, I don't have much choice, do I?' He put the phone face down on the table. Then he looked towards the restaurant kitchen and checked his watch.

'That was my wife,' he said. 'We're separated. Her speciality is changing arrangements at the last moment.'

He took off his glasses and laid them on the table. His eyes were heavy-lidded and tired.

'Sorry,' he said. 'I don't mean to be disrespectful. I'm sure I annoy my wife equally.'

'I wasn't offended.'

'Did you and Cobain have children?'

'No.'

The waiter came with a plate of fish fried in batter, which he put on the table, together with a wicker basket of bread and a bowl of olives.

'For you, signora, alivi scacciati,' said the waiter with a small bow.

'These are cracked green Sicilian olives marinaded with garlic, oregano and parsley.'

'That sounds delicious,' said April.

'*Grazie,*' said Luca Mazzotta. He picked up the half-lemon at the side of the plate and squeezed it over the fish.

'So how is your investigation going?' he asked. 'Have you made any progress?'

'I'm still trying to untangle the knots within the family. It's more complicated than I anticipated.'

'Families always are. Especially old families. They've had the time to accumulate plenty of skeletons.'

April ate an olive. It zinged with flavour. She took another.

'And I bet,' continued the inspector, 'there are allegiances and jealousies and people jostling for attention and affection and nobody ever says exactly what they mean.'

'How do you know all that?'

'Experience. I'm describing my own family.'

April's family had been small; just her and her mother after her parents separated. It had been a relief to go to boarding school and escape from her mother's bitterness.

The inspector speared a fish on his fork, and put it in his mouth, battered head, fins and all.

'*Ottimo!*' he said. 'How are the olives?'

'Divine.'

He took a drink of wine.

'If you know that the Alfa Romeo wasn't examined, then you've read the Irene Borgata case notes,' said April. 'What do you think, Inspector? Do you subscribe to the theory that Enzo Borgata killed his young wife thirty-five years ago?'

'I subscribe to no theories. My plan is to go through the witness statements again and look for anything that might have been missed the first-time round. How about you?'

'I'm not ready to theorise yet either.' She ate another olive, then said, 'I don't suppose you've had any dealings with a young man called Tonio Oliveri? All I know is that he hangs about the villa, smokes weed and brings supplies to the Borgatas' housekeeper from his father in Salgareale.'

'There are no big-time criminals from Salgareale called Tonio Oliveri that I'm aware of. What is it about him that worries you?'

'He sneaks about. But Donatella, the family matriarch, doesn't know that he comes. She doesn't approve of the Oliveris, so he has to be surreptitious. That's what I was told, at least.'

'Right.'

'And I think he and Elissabeta, Sam's daughter, might be going out with each other.'

'So there's a lot of deceit going on.'

'As long as Tonio's not bad news, I guess that's none of my business.'

The inspector finished the last of his fish and wiped his fingers on his napkin.

The waiter removed his plate and returned with two dishes. One contained nothing but three pieces of fish flesh in a pale-coloured sauce. Coils of spaghetti were heaped on the other, shining with oil and flecked with parsley and chunks of tomato.

The inspector passed the pepper pot to April.

'Enjoy your meal,' he said, kissing the tips of his fingers. *'Buon appititu.'*

'Thank you. One of the things I wanted to ask you was—'

'Not now,' he said. 'Eat, don't talk. That's the Sicilian way.'

So, she ate.

38

When the inspector asked April if her pasta dish was okay, she confirmed it was one of the most delicious meals she had ever eaten. Perhaps it tasted so good because all her senses were firing at a faster rate than they had been for months, because she was more attuned to the world around her. She was waking up. She was conscious of the warmth of the air, the faint stripes of green and white on the table caused by the sun shining through the awning, the clattering sounds from the kitchen; the clean, woody smell of the oil used on the planks of the decking; the pleasure of being somewhere different; the thrill of working again, of sharing information with a fellow professional.

Luca Mazzotta steadfastly refused to pick up the conversation about the investigation until they had finished their food. Only when the dishes had been cleared, the proprietor mollified by the fact there wasn't a scrap left on the plates – if Cobain had been there he'd have said, 'They don't need washing,' – only then did the talking resume.

'Who was it within the family asked you to come to Sicily and carry out your investigations?' the inspector asked.

'Maddalena, who was with me yesterday. Enzo's daughter with his first wife. We were at school together and we used to spend our summer holidays with her father in Sicily. You know that he had a heart attack?'

'Yes.'

'Obviously, Enzo is the prime suspect, but as far as I can tell there's no compelling evidence to suggest that he was to blame.'

The inspector nodded. 'Conti is backing his allegations up with unrelated facts. He'll use domestic violence statistics to lead his viewers to the assumption that Enzo is guilty.'

'The family is already getting grief from local people.'

'That's what happens.'

'But if it wasn't Enzo, then who? Nobody in the family believes the Mafia had anything to do with Irene's disappearance.'

'I don't think so either. You know about the meeting being hosted at the Villa Alba that evening? The family heads would never condone Irene being abducted while they were accepting hospitality from her in-laws. It would go against their "codes of honour", and send out the wrong message. The Cosa Nostra business model was – *is* – based on intimidation. "If you don't do what we say, we'll hurt your family." The Borgatas were co-operating. You could almost say they were collaborating. So, for Irene to come to any harm on their watch, so to speak, would be unthinkable.'

'That doesn't rule out an opportunist kidnapping though.'

'That doesn't add up either. The car was worth a mint, and Irene had her bag with her, her jewellery and so on. If it was an opportunist, why not grab the saleable items and run? Irene was in no position to stop them. Why go to the trouble of taking a human being who did not want to be taken, and furthermore was pretty immobile, when they could have just stolen her possessions? And why take her and then not demand a ransom?'

'Perhaps something went wrong.'

'Maybe.'

There was a pause as the coffee was delivered to the table.

The inspector opened his briefcase and took out a slender file. He passed it to April.

'Case notes?'

'Copies. I've kept the originals.'

'There's not much.'

'It's all there is. My colleagues were convinced that Enzo had killed his wife, and hidden her body in a shallow grave somewhere on the mountain, but with no evidence were in no position to progress the case.'

'Right.'

'There is always another possibility: that Irene isn't dead; that she left of her own accord,' said the inspector. 'Nobody considered that in the first investigation.'

'But how could she have? She'd lost a leg a few weeks previously. She was in the middle of nowhere with no means of contacting anyone.'

The inspector shrugged. 'My colleagues thought it unlikely too.'

He took a drink of coffee and checked his watch. His demeanour suddenly changed.

'I have to go.' He rubbed his fingers together to signal that he wanted the bill.

'You must let me pay half.'

'I won't hear of it.'

He pushed back his chair, stood up, put on his sunglasses, took his jacket off the back of the chair and hitched it on over his shirt.

The waiter brought the bill on a tray and the inspector gave him his card.

'Tread carefully, Mrs Cobain,' the inspector said. 'Remember, it's possible there is a murderer in the villa watching you and keeping tabs on how much you know.'

He said this lightly but April recognised the warning.

'I'm not afraid, Inspector.'

'Even so. Take care. And stay in touch.'

39

IRENE

On the way back from Palermo, we stop in Gibellina. It's a thriving, busy town, tumbling down the slope of one of the hills. Enzo goes to seek out a man, a mechanic he wants to employ to adjust the engine timing on his beloved Alfa Romeo. While they are occupied, I wind my way up to the top of the town, nodding to the old people sitting on chairs outside their doors.

Many of the houses have a downstairs, an upstairs, and another floor above that; almost all have balconies outside every window and the balconies are full of plants growing in old olive oil and tomato tins. There are little alleyways, steps, gardens enclosed by walls, arches; shops. I suppose this ancient architecture makes the most of the light and the views and perhaps it helps keep the lower storeys cool. I don't know. What I do know is that everyone must know everyone else's business because all the doors and windows are open and you can hear the sounds of radios and people talking and laughing and singing inside the houses. Living here must be like being part of one great big family.

The street lights are suspended from wires strung between the buildings and delicious cooking smells waft out of the doors.

I wish Enzo and I lived up here, in the town, amongst the people, rather than down in the valley, in our grand isolation. The sunlight must last longer here. Life must be brighter. As I'm thinking that, a voice says, 'Hello, Miss Irene.' I turn and it's Quintu, the Borgatas' stable hand. He lives in the cottage close to the stables at the villa, but Patrick has told me that he has family up here and spends his free time in Gibellina.

I am not pleased to see Quintu. I don't like the way he looks at me, rudely, blatantly and with a kind of disdain. I know a little more about him now. Patrick told me he was close to Alia; nothing to do with horses; rather their families are connected via marriage and they also share business interests. Perhaps he dislikes me out of loyalty to her.

'Good afternoon,' I say, and I turn and walk back down the hill.

As I stand in the little piazza outside the church, a young woman in old clothes and shoes comes up to me holding a basket. There are gaps in her smile where teeth are missing. She takes a greenish-blush coloured fruit about the size of an apricot from the basket and offers it to me. I have no idea what it is.

'Ficu,' she says helpfully. She points to a tree growing behind a wall behind her that has large leaves, shaped liked hands.

I'm none the wiser. She takes a second fruit and bites into it. I copy her. The skin is soft and warm, slightly velvety, and inside is a delicious, seedy sweetness – a taste like honey. I have never eaten anything quite so delicately flavoured. 'Oh!' I cry. 'Deliziusu!' and the woman smiles.

40

_____

April called Maddalena, who answered her phone so quickly she must have been holding it in her hand. She had left the hospital. She was in the shopping district, the Centro Commerciale Forum, picking up supplies for Giuseppa, but she'd make her way back and meet April at the seafront.

April followed the signs, emerging from a small, dark alleyway to find herself facing a spectacular view. Brilliant blue water was lapping the shore of a small beach and just a few metres behind was the Byzantine architecture of the grand buildings that looked out over the sea. Starlings were calling from amongst the branches of trees.

She sat on a bench on a neatly lawned area, where a welcome breeze breathed away the heat, and she opened the slender file that the inspector had given her. It contained some two dozen sheets of paper, mostly witness statements taken at the time of Irene's disappearance. They were in Italian, handwritten in a script that was difficult to read although she could pick out certain names and locations.

There were also copies of photographs including a poor quality black and white image of Enzo and Irene Borgata together, taken outside a restaurant, presumably in Sicily. It was difficult to make out any details.

Other photographs showed members of the Borgata family: younger versions of Daria and Sam and men and women April assumed were villa staff. One face bugged her for a while until she realised it was Giuseppa. Thirty-five years ago, Giuseppa had been an attractive young woman, with black wavy hair and strong dark eyes.

'April! There you are! Hi!'

It was Maddalena. She leaned down to kiss April and dropped onto the bench beside her. She had a bottle of water in her hand.

'How did it go with the inspector?'

'Better than I was expecting. How's Enzo?'

'Asleep. He had another mini-heart attack in the night.'

'Oh no, Maddi, I'm sorry.'

'He's not getting better, April. He's getting worse. I don't know what to do.'

'You're doing everything you can.'

'It doesn't feel like it's enough. But anyway, distract me. What's that?'

'This? It's a copy of Enzo and Irene's marriage certificate.'

'Can I see?'

April passed it to Maddalena.

'Westminster Register Office, London,' Maddalena read out loud. 'The nineteenth of February 1963. It was only a few weeks after they met.'

'How did they meet?'

'Papa was stuck in London over Christmas because of the 'flu and Irene, who was working in the hotel where he was staying, looked after him. He got better but then he couldn't get home because of the weather; the airports were snowbound and the roads were closed. He ended up spending weeks in London and he and Irene fell in love. We can blame all of this, where we are now, on a high-pressure system over the Northern Atlantic.' She took another drink and looked at the certificate again.

'There's the name of my grandfather, Patrick Borgata: horse breeder. What about Irene's father?' Maddalena held the paper at arm's length to better interpret the old-fashioned handwriting. 'Arthur Weatherbury, Mining Engineer from Beal, in the West Riding of Yorkshire. I've never heard of Beal.'

'There's a big colliery there.'

'Do you think Irene left Yorkshire to come to London for the hotel job?'

'That's what it looks like. Do you know which hotel it was?'

'The Pimlico Hotel in Victoria. Last time I came to London I went to look for it, but it was gone. Demolished to make way for flats.'

'What did Irene do there?'

'She was a waitress.' Maddi sighed. 'I always thought it was romantic, Enzo and Irene getting to know one another in the hotel, over Christmas with nobody else around, but now I think about it, it sounds rather...'

'What?'

'I don't know... lonely.'

41

IRENE

'Figs,' Enzo tells me later, when I show him the fruit in my handbag that the young woman from Gibellina insisted on giving me. 'The trees grow like weeds here. We have plenty of our own in the villa garden.' He glances at me. 'She didn't ask you for money, did she?'

I don't reply.

'Oh, my little Irene!' Enzo says fondly. 'You have a lot to learn. How much did you give her?'

'Nothing,' I say.

It had only been a couple of notes, but the woman had seemed very pleased. Obviously, it was too much.

We are in the car, driving down the hill, back towards the villa. I don't like being called 'Little Irene.' It's patronising. I don't like the fact that Enzo thinks I was taken for a fool. I feel edgy now, and tense.

'Why shouldn't I pay that woman if I wanted to?' I ask. 'She was nice to me.'

'Oh, sweetheart,' says Enzo, 'I'm not scolding you! I just don't like to think of anyone taking advantage of you.'

It occurs to me, then, that for the first time in my life, I have no girl-friends. Nobody my age with whom to chat and laugh and have fun. No other young wife with whom to compare notes about our husbands. Nobody I can be honest with; nobody I can talk to about you, Jack.

I love Maddalena. I care for Sam and Daria, and I'm fond of Enzo, of course I am, but the thought of the family being all I shall ever have, is crushing.

And also, Enzo is wrong about the fruit. They can't be figs. Back home, my mother always used to produce a box of figs at Christmas as a treat. They tasted wizened and leathery; they stuck to the teeth. I take one of the fruits out of the bag and realise that what I'm used to are dried figs; these are the fresh variety, picked directly from the tree.

I feel foolish then. Enzo is right. There is so much I don't know.

I don't miss England. I don't miss the rain, or the coldness, or the grey skies; the wet pavements; the smell of damp wool; the buses; the fried food; the newspapers; the fruit that only comes in tins, the dried figs.

But I miss you, my darling.

Don't think for a second I've pushed you aside.

You still occupy all of my heart.

I will never stop missing you.

If only you were here, really here, not just the version of you that I carry in my heart. I sometimes dream that if I wish it hard enough, I might be able to bring you back to life.

42

Maddalena insisted that she show April some of the delights of Palermo and April felt it would be churlish to say that she'd rather be alone somewhere to pore over the case notes.

By the time they had walked along some of Palermo's finest streets, and sat outside a café for a cold drink and a piece of Torta Setteveli – a chocolate and hazelnut delight that, Maddalena told April, was named after Salome's famous dance of the seven veils – the afternoon was growing late. It was a trek back to Maddalena's jeep and then they hit the commuter traffic coming out of Palermo. All in all, April was glad when they found themselves on the Gibellina road again. Maddalena had turned on the radio, the windows were down and the sun was low in the sky, painting the countryside gorgeous shades of vermilion and apricot.

Once again, they drove past the Cretto di Burri that covered the ruins of old Gibellina, and once again April was affected by a profound sense of sadness and loss.

The jeep bumped over ruts in the track. April wondered how difficult it would be to hide a body in this desolate landscape. It would be a challenge to dig a hole big enough to constitute a grave, certainly, especially in the summer when the ground was dry and hard. But if one were to roll the body down a steep section of the hill, it would be straightforward to disguise it with rocks and fallen branches.

In May, when Irene went missing, the river would have been in flow. April was no expert, but she thought it likely a body fallen from a bridge would end up caught on the bank, or amongst the rocks downstream. It would have been found.

Back at the villa, Maddalena and April found Sam at the gates with Tonio Oliveri. Tonio was sitting astride the wall and Sam was standing beside him, with an open toolbox at his feet.

'Tonio brought us a security camera,' Sam explained.

'What a great idea!' said Maddalena.

'Yeah.' Sam indicated shards of broken glass swept into a pile. 'The ghouls have been up here again. Hopefully this will be a deterrent.'

'What about the top entrance, by the stables?' April asked.

'Hardly anybody knows you can get in that way,' said Maddalena.

'I still think you need to look at making that secure too.'

April helped Maddalena carry the shopping bags into the kitchen. Giuseppa had her sleeves rolled up and her hair held back with a head-scarf, and was standing at the sink washing something with mottled blue flesh.

Maddalena put the bags on the counter. 'I'll unpack for you, Giuseppa,' she said. 'What's for dinner?'

'Sam's favourite dish,' Giuseppa said, wielding a large knife. 'Octopus. I'm going to cook it with garlic, chilli, potatoes and lemons.'

She plunged the knife into the octopus and the flesh fell apart. April had watched a documentary about octopuses with Cobain. They were sensitive, highly intelligent creatures. It made her queasy to see the animal being butchered like that.

Maddalena stacked the shopping in the fridge and the larder. Then she said, 'I'm going upstairs for a shower. Are you okay, April?'

'I'm fine.'

'See you at dinner, then,' Maddalena said, and she disappeared.

'May I help myself to a drink?' April asked Giuseppa.

'Of course.'

April found a can of San Pellegrino lemonade inside the voluminous and ancient fridge. She stood close to the window, facing Giuseppa and asked: 'When did you first start working here?'

'Straight out of school.'

'Was it what you wanted to do?'

Giuseppa didn't answer the question. 'Signora Donatella needed a new maid,' she said. 'She could have chosen any of the girls in Salgareale, but she picked me. My mother was pleased.' Giuseppa gathered chunks of octopus into a colander and rinsed them vigorously under the cold tap.

April popped the ring-pull on the can.

'Did you enjoy working here?'

'Work is not supposed to be enjoyed. If my family had been rich, then I wouldn't have had to come here, cleaning up after other people.'

'No.' April took a drink. 'Were you at the villa when Enzo brought his new English bride home?'

'Yes.'

'What did you make of her?'

'Irene? I didn't make anything of her.'

'Did you like her?'

'It wasn't up to me to have an opinion about her. What was up to me was to make the beds and mop the floors, clean the glassware, scrub the lavatories and hang out the laundry. Things were different then,' said Giuseppa, stirring the contents of the colander robustly with her fingers. 'There was more of a distinction between family and staff. Now, I do everything for Donatella; I call her "Donatella". I take care of her personal matters. We are almost like friends. Then, we were mistress and servant. We had our roles and our boundaries. I'll tell you something though, Donatella wasn't thrilled about Irene.'

'Oh?'

'Not at all. Her husband, on the other hand, Patrick, *he* thought the sun shone out of Irene's backside. Those two, Patrick and Irene, got on like a house on fire.'

She lifted the colander and shook it to remove the last of the water.

'Why didn't Donatella warm to Irene?'

'Enzo has always been her golden boy, her favourite child by a country mile. She preferred Enzo's company to that of her husband. After his first wife, Alia's death, Donatella had Enzo to herself. They used to do every-thing together. Then Irene came along and Enzo didn't want to spend time with his mother any more.'

She drained the sink. Suckers and tiny pieces of skin circled above the plughole.

'What were Irene and Enzo like, when they were together?' April asked.

'He was besotted. It was as if he couldn't believe that someone like Irene would marry someone like him.' Giuseppa sniffed. 'He was down here every morning making her a cup of English breakfast tea before he left for work. He used to order it in from some fancy shop in Palermo that imported it from London. Cost an arm and a leg, but he got it because coffee wasn't good enough for her majesty, no. He'd prepare it as she liked it, with cold milk and sugar, and he always cut a flower from the garden and took it up to her in bed.'

'That's very sweet.'

'If you saw him you wouldn't have said "sweet". It was more like he was desperate.'

'Oh?'

'Desperate to hold onto her. You could see it in his eyes, right from the first day he brought her back. It was as if he knew he'd lose her, one way or another, but he married her anyway.'

'You didn't think the marriage would last?'

'No. I didn't expect it to end as it did, mind. But they were never suited, as a couple.'

Giuseppa lit the gas on the hob with a match and busied herself with a pan and some oil.

'What about Irene. Was she happy?'

'She was happy when she was up at the stables with her father-in-law, seeing to the horses; riding them, grooming them. And Patrick loved the bones of that girl. She was the kind of daughter he'd have liked to have had, the opposite to the one he did have.'

'Daria.'

'She's a watered-down version of her mother, too timid to step out of Donatella's shadow. Irene, on the other hand, had roses in her cheeks and her eyes were bright and she liked to be happy. He gave her a horse, you know.'

'Patrick did?'

'That's right. She was looking after a foal that had been bred here but it wasn't old enough to be ridden and none of the other horses was right for her. Patrick had heard about this stallion, Turi, that was up for sale and he drove Irene all the way to San Fratello to look at him. The owners let her try him out and she loved him and they brought him back in the horsebox. Dark brown he was, high-stepper, wild-eyed, an absolute beauty! You should have seen Donatella's face when she heard how much Patrick had paid for him! See, the money wasn't Patrick's. It was Donatella's. All the money came from the tuna business, and that had been established by Donatella's family, going back generations.'

Giuseppa took an onion from the string hanging from a rack, and began to chop it with a large knife.

'Goodness,' said April. 'It sounds as if Irene coming here caused some tension within the family.'

Giuseppa snorted. 'That's putting it mildly.'

She turned the onion and chopped it the other way.

'You asked me about Irene and Enzo's relationship. Well, I'll tell you. Enzo loved Irene, but Irene, she loved being up at the stables. That was her priority, not her husband. Everyone could see it. Enzo must have known. Deep down, he must have known that he was never her number one. And imagine how it must feel to love someone as much as he loved Irene, and to know that she didn't feel the same way.'

She scooped the onion into the pan.

'I've never been married, but I know what a marriage should look like. And it shouldn't look like Enzo and Irene's. It shouldn't look like that at all.'

43

IRENE

September 1963

I've been in Sicily for six months. It's almost unbelievable. The individual days pass slowly, but when I look back on the time, it feels as if that half-year has flown by. And what has happened in that time, Jack?

Many things have happened.

Do I love you any the less?

No.

It is my birthday. I hadn't mentioned it. I hoped Enzo might have forgotten, but he hadn't. Tonight, when he came home from work, he presented me with a beautiful cardboard box, secured with a thick white ribbon. I had Maddalena help me open the box, and amidst many 'oohs' and 'aahs' I pulled out a new dress. A long, long-sleeved, salmon-pink dress with a pleated skirt and a high neckline. It is the kind of dress my grandmother would have worn.

'Enzo!' I said, trying to keep the dismay from my face. 'You really shouldn't have.'

'Do you like it?' he asked, his eyes so eager for my approval that I simply didn't have the heart to tell him how hideous I found the dress. I've no doubt it

cost a small fortune, but I'd have been far happier if he'd let me choose some fabric and make my own or better still, if he'd simply bought me some new riding clothes.

'It's gorgeous,' I said, holding it up against me, hoping he would see how badly the colour looks against my skin, how unflattering the collar, but he just beamed and kissed me.

'My mother chose it from her favourite shop in Palermo,' he said. 'She said that it would suit you very well.'

I'm wearing the dress now; standing in front of the mirror in our bedroom. My skin is tanned from the sunshine, Jack, and my arms and legs are strong from working with the horses. When I lost you, I faded, as if I'd lost something of myself too. I became smaller, less significant somehow. But now I'm coming back to how I used to be, when you loved me.

You wouldn't love me in this dress. I look like the kind of tasselled lampshade my aunt, Hilda, would have favoured. Even so, I shall wear it for dinner to please Enzo and so as not to humiliate him in front of his mother. Perhaps I could 'accidentally' stand too close to a candle, and catch my sleeve in the flame, and scorch the dress. Perhaps I could trap the hem in the door and tear it. Perhaps I could do what Maddalena did, and spill ragu over it. There must be a hundred ways to sabotage the gift. Sooner or later, I'll find one.

44

When April came down for dinner that evening, she could hear piano music playing somewhere in the house. She followed the sound to a room she hadn't seen before: a circular, domed space at the far side of the villa, with floor-to-ceiling windows opening into the garden thrown wide. The pianist was Maddalena, playing the baby grand barefoot and wearing a gauzy blue dress with shoestring straps. Moths were flitting around the candles burning on the tables outside, making crazy shadows on the curved, inner walls, which were naked, save for the old terracotta plaster.

It must have been something to do with the light and the movement of the insects, but April was almost certain she glimpsed a young woman leave the room via the French windows as she entered from the hallway. The young woman glanced back at April, before slipping into the darkness of the garden.

At last, April thought, she was beginning to understand Irene Weatherbury. She had an idea, now, of how difficult it must have been for Irene coming here, to this great old villa with its high ceilings and its thick stone walls. What a journey from, presumably, a fairly modest house in a mining town in the Ridings of Yorkshire via a businessmen's hotel in London.

Fate had brought Irene and Enzo together in the Pimlico Hotel. Enzo was a softly spoken man, not the kind to oversell himself, or his background. Perhaps Irene had been impressed by the combination of his wealth and humility; thrilled that she, a working-class girl, was being befriended by this quiet Sicilian. Or maybe she'd simply been lonely. Looking after Enzo while he was sick might have given her a purpose. And when he'd recovered, she would have been delighted when he suggested they go for a walk together, to wonder at the frozen river, or perhaps he offered to buy her dinner one evening as a 'thank you'. However their affair had started, April was sure it would have been gently.

Irene had been very young. She must have been flattered when Enzo proposed to her. Or had she been overwhelmed? Enzo wasn't a pushy man. If Irene had wanted to say 'no', he would have made it easy for her to do so. What if she'd been searching for an escape route? She could have been running from a situation; from a man, or a debt, or something else altogether.

If only I could talk to you, Irene, April thought.

You must have been in this room a thousand times. Were you happy? Were you glad you'd taken the path that led you here or did you have any regrets?

This strange room would have looked exactly the same forty years ago. Irene's eyes would have seen what April was seeing now. The same old jasmine would have been flowering outside. Someone would have played this same piano. It was easy to picture the child Maddalena perched on the piano stool where the adult sat now, picking out the notes of 'Twinkle Twinkle Little Star' under the doting gaze of her father, while, surreptitiously, Irene pulled faces at her, trying to put her off.

On cue, Maddalena looked up.

'Do you remember this music?' She asked April. 'It's the "Prelude in E Minor" – the piece I had to learn for my piano exam at school.'

'I don't recognise it.'

'You do! You must have heard it a thousand times.'

'I don't recall you ever playing anything so melancholy.'

'That's because I didn't do melancholy back then. I used to race through it as fast as I could.'

As she listened, April stood by the open windows and inhaled the muskiness emitted by the jasmine flowers tumbling from the stems wound around the pergola. Sadness came creeping up to her; she embraced it, wrapped it round her like a cloak. The music was pulling at her emotions; it was reminding her of feelings she'd suppressed these last months; memories of Cobain too painful to revisit.

Maddalena finished the piece with a long, mournful chord.

'Don't stop playing, Maddi,' said April.

'I've exhausted my repertoire.'

'Play that last one again, then.'

'No. Something upbeat.'

She began to play 'Chopsticks'.

Troy, who had been lying beneath the piano, raised his head. His ears were pricked, the hackles on his honey coloured shoulders raised. Elissa and Tonio appeared around the corner of the villa and walked across the open windows.

Troy growled softly.

'Shhh,' said Maddalena, 'silly old dog. You know who they are.'

Neither Tonio nor Elissa looked into the house as they passed by and disappeared into the darkness.

'They're together, aren't they?' April asked.

'It looks that way,' said Maddalena.

'But he doesn't come into the villa.'

'My grandmother wouldn't allow it.'

'Because he's an Oliveri?'

'Yes.'

April dropped down onto an old chair close to the piano, and rested her chin on her hand. She gazed up at Maddalena. 'Why do the Borgatas and the Oliveris hate each other?'

'Because my mother, my *real* mother, Alia, was an Oliveri. And the two families fell out irreparably after Alia's death.'

45

IRENE

I've decided to go the whole hog. As well as the dress, I've put on the ruby brooch, and the hated tiara. Sod Donatella, *I thought,* she can have the full works.

Maddalena comes into the bedroom.

'What do you think?' I ask her, turning in the dress.

She wrinkles her nose.

'Exactly,' I say.

We go down to dinner.

Maddalena and Sam have bought me a present between them. It's an Italian Serie A footballing annual. It pleases me very much because I don't know much about Italian football and those involved, but this will help me learn. It will also expand my vocabulary.

My gift from Daria is a bar of soap, made from honey produced by local bees. It's designed for sensitive skin, and the gift also pleases me no end.

Giuseppa has set the table for a special meal, and I am touched that the family has gone to this trouble on my behalf. Patrick and Donatella turn up, he in a black suit with a bow tie, she in a gown far more glamorous than mine. She makes up her eyes like Cleopatra, outlined in black and with wings at the edges.

Patrick takes his place at one end of the table. His cheeks are flushed. He and I are going on a road trip tomorrow to look at a horse he's thinking of buying. Donatella is opposite him. Queen Bee. We say grace and we sit down to eat.

I can understand more of the language now, Jack. Being here, immersed in the Sicilian dialect, means it has made its way into my mind. I dream in Italian some nights. Sometimes I accidentally answer a question without thinking. I am not fluent by any means, but I'm improving.

That's why I know what Donatella says, when, as we are eating the spaghetti Norma that Giuseppa has cooked especially for me, she turns to Enzo and asks: 'Any signs that a baby is on the way yet?'

I bristle. I do not like her tone, nor the way she asks my husband about something that concerns me so intimately. Whether or not we are trying for a baby is none of her business. Neither is my reproductive system a suitable topic for discussion at the dinner table.

I exhale slowly and put down my fork. Enzo puts his hand on mine.

He squeezes.

It's such a small show of solidarity; not enough for his mother to notice, but I am grateful for his sensitivity.

Then he answers Donatella's question: 'Not yet, Mamma, but hopefully it won't be too long until we have some good news for you.'

Oh, really?

He dabs his lips with the napkin, and then takes a drink of his wine. He's a prissy drinker, not like his father, who knocks it back. I feel giddy and angry and sick, dressed up in a dress that I hate, feeling that I am being talked about as if I am a prize cow, my husband paying lip service to my feelings, but, every time, every single bloody time, siding with his mother.

46

'Can we talk about your mother's death, Maddi?' April asked.

Maddalena shrugged. 'I don't mind. I can only tell you what I've heard.'

'That's okay.'

'I know that Alia had a couple of late miscarriages before she was expecting me, so everyone was anxious as the pregnancy progressed. Alia's mother, my grandmother Oliveri, wanted to take her back home to Salgareale, so she and the local midwife could look after her. Donatella said she should stay here in Villa Alba. Donatella got her way, of course. The pregnancy went smoothly under Donatella's supervision right up to the birth. I was a big baby, and I was breech. Donatella had paid a top doctor to come and oversee the delivery, and she was certain he'd got everything covered. He wouldn't let the Oliveri's midwife into the room.'

'What happened?'

'Well, he got me out in the end. Alia was exhausted, but that was only to be expected. The next day the Oliveris were invited up to the villa to marvel at the newborn me. The bedroom was full of people taking turns to hold me while Alia was propped up in bed in a clean nightie putting a brave face on things. It looked as if a happy ending was on the cards.'

'But your mother was ill?'

Maddalena nodded.

'She was bleeding internally. The doctor hadn't realised and I imagine Donatella would have been so determined that everything was going to be perfect, that she wouldn't countenance the possibility that something might have gone wrong. Alia died within the week.'

'I'm so sorry.'

Maddi shuddered. 'I don't even know if she knew she was dying. But from the Oliveris' point of view, I can see it looked as if their beloved daughter had been neglected when she was at her most vulnerable.'

'It must have been awful for them.'

'That wasn't even the end of it,' said Maddalena. 'They wanted Alia's body back, so they could bury her in the municipal cemetery, but Donatella wasn't having that either. According to her, Alia, even dead Alia, belonged to the Borgatas. She was buried in the family tomb, in the graveyard here, at the villa, which, of course, made it difficult for the Oliveris to visit her.'

'What about you? Did you spend time with your Oliveri grandparents growing up?'

'When I was little. But as soon as I had a say in the matter, I chose not to go.'

'Why?'

'I was scared of them. Because they didn't see me that often, when they did see me, the visits were so intense I felt suffocated. I hated going to stay with them. Even though I was no more than a couple of miles away, I used to get desperately homesick.' Maddalena shook her head. 'Of course, Donatella used to tell me stories about the Oliveris, stories designed to turn me against them. She can be quite wicked when she sets her mind to it. By the time I figured out that I'd been manipulated, it was too late.'

'It's a sad story.'

'Irene, to her credit, tried to build bridges between the two families but Donatella regarded that as disloyalty, and put a stop to it. And then Irene disappeared. It's no wonder the people in Salgareale regard the Borgatas with such suspicion.'

'No.'

'I keep thinking that I ought to do something to make things better,' said Maddalena. Perhaps, if Elissa and Tonio make a go of things, that'll be the relationship that heals the rift.' She smiled. Then added: 'Tonio wasn't born an Oliveri.'

'No?'

'Both his parents died in the earthquake, and he was adopted. His blood isn't Oliveri blood. Not that that does anything to redeem him as far as Donatella's concerned.'

The drapes hanging at the window lifted then, as a warm draught of air came into the room. It must have blown down from the hill, coming through the trees and the little dark cemetery where Maddalena's mother lay buried.

47

IRENE

'Well,' says Patrick. 'What do you think?'

We are leaning on a fence that surrounds an exercise paddock, outside a grand stable building on a horse-trainer's compound high in the mountains, watching a young stallion being put through his paces at the end of a lunge line. He's a lovely creature, some sixteen hands high, chestnut in colour with a white flash on his forehead and four white socks. He holds his feet up something lovely and his gait and stride are a sight to see.

'I think he's perfect,' I say to my father-in-law.

Quintu, who has come with us, mutters something. He is not keen on this horse, he's already said. He finds Turi, that's the horse's name, hard to handle. I watched him tacking up, saw how clumsy he was, how rough, and I thought no wonder Turi doesn't like him. Quintu treats horses as if they don't have feelings and that's wrong. He thinks he can control them by showing them who's boss. Idiot.

This is a beautiful spot; breathtaking. The high slopes stretch around us. The air is cooler up here. The colours are muted. Around us are large fenced paddocks, with horses grazing; beautiful, healthy, content horses. You would love it here, Jack. You'd absolutely love it.

'Do you think you could do something with a horse like that?' Patrick asks me as the handler slows Turi to a fine extended trot.

'What do you mean?'

'Have some fun with him?'

I picture myself riding that beautiful animal. I try to imagine the two of us, out together in the Sicilian countryside, galloping like the wind, he with his handsome tail arching, his ears pricked forward.

'I'd love to get to know him,' I say.

'Good,' says Patrick, grinning, showing off his charming, crooked teeth, 'That settles it then. I've made up my mind to buy him.'

48

That evening, the atmosphere in the Borgata household was more relaxed.

Conti did not make an appearance on the *Serata* television programme. April had fully expected him to be filmed standing triumphantly beside the bloodstained passenger seat from Enzo's Alfa Romeo. Instead, there was a long item about a famous singer, who had unexpectedly arrived off the coast of Sicily in a luxury yacht and had been spotted dining in a restaurant at Taormina.

It also helped that Tonio and Sam had successfully set up the security camera at the front gate. It was motion-sensitive and recorded directly to video. Hopefully its presence would act as a deterrent to any potential troublemakers.

After dinner, Donatella said she felt well enough to take her coffee outside, on the terrace. The rest of the family was clearly expected to keep her company. April was glad to be able to say goodnight to the group and go upstairs to her room alone.

On the landing, she stood for a few minutes beside the door to Irene's room, listening. There was no sound from inside, no hint of movement, nothing at all.

April went into her room, changed into her short, cotton pyjamas, took off her make-up, turned on the lamp on the desk, and sat down. She opened her laptop, returned to the file she'd made about the Borgata family, and filled in the blanks with information she'd amassed during the day.

While she was doing this, her phone pinged with an incoming message. It was from Inspector Mazzotta.

Looking at case notes now. Let me know if you find anything of interest.

April replied:

Will do. Thank you for lunch.

Then she did what she'd been longing to do ever since she and Maddalena left Palermo six hours earlier and returned her attention to her set of case notes.

She opened the file, turned the sheets until she reached the copy of Enzo and Irene's marriage certificate, the last document she'd already examined. Paperclipped to the back of the certificate were two more pieces of paper.

The first was a copy of a typewritten letter from Inspector Steven Hathaway of the West Riding of Yorkshire Police addressed to a colleague in Palermo. The letter was dated Wednesday, 12 June 1968, and was in English.

Dear Inspector Costanzo,

Thank you for your telegrams of 2, 3 and 5 June. Following our subsequent telephone conversation, I dispatched a colleague to visit Mr Arthur Weatherbury and his wife, Elsie, at their home in Halifax Row, Beal, this morning as per your request. Constable Elphick spoke to both Mr and Mrs Weatherbury, who informed him they had received no letter or other communication from their 'headstrong' daughter, Irene, since an argument in January, 1963, when she informed them on the telephone of her intention to marry a suitor of whom they disapproved – the second time this situation had occurred.

Oh, April thought, *they weren't happy about the wedding, then.*

And what did that last part of the sentence mean? The second time what situation had occurred? Irene planning to marry someone her parents didn't like? She was only nineteen, had she already been engaged before she met Enzo?

She read on:

Mr Weatherbury stated that the potential groom was foreign, and also a decade older than Irene, which he and his wife considered an unacceptable age gap.

Mr Weatherbury is a respected member of his community, being chairman of the bowling club, senior warden at his Masonic Lodge and a regular attendee at St John the Baptist Church in Selby where, he says, any member of the congregation would vouch for his good character.

He started work as a mining apprentice when he was fourteen, later retraining as a mechanical engineer, maintaining and fixing the operating equipment, including lift mechanisms, pumping engines and conveyor belt systems. He is a dab hand with motor car engines too. His good lady wife is a regular churchgoer and a stalwart of the local Women's Institute group.

When they last spoke to their daughter, Mr and Mrs Weatherbury had vigorously urged her not to marry Signor Borgata, they being of a belief that such a union would not end well. Mr Weatherbury pointed out that Irene's subsequent disappearance proved that they had been right.

'Charming!' whispered April.

The second piece of paper was a copy of a cutting from the London *Evening News*, with a handwritten the date at the top: 4 November 1962.

The headline read:

Hero dies in child rescue bid.

The article was brief.

A man has died after selflessly leaping into freezing water to rescue a drowning child.

The tragedy came about after schoolboy, Eddie Greene, 10, of Nursery Road, Lambeth, climbed onto an icy wall, lost his footing and fell into the River Thames, close to London Bridge.

A passer-by, one Jack Harding, 21, on his way to work as barman at the Pimlico Hotel in Victoria, saw the boy enter the water at about 4 p.m., just as dusk was falling. Without any consideration for his own well-being, Mr Harding took off his coat and boots and jumped in. He managed to bring the child to shore, but was too weak to scramble up the bank himself, and, despite the best efforts of those people who tried to help him, slipped underwater.

A body was later retrieved some distance downstream.

Jack Harding was working in London, but originally came from Knottingley, a mining community in North Yorkshire, where his parents, Jean and Howard, still live. Before moving to London, he was employed at the William Marrs racing stables, where he rode out the horses and helped with training. He was engaged to be married to former stable hand, Irene Weatherbury, 19, also from North Yorkshire, but currently living in London and also working at the Pimlico Hotel, Victoria.

April laid down the piece of paper and rested her face against the palm of her hand.

No wonder she had felt a connection with the disappeared Irene. The young woman had also lost the love of her life.

Her heart must have been breaking too.

49

IRENE

I'm leaning forward in the saddle, almost standing in the stirrups, and beneath me Turi gallops along the track that leads up the hill. His hooves thunder, scattering pebbles, clouding the dust, I can hear his panting, and I can smell the heat of him as he pounds the ground. The warm air is in my face, my hair streams behind me. I feel as if Turi's muscles extend into my back, as if we are one being; we are so perfectly balanced. And his neck stretches out ahead of me, his ears pricked, his mane flying, and his shoulders rising and falling and I remember you telling me how good it feels to gallop a keen horse and at last I know what you mean.

I've never ridden like this before. Bill Marrs wouldn't let me take out the racehorses at the stables where we met, no matter how I begged him, do you remember? He said it was too dangerous 'for a girl'; that the gallops were men's work.

I wish Bill could see me now! I'm flying, Jack, flying!

Turi runs like the wind. He's like the tide rushing into the bay. He is a force of nature.

We're alone, he and I. We're racing through the hills, across miles and miles of barren land. It's like the wild west. It's like being immortal. I could stay out here forever. I have never felt so free. No, that's not true. I felt free when I was with you, my darling. I had that same feeling of joy.

What a gift Patrick has given me. Oh, God, this is better than diamonds, or gowns. He has given me freedom. He's given me a friend.

Patrick warned me not to go too far. There are bandits around, he says, but I'm not afraid. Turi could outrun any horse and no car or motorbike would manage this terrain. Turi is fleet and strong and sure-footed and brave. He has a big heart. There's dust in my mouth and the blood is pumping in my veins.

I'm more alive than I have been since that awful evening when the police came to the Pimlico Hotel.

That evening when they sat me down in front of the gas fire in the guests' lounge and held their hats in their hands and told me, 'Sorry, Miss,' that you were dead.

I won't think of it again.

I'll think of you, but not that night. That's the past. This is now.

I'm back to my old self, Jack. I'm galloping with this beautiful creature, beneath this big, bright sun and this high, wide sky, with Patrick's cowboy hat on my head and I'm thinking of you, and, honest to God, it's like you're here with me, beside me in the wind.

50

THURSDAY 14 AUGUST 2003

Two days until Conti's TV exposé

April had another restless night. There were no noises, this time, from the room next door to hers, no footsteps on the path below her window, but she couldn't settle to sleep. She kept replaying Irene's story in her mind and feeling a combination of pity and admiration for the young woman. She imagined her in some small room in the eaves of the Pimlico Hotel, trying to keep warm beside an inadequate coal fire, chilblains on her toes and her back aching from the waitressing work, wondering how she was going to get through the rest of her life without her drowned sweetheart.

Did Irene identify the body, April wondered, or was she spared that ordeal? Normally, the authorities insisted on a spouse or a close relative. They might have sent for Jack's parents instead.

And what about the inquest? There would have been one, but probably by that time Irene was here in Sicily, with Enzo.

Irene's reasons for marrying Enzo were crystal clear to April now. She had needed a route away from her old life. She was too proud to go back to her parents – April could imagine how they would have taken satisfaction from their daughter's despair, thinking it served her right for going against their wishes. Marrying a wealthy Sicilian must have seemed like the answer to Irene's prayers.

But was any of this relevant to what came later, to Irene's disappearance?

April turned over in the bed, the fan turning above her. It clunked softly at each rotation and the sound drifted into April's consciousness and became a kind of rhythm to her half-sleep; like a heartbeat.

* * *

In the morning, when the light coming through the window was strong enough to wake April, she got up, showered, fetched her swimming things from the balcony, and went downstairs. She went through the villa and out to the pool, which was empty save a few fallen bougainvillea flowers turning slowly on the surface, and a large bee, swimming frantically, which she rescued and placed on a rose to dry out.

In the bright early morning light, she climbed down the steps, catching her breath at the coldness of the water, and then dropped in until her body was submerged and swam with silvery dragonflies dipping around her. She counted to thirty lengths and then, feeling warm, with her blood pumping, and more awake, she came out of the pool to dry off and change back into villa-appropriate clothing.

She had a towel wrapped around her head and was almost dressed when she noticed a thin curl of smoke rising up from amongst the cypress trees and the giant Indian fig cacti that climbed the side of the hill around them. It was only one single wisp, and then it stopped, but it was out of place.

April finished dressing, put on her sandals and set off across the garden in the direction of the smoke. She followed a narrow path through a hole in the rosemary hedge and walked steeply upwards through a pine woodland. The ground underfoot was hard and rocky, slippery with pine needles and cones. Eventually she came to a clearing, a patch of land that was used as a dumping ground for old furniture and other rubbish from the villa; it was piled together in a heap, broken chairs and an old standing lamp with a huge, crumpled shade, a microwave oven, a vacuum cleaner, a refrigerator. All the things, thought April, that had probably been meant to be taken away to be recycled, or to a municipal refuse facility, but that nobody had ever got round to removing. Three large wooden compost bays at one corner contained garden and kitchen waste in various stages of decomposition, although none looked as if they'd been touched for a while. There was a rusty wheelbarrow, and several old oil drums. One of these was the source of the smoke.

It was some distance away from April. Beside it was a plastic container of the kind used to carry petrol and decant it into cars. Also beside it was a figure, with its back to April: Giuseppa.

April stayed back, amongst the trees, and as she watched, Giuseppa picked up the can and sloshed some of its contents into the smoking drum. There was a flash and an explosion as the stuff ignited. Giuseppa stepped back, lifting an arm to her forehead, to protect her eyes from the heat. It had been a horribly dangerous thing to do.

April withdrew back into the woodland, sat on a stump and watched and waited until the flames had burned low. Now Giuseppa, fanning herself with her hand, peered into the drum and, seemingly satisfied, covered it, containing the smoke inside. She took the plastic can into a rickety old tool shed, then headed back towards the villa.

April waited until Giuseppa was out of sight, and then came out of her hiding place and went to the oil drum. The air around and above it shimmered as she drew close, and she could feel the heat pumping out. She used the handle of a rake to lift the lid. Thick smoke gushed into the sky. April let it disperse and then she stepped forward and peered inside.

She did not know what she was expecting to see, but, certainly, it was not what she found. Because there, in the drum, were the disassembled components of the seat of a classic Alfa Romeo sports car. The leather upholstery had shrivelled horribly and hung in strips like charred meat. It was so burned that it was quite impossible to tell whether or not it had ever been stained with Irene Borgata's blood.

51

IRENE

January 1966

The years are slipping by — can you believe Enzo and I will soon be celebrating our third wedding anniversary? Everything is changing, Jack, except my love for you. That remains the same. Time doesn't diminish it, not at all. You are a diamond that I keep in my heart. When I take out my memories, and hold them up to the light, they shine as brightly as ever.

    Maddalena is eight now. What a darling child she is! A total tomboy, much to her grandmother's chagrin, and my delight! She's clever too. When Enzo is here, she is compelled to play the diva, showing off and playing up as if to prove to me that he loves her more than he loves me, no matter how badly she behaves. But when he's away, like now, she seeks out my company. In the cold months, she'll bring her book, or her colouring pencils, and sit beside me, reading or drawing while I read the horse magazines I've ordered to be sent from Britain. In summer, we'll go into the pool together and play chaotic games, one of us being a shark or a crocodile, chasing the other. Donatella dislikes the noise. She has also forbidden me to take Maddalena riding. She says she's concerned for the child's safety. I think, really, that she's afraid Maddi will turn into a mini version of me rather than the little Donatella that her grandmother would like her to be.

Now that it's winter – and God! Jack, the winters can be cold! – Maddi and I sit by the fire and chat about this and that. I can make her laugh by being irreverent. I teach her some jokes. I talk about you, although I never tell her your name. 'My amazing friend,' I say, 'who worked with me at the stables,' and I tell her stories about the things we used to do; the fun we used to have; riding in the horseboxes; bringing in the hay; getting up before dawn to prepare the horses for point-to-points.

James, by the way, has grown into a beauty; a good seventeen hands high but gentle as a lamb. Patrick and I are handling him together and he's coming on a treat.

The only fly in the ointment is Quintu. I saw him, the other day, whipping James with a length of stick because he wouldn't go into the stable. I should hate to see him treating any horse in that awful way, but James is so close to my soul that I literally couldn't bear it. I wanted to tear off Quintu's head! I challenged Quintu – he pretended he couldn't understand what I was saying, so I fetched Patrick and told him. There was a big row, Patrick shouting at Quintu, and Quintu shouting back, pointing at me, gesticulating. And James, who is the sweetest soul, stood in his stable (where he'd gone meek as a lamb when I asked him nicely), chewing his hay.

Afterwards, Patrick said he's had enough of Quintu. He said he'll look out for a new stable hand.

'You could employ me,' I said. I had a little fantasy, imagining myself moved into the cottage by the stables, out of Enzo's bed, living an independent life; me and the horses and Patrick and my memories. I thought that Maddi could come and stay with me on the days when Enzo was away on business; and Sam too, if he wanted. I imagined me, pottering around in my own space, free to spend as much time as I wanted with James, telling him about you. Perhaps, I thought, I could learn to drive; take myself off into Palermo; make some new friends.

All these thoughts flashed through my head in the smallest moment.

Then Patrick looked at me, as if to check that I was joking. I grinned, to show that I was.

52

At breakfast, Giuseppa was her usual, busy self, fussing around the family, replenishing the coffee pot. She had changed into a clean dress and there were no obvious smuts on her face to indicate what she'd been up to that morning, neither did she appear out of sorts. Donatella did not put in an appearance.

April had no appetite. She had been profoundly unsettled by what she had witnessed in the clearing. It hadn't been Conti interfering with the potential evidence, but a member of the Borgata household. Why? What was the older woman afraid might be revealed by the bloodstained seat?

As soon as she politely could, she left the others with their coffee, sitting in the sunshine, and went back up to her room where she sat on the bed and called Inspector Mazzotta. The phone rang a couple of times and then diverted to voicemail.

She cut off the call, and at the same moment Maddalena appeared.

'Would you like to come and see the cursed portrait of Irene?'

'Now?'

'Why not?'

'Okay. Sure.'

They went down to the grand living room. Light was streaming through the dusty windows, making rectangles and lozenges on the floor-boards, highlighting the threadbare nature of the enormous tapestry rug and sparkling from the spangles of the chandelier.

'Over here,' said Maddalena.

She tugged at the head end of an enormous old chaise longue, placed in front of a cupboard.

April went to help her and together they shifted the chaise far enough for Maddalena to unlock and open the door behind it to reveal a large cupboard built into the alcove. She stepped half inside and tugged at an object about a metre high, wrapped in an old grey dustsheet and pushed behind boxes of jigsaws and board games.

They managed, between them, to manoeuvre it out and propped it against the chaise. Carefully, Maddalena uncovered it.

'Can you see it? Shall we move it into the light? There!'

It was an oil painting; a picture of a young woman wearing a pale blue dress with a bow over one shoulder. The portrait showed only the top half of her body. She was gazing out of the frame, directly at the artist. Her hair was honey brown in colour, with the ends flicked out on either side over her shoulders. Her eyes were apple green, and her upper eyelashes were heavy, as if she was wearing false eyelashes, and the artist had attempted to reproduce the cosmetic effect without making it obvious. Her head was held high, her shoulders straight, and there was something almost confrontational in the directness of her gaze. She was not simpering, or flirting, or trying to show her best side. She was saying: *Here I am, this is me, take me or leave me.*

The image was striking, but even more so was the fact that the canvas had been slashed in several places, one of the cuts tearing across the young woman's cheek, one diagonally across her lips, the largest and most violent slash in the place where her heart would have been. The vicious deliberateness of the desecration, the obvious symbolism of the posi-tioning of the cuts, sent a chill through April. Whoever did this had acted out of hate. It was as if they were saying to the woman in the portrait: *I'm going to defile and destroy you.*

'Wow,' she said softly. 'There's a lot to take in here.'

'I know.'

'When was the portrait painted?' April asked.

'Enzo had it done as a present for Irene on their first wedding anniversary.'

April leaned down to look at the slashes. The canvas was hanging from Irene's cheek, exactly as if her skin had been cut.

'Do you know who vandalised it?'

'Nobody knows. Enzo wanted to have it repaired but Nonna wouldn't let him.'

'Why not?'

'Imagine what would have been said if he had turned up at the restorer's shop in Salgareale with a portrait of missing Irene slashed to shreds when people were still unhappy about the circumstances of Alia's death.'

'I can see that would have been difficult.'

'All their darkest suspicions about the Borgatas would have been vindicated.'

April smiled. 'So when exactly did this damage happen?'

'Around the time of the earthquake.'

'A few months before Irene disappeared.'

'Yes.'

'And it was slashed while it was here, in the villa?'

'Yes, it used to be hung here, in this room over the fireplace, where the picture of Selinunte is now.'

April knelt in front of the picture so that her eyes were on a level with Irene's. Carefully, she moved the torn canvas with a tip of a finger, so she could look behind it. The blade that had been used to pierce the material had been wielded with such force that it had marked the board behind, making a deep scar across the wood.

'It's creepy, isn't it?' said Maddalena.

'Disturbing.'

'We'd better put it away before anything bad happens.'

'You don't really believe it's cursed?'

'I just don't like looking at it!'

They re-covered the portrait with the blanket and manipulated it back into the cupboard, shut the door and Maddalena turned the little key in the old lock.

She padded over to the drinks cabinet in her bare feet, took the stopper out of a heavy, cut-glass carafe and sniffed the contents. 'I'm not sure what it is but it smells okay. Do you want one?'

'It's a bit early for that, isn't it?'

Maddalena shrugged. 'That picture freaks me out. I'd forgotten how bad it was.'

April sat on an elaborate sofa. She watched a dragonfly dart into the room and hover in front of one of the huge mirrors, as if admiring its own reflection.

Maddalena blew dust out of a shot glass and filled it with drink.

'Giuseppa told me your grandmother wasn't keen on Irene,' April said.

'She wasn't. Irene wasn't at all the kind of woman Nonna would have wanted Papa to marry. She wasn't Catholic, she wasn't even religious, neither was she Sicilian, nor the daughter of a business associate, or a politician, or some other person of status. The way it happened didn't help… Papa going to London on tuna-selling business and coming back with a much younger English wife he'd met in a hotel. She didn't tick *any* of the boxes. Also, Irene was one of the few people in the entire world who wasn't scared of Donatella.'

Maddalena sat down beside April and tucked her feet up to one side. She took a sip of her drink, pulled a face, and drank again.

'Was Donatella really that scary?'

'She was like an angry crow. I used to have nightmares about her. She said she could read my mind and I believed her because she always seemed to know what I was up to.' She laughed, as if this were a happy memory, but her eyes told April that it was not. 'She used to tell me stories about how terrible things happened to disobedient girls. Irene said that wasn't true. She said Nonna was trying to bully me into being obedient, which was a highly overrated quality.'

'Donatella wouldn't have liked that.'

'No. She didn't know how to handle Irene. She wasn't used to having a dissenter in the ranks. Then after the earthquake, when Irene lost her leg, well, for weeks Nonna walked around with an expression on her face which was kind of: *Well, she got exactly what was coming to her.*'

Maddalena lay back and draped one arm over the side of the sofa.

'And it was even worse after she disappeared. Nonna was practically exploding with self-righteousness. Papa went so deep into his shell that I thought he'd never come out, and Sam went really weird too, he was no fun any more, and there was so much trouble from the people of Salgareale pointing fingers at us, saying losing one wife was bad enough, but two was proof of evil at work.'

She sighed, and ran her fingers through her hair.

'That was why they sent me to boarding school in England, to keep me away from all the suspicion and finger-pointing that happened after Irene disappeared, and that's why I used to hate coming back here in the school holidays. Why, if there was a choice, I would always choose to stay at school. Of course, I loved it when the two of us went to the summer house with Papa. But not here. I didn't like coming here after Irene disappeared because here was awful. Toxic. I spent as little time here as I could and if I could have stayed away for ever, that's what I would have done.'

53

IRENE

Oh, Jack, guess what! The magazines I have sent over from England arrived this week. And, in Groom and Jockey, *there is a feature about the William Marrs stables! Six pages of it! My hands were shaking as I turned the pages, Jack. 'Please,' I was begging, 'please let there be a photograph,' and there was! There we were, all the staff, lined up in the yard. It was the same picture Bill used to have hanging in the mess room, the one taken that summer after Billy's Venture won the Gold Cup, with us posed in rows, short-arses at the front, tall ones at the back, and the horses looking out of their stables behind us.*

Oh, your face, your beautiful face! Your smile! That lopsided smile you used to have when the sun was in your eyes and you were squinting.

I remember that photograph being taken. I remember how we all messed around, trying to make one another laugh. I remember afterwards, you in the feed room measuring out the buckets, and the dust and the sunlight and us not realising how happy we were.

Can you imagine how I felt, seeing us pictured together in that magazine, my love? I want to cut out that page, have it framed and hung in the bedroom so I can look at you, us, before I go to sleep.

I can't, of course. I can't have your face on display here. Instead, I tear the page out of the magazine, and I fold it carefully, so that none of the creases are on the image of you, and I take it up to the stables and tuck it in the crack in the wall of the end stable, Turi's stable.

Now when I am up there, with him, and nobody else is around, I can take out the sheet of paper and open it up, and I can look at you; me; us. I can look into your face. I can remember the warmth of your shoulder, next to mine.

I can remember how it felt to be perfectly happy.

How I wish we had realised what we had, at the time.

54

April went into the garden. The sun was high in the sky and the air was hot, a warm breeze whispering. The silvery greens of the foliage, and the pale golds of the seedheads of the herbs that grew amongst the purple and dusty pink phlomis and lavender, were beautiful but unfamiliar. This Sicilian garden, with its low walls and its potted palms, its espaliered peach trees and ancient olive trees, must have been anathema to Irene. She'd have been brought up with allotments and greenhouses and people keeping a couple of chickens in coops in their damp back yards, and beyond would have been the moors: green and purple and grey; boggy and cloudy and cold.

Her phone rang, jolting her out of her introspection. It was Inspector Mazzotta.

He was brisk.

'I missed a call from you this morning.'

'I wanted to update you on a couple of—'

'Have you read all the witness statements yet?' He was walking. April could hear traffic noises behind him and he was breathing heavily, holding the phone to his ear.

'No, but I read the letter from the Yorkshire police and—'

'There's a disparity. Look at Daria's statement and then at Sam's. Or vice versa. One of them was lying.'

'Okay, thanks, I—'

'Got to go. I'll speak to you later.'

The line went dead.

55

IRENE

May 1966

Enzo and I argued today. He's been away on business, and he wanted us to spend the day together. But I haven't been able to ride Turi for two weeks because he's been lame and he needs some gentle exercise.

I told Enzo that I needed to see to Turi. I said we could have dinner together this evening, that we could maybe go into Salgareale, just the two of us, and eat at a restaurant, but he said: 'No, we can't do that. Quintu shot a boar at the weekend, and Giuseppa has butchered it. Mother has asked Giuseppa to cook something special for the whole family.'

And she, Donatella, who was in the room with us (she's always in the same room as Enzo), she looked at me over the top of her reading glasses and said: 'I'd have thought you'd be pleased to spend some time with your husband when he works so hard to support you, Irene.'

I don't think Enzo actually does support me. I think it's the family's existing supply of money that does that. But that's splitting hairs.

What's mithering me is that he can bugger off for a week leaving me here, and then expect me to do exactly what his mother wants me to do when he comes back. Why doesn't he tell her that my life is none of her business? Why doesn't he stand up for me?

Also, the baby issue has raised its ugly head, <u>again!</u>

Donatella wants me to see a doctor. I said absolutely not, no way.

Now, Donatella tells Enzo about this exchange. Enzo's face is a picture of awkwardness; her on one side, me on the other, both of us in a stand-off and he not knowing which of us to favour.

'I don't need to see a doctor,' I say, and I reiterate, for both Enzo and Donatella's benefits: 'There's nothing wrong with me.'

Donatella's lips are thin and tight. 'You've been married three years,' she says. 'You should have fallen pregnant by now.'

Enzo sees the murderous look on my face.

'Dear Mother,' he says, 'I know how badly you want our family to grow, but Irene's not even halfway through her twenties yet. There's plenty of time for babies.'

He looks at me then like he deserves a medal for sticking up for me. I glare back.

Why doesn't he understand how humiliating this kind of talk is? I wasn't put on this earth to produce children to make other people happy! It's not my duty!

'Irene doesn't want to wait much longer,' says Donatella, speaking about me in the third person as if I wasn't here. She adopts a concerned look. 'The older the mother, the more likely that things will go wrong.' Which is nonsense. My auntie, Hilda, was forty-six when her Stanley was born and she had him no trouble.

Enzo has never asked about my love life, if there was anyone before him. He assumes he is my first lover; he likes to think of me as being naïve and innocent; someone he can mould. He is confused by my refusal to be moulded.

Sod Enzo. Sod Donatella. I've come up to the stables anyway. Turi is pleased to see me. He whinnies and blows into my hair while I'm grooming him; feeding him pony nuts from my pocket, kissing his warm cheek. I love every inch of him. He rubs his head against the knuckles of my hand. The two of us are so deeply connected.

Oh, Jack... I'm finding it tough, these days, to keep going. To keep being Enzo's wife, I mean. I know I put myself in this situation, and I don't really have *the right to complain, but I'm finding it harder and harder to be nice to him. Harder and harder to look interested when he tells me some interminable, boring story about bloody tuna. And, since I know you're wondering, almost impossible to show even the tiniest bit of enthusiasm when he reaches across the bed to me at night.*

I won't have a child with him.

I can't.

It would be the worst thing I could do.

56

April opened the windows in her room as wide as she could and she sat at the desk and read the Borgata family's witness statements while the gauze curtains billowed gently to one side.

She read Sam's first – having already spoken to him, she thought it would be easy to spot any differences between the written account and the verbal account he'd given her previously; but the statement pretty much backed up what he'd told her before.

'Okay,' said April, laying the statement to one side. 'Let's see what you had to say, Daria.'

Daria's statement said that Daria had been at work for most of that day. She was an assistant at Franco's pharmacy in Salgareale and had worked from 9 a.m. to 5 p.m. At 5 p.m. she had driven home in her Cinquecento. She'd left the car by the villa gates, at the far end of the drive, because she knew her parents were expecting a number of visitors that evening and she didn't want her car to be in their way, neither did she want it to be trapped in. She'd helped herself to a slice of pizza from the kitchen, and then gone upstairs to her bedroom to wash and change – so Daria must still have been living here, in the villa at that time. At 7 p.m. she'd gone downstairs, at her mother's request, to help serve refreshments to the guests.

Not long after that, Enzo came to find her. He was 'panicky and covered in dust'. He said his car had broken down near Gibellina and he'd left Irene in it while he came back to the villa to get help. Daria picked up her car keys and told him not to worry, she'd drive him back to Gibellina at once.

As they were going back along the drive, past the cars of her father's guests, they encountered Sam coming the other way. He was pushing his bicycle. They didn't talk to him because they were in a rush to get back to Irene, but Sam was in a state. He'd tried to hide it, but he looked as if he'd been crying.

57

IRENE

June 1966

Quintu has moved out of the cottage by the stables. Hurrah!

He packed his belongings (minimal) into the back of his smelly old truck and buggered off back to Gibellina. Tomorrow he is getting married to a girl he's known since they were both at school. They're going to set up home in Gibellina and he will drive down to the villa each working day to do his handy-manning.

I am SO relieved that he won't be around so much any more, Jack. I dislike everything about that man. He has a nasty streak inside him that manifests as cruelty to the horses. Patrick hasn't let him near them for months, and I know Quintu (rightfully) blames me for that, but tough. He spends his days now fixing the mortar in the walls around the villa, replacing ancient pipes, tending to the garden and burning rubbish.

I would prefer him not to be in the villa at all, but Patrick says Donatella regards him as part of the family. Quintu's family and her family go back a long way. Those kinds of connections are important round here. It's like the Masons back home, but with bells on.

Quintu spat on the ground, close to my feet today, while I was up at the stable yard, and he was clearing out the cottage. His spit made a dark patch in the ochre dust. Then he looked at me, as if willing me to make something of it.

'Off you fuck, you horrible man,' I said to him in English, smiling my sweetest smile, flicking back my hair. 'And I hope to God your poor wife-to-be knows what she's letting herself in for.'

Good riddance. If I never saw him again, it would be too soon.

58

Giuseppa was kneading dough at the kitchen table when April walked in. Behind her, something that smelled deliciously of tomato and garlic was bubbling inside a huge pan on the hob and a tray of pastries, golden brown and fluffy, was cooling by the window.

'Ciau,' said Giuseppa. 'Are you hungry?'

April had been at the Villa Alba long enough to know that the correct answer to this question was always: 'Yes.'

'I am a little now you mention it.'

Giuseppa tried her best to look put upon, but her pleasure at this response was evident. She began to dust the flour from her hands.

'I made a tomato salad earlier, and there's some fresh-baked ciabatta. How does that sound?'

'Divine,' said April, truthfully.

'Sit down,' said Giuseppa. 'I'll bring it to you.'

The kitchen table was enormous, quite large enough to accommodate Giuseppa's bread-making at one end with several people sitting down to eat at the other; and it was so old it might have been medieval.

'Could you tell me a little more about Daria?' April asked Giuseppa as the older woman busied herself with a bowl, cutlery and a napkin.

'What do you want to know?'

'How did she and Irene get on?'

'They didn't have much to do with one another.'

'But they were close in age, weren't they?'

'That's right. Daria must have been sixteen or seventeen when Enzo and Irene were wed.'

'Was she already working at the pharmacy?'

'Yes.'

'So she was out during the days?'

'Yes, and she kept herself to herself in the evenings, up in her bedroom. She's always been like that, mind. Always a bit of a loner. Enzo too. Sam was the only really friendly child, the one everybody loved. He's still the same now.'

Giuseppa took a bowl out of the fridge and placed it on the table.

April asked, 'Do you remember the evening that Irene disappeared?'

'I'm hardly likely to forget an evening like that one. I'd had to prepare refreshments for twenty-four guests. Twenty-four! And Donatella was insistent it was the best quality everything. I'd ordered a huge flank of beef; spent heaven knows how much on shellfish and butter. I'd been cooking all day and I was rushed off my feet, all the comings and goings; people turning up in cars. It wasn't just the men who'd come for the meeting – half of them had drivers who were hanging about on the terrace, smoking and drinking coffee. Some of them had brought their wives. They needed attending to as well. Food and drink. Always someone wanting something. All the time.'

'Sam told me he'd been out hunting rabbits that day with a friend.'

'That's right.' She put bread on the table, and the pepper pot. 'They called it "hunting" but they never caught anything. They'd go out with their shotguns and walk through the mountains all day, until they got so hungry they came back.'

'What time did Sam return that evening?'

'About seven o'clock. He was sitting at this table, right where you are now, eating his soup when Enzo came in.'

'Okay. And how was Sam?'

'What do you mean: "How was he?" He was the same as he always was after a day out "hunting". Tired, hungry, in need of a good bath.'

'But he didn't seem upset about anything?'

'No. He was on fine form. Why are you asking? Has somebody said something to you about Sam that night?'

'Nobody's said anything to me, no. But in Daria's witness statement, she said Sam wasn't home until after Enzo, and that he, Sam, seemed distressed.'

'Well, she was wrong. He was tired, certainly. And dirty. But not distressed. No.'

'And he was definitely home before Enzo came in?'

'Well before. At least half an hour, I'd say.'

59

Jack, you won't believe what's happened now! Donatella has only gone and bought me a doll! A baby girl-doll with real yellow hair and eyes that open and shut, and even eyelashes (ugh!) and rosebud lips with a little hole in the centre, into which you could, if you were so inclined, insert the tip of the feeding bottle that came with her.

When you bend her forwards, she says: 'Mamma!'

She was presented to me in a big box, beautifully gift-wrapped. When I opened the paper and saw what was inside, I thought it must be some kind of joke. Daria, who was in the room with me, didn't understand what was going on either.

'Is this meant for Maddalena?' I asked.

'No,' said Donatella. 'She is for you.'

'I'm a little old for dolls, Donatella.'

'It's a special kind of doll, designed to promote maternal feelings. She's been on order from a shop in Rome. Each is individually made, like a real baby. I asked for a doll that would look how your and Enzo's child might look when he or she eventually arrives.'

Really?

Daria, perched on her chair, put her elbows on her knees and her chin in her hands. She was observing the scene unfolding with a kind of appalled fascination; in the same way I once watched a gull drown a pigeon. I am horrified, but at the same time impressed by Donatella's brass neck. She would give my mother a run for her money.

'She's called Bella,' said Donatella.

I don't even get to choose her name. I caught Daria's eye. Daria didn't blink. She was not prepared to ally herself with me.

There was nobody else I could turn to for support, there being only me and her and Donatella in the living room, with the wrapping on the floor and the doll in her box between us.

Donatella produced a wicker basket. 'These are for her too.'

The basket contained a layette for the doll: exquisite, tiny knitted clothes, dresses, bonnets, bootees, nappies, even plastic pants and nappy pins and talcum powder. Real baby clothes!

'You want me to play with her?' I asked.

'I want you to look after her. Treat her as you would treat a real baby. Nurture her. You will be surprised how quickly your body starts to respond.'

I am like a ewe that has lost her lamb, being presented with an orphan lamb wrapped in the pelt of her dead offspring.

'Thank you,' I said to Donatella, because what else could I say?

I took the doll and the basket and brought them upstairs and put them in the dressing room behind the bathroom at the back of our bedroom.

And now, I sit on the bed and look at the photograph of Alia, looking back at me with that serious expression on her face, and I think: You could have warned me.

The rest of my life is going to be like this, isn't it?

What am I going to do, Jack? How am I going to bear it?

I thought I was marrying into a dream. It's turning into a nightmare.

60

Giuseppa went back to her kneading. April ate for a few minutes – the food really was delicious – before she resumed her questioning.

'Daria was still living here, in the villa, at the time of Irene's disappearance, wasn't she?'

'Yes. She didn't move into the cottage until later in the year, after Patrick sold the horses.'

'Why did he do that?'

'His heart wasn't in it any more. Even looking at them made him sad. He said they reminded him too much of Irene.'

'So the cottage was empty until Daria moved in?'

'It had been empty since the earthquake, yes. Before the earthquake, the stable hand was living there.'

'Oh? I didn't see any mention of a stable hand in the police case notes.'

'You wouldn't have. He died in the earthquake. He was in the stables with Irene when the wall collapsed.'

'Irene and the stable hand were there together?'

'Yes.'

'How come?'

'The horses had been brought in at night on account of the cold. They were moving them back out into the paddock, where they'd be safer.'

April thought for a moment. Then she said, 'The earthquake was in the early hours of the morning, wasn't it?'

'The first tremor was, yes.'

'So... just so I'm clear in my mind, Irene went up to the stables *after* she'd been woken by the quake?'

'No. She was already there.'

'Why?'

'Turi, her horse – she adored him! – had been behaving oddly all day, and she couldn't sleep for worrying about what might be wrong so she'd left Enzo sleeping and gone to the stables.' Giuseppa lifted the dough into a bowl and covered it with a cloth. 'Animals have a sixth sense for natural disasters, you know. There were lots of stories about creatures acting strangely in the hours before the earthquake. Trouble was, people were too stupid or too busy to pay them any heed.'

April tried to think of a sensitive way to phrase the next question.

'I suppose Irene would have been good friends with the stable hand, she being so involved with the horses?' she asked.

Giuseppa was silent for a beat too long before she answered.

'He and Irene spent a lot of time together, yes.'

* * *

The day was drawing on. The villa was quiet. Sam, Elissa and Maddalena were in Palermo, Daria was at work. April decided to go back to the stables.

She went to her room to fetch the camera, and while she was there, she started to write a text to Inspector Mazzotta.

Borgata housekeeper confirmed Sam's version of events. Hinted that Irene was—

That she was what? Involved with the stable hand? Having an affair with him?

Giuseppa hadn't actually said anything. All she'd done was answer a slightly leading question of April's with a response so subtle in its insinuation that, if anyone were to ask Giuseppa what she had meant by it, she could easily deny that she meant anything at all.

April deleted the words she had written.

She put the camera strap over her shoulder, and left the house.

The breeze had dropped and the afternoon heat was stultifying.

She walked on, following the path that led up to the stables, the same route that Irene would have taken. She too would have walked in and out of bright pools of sunlight and alternating dark splashes of shadow. She would have disturbed the lizards basking on the stone, heard the doves cooing in the trees, and the wrens would have been darting in and out of the shrubs, keeping her company.

Now, with that tiny, tiny hint of Giuseppa's, April's mental picture of Irene had changed again.

Did the young woman come up this path in her jodhpurs and riding boots, itching to see her beloved Turi again, to tack him up, and ride him over the tracks that criss-crossed these wild blue mountains? Or, when she walked up these steps, was it a different kind of pleasure she was anticipating? A different freedom?

April was out of breath, sweat running down her back. She reached the top of the path and walked into the stable yard. Everything was as it had been before: swallows hunting around the barn, insects catching the sunlight in their wings. April turned, shielding her eyes from the glare of the sun, and gazed back towards the villa. It was a long way below. There was no way anyone down there could spy on someone up here. Whether or not there had been anything between Irene and the stable hand, the two of them would have had their privacy when Patrick wasn't around. If they had gone into the dry darkness of the barn, they could have held hands, they could have kissed, they could have done anything, without being seen.

April closed her eyes. She tried to feel what Irene might have felt. She imagined the stamp of hooves against the stone of the stable yard, the smell of warm hay, a whinny. She imagined Irene's heart racing in antici-pation, that dry-mouthed, thrilling sensation of being close to someone who made her want to take her clothes off; someone whose body she couldn't wait to feel pressed against hers, skin on skin.

If what Giuseppa had hinted at was true.

But how could anything be proved, one way or the other, now?

And if Irene had been having a love affair with the stable hand, what were the implications for the investigation? Did it make it less likely that Enzo had killed her, or more likely? The stable hand had died in the earthquake, Giuseppa had said, four months before Irene disappeared. Superficially, it would seem that, no matter what Irene's relationship had been with the man, it couldn't have had anything to do with what became of her. But... what if, on the drive back from Palermo on the day of Irene's disappearance, she and Enzo had argued and Irene had told Enzo what had been going on?

What then?

61

IRENE

'Don't you like Bella?' asks Maddalena.

She is sitting on the bedroom floor, with the doll undressed beside her, and the doll's clothes spread out all around.

'I never was one for playing with dolls,' I tell her. That's one thing I will say about my parents; they never tried to make me into a girly-girl. They believed in hard work and godliness and paid for me to go to secretarial school. The plan was that I'd go to work for one of the colliery managers, and marry him. It was a shock for them when I got a job at Bill Marrs' stables instead, although it shouldn't have been. I'd always wanted to work with horses.

They didn't think working in a stable was a respectable job for a young woman, but at least it was steady work. They weren't to know that I was about to meet you, Jack, and fall so completely, madly in love.

When we found out I was pregnant, do you remember the state we were in? A mixture of panic and pride. That's why we ran away to London. I couldn't bear the thought of having to tell my parents, and yours; of the shame and humiliation that would ensue. We knew exactly how they'd react, and I didn't want to bring a child into this world under a cloud of disapproval. We decided to run away to the city. We saw the Pimlico Hotel jobs advertised in the newspaper. The proprietor, Mr Fartingale, was looking for a 'young married couple to carry out a variety of tasks'. Bed and board was included.

You bought me a ring in Woolworths. We caught the train to London. En route, I stopped being Irene Weatherbury and became Mrs Jack Harding. We walked all the way from Kings Cross to the Pimlico Hotel and went to reception where old Fartingale was standing, a cigarette burning in the ashtray on the counter. 'We're Mr and Mrs Harding,' you told him. 'We're looking for work.' Fartingale was so desperate for staff that he asked no difficult questions. He took us upstairs. 'These are your quarters,' he said.

Our room was small and dark and cold and you couldn't even stand up straight on account of the sloping ceiling. We had to share a bathroom with the other hotel employees, and there was a communal cooker on the landing. The curtains in our room didn't close and the bed springs creaked and we didn't even have a wardrobe for our clothes and yet – oh! It was perfect!

You did everything in that hotel, didn't you, Jack, from unblocking the drains to carrying the businessmen's suitcases up to bedrooms. I was a waitress, chambermaid, and occasionally one or the other of us would do shifts on the reception desk too. It was awfully dull, boring work after the horses. I was forever being propositioned by the guests. I showed them the ring on my finger. 'I'm married,' I said. I said it so often that I began to believe it. I had to wear a uniform; a black dress with a white pinny. After a few weeks, it began to get tight across my belly.

We were apart during the day, you doing your work, I doing mine, but at night we were together in our room in the hotel eaves and we made one another laugh with the stories of how our days had gone. We slept in that uncomfortable little bed, our arms wrapped around one another and although we didn't have anything, what we had was enough. We made plans. We talked about our future. We both thought the baby would be a boy, and we were going to call him James, after James Coburn who was our favourite character in the film, the Magnificent Seven.

We started work at the hotel in September. In November, I started to bleed. We couldn't tell old Fartingale what was going on, so you said I had a stomach bug, and I took half a day off work. You kept coming up to check on me. 'It'll be all right,' you said, kissing my forehead, 'everything's going to be all right.' But it wasn't.

By the end of that day, I was no longer pregnant.

That evening, you brought two bottles of stout up to the bedroom and some fish and chips, and we sat on the floor, with our backs against the bed and the gas fire burning our knees.

I felt sore and tired and sad. I was trying not to make a fuss, but my head was full of James, and all the things that wouldn't happen now. I don't know when I started loving him, but by the time he was lost, the love was there.

'I'll never get to take him to school,' I said. 'Never teach him to ride a bike. Or a horse.'

You put your arm around my shoulders. You kissed the top of my head.

'James wasn't meant to be,' you said.

'No,' I said.

'We'll get through this, Irene. We'll be grand.'

'I know.'

'Eat up,' you said. 'I want to see them roses back in your cheeks.'

We decided we would stay at the hotel until we had saved up enough money to get married and rent a place of our own. We might even go back to Yorkshire. You'd been in touch with Bill, and he'd said he'd welcome us back to the stables. We thought it best to be properly married before we returned, for everyone's sake.

We would have been all right. We would have had a good life.

And then that young boy slipped and fell into the river.

And you, you could have let someone else play the hero, Jack, but you didn't.

You heard his mother's scream and you ran to the wall and looked over and saw the child flailing in that black, greasy water. You saw him going under.

You took off your jacket and your boots, and you went in after him without a thought for yourself. I know this because the boy's mother told me. She brought me some flowers and some fairy cakes she'd made, in a coronation tin. 'I'm so sorry for your loss, Mrs Harding,' she said. 'Your husband was a hero.'

I fed the cakes to the pigeons.

You left me, Jack. You left me! How could you do that to me?

'Irene? Irene!' Maddalena's voice brings me back to the present. And I've been so lost in the past that I am, for a moment, disorientated.

'Sorry, Maddi. Sorry, pet. I was miles away.'

She holds up the doll.

'Do you like how I've dressed Bella? Do you think she looks nice?'

'She looks a picture,' I say. 'You've done a grand job.'

Maddi smiles. I pull her close and I kiss the top of her head, as you once kissed mine, and I try to be grateful for what I have, and not to dwell on what I have lost.

62

April had a quick look at the cottage. It was set into the hill, lower than the stables, and was a small, functional building with plastered walls, and a slab roof covered in red tiles with a water tank on top. There was only a tiny patch of garden. Daria's laundry was pegged to a washing line that ran from the side of the house to a post, and back again. Situated as it was, with two of the walls facing the slope of the hillside, and the others close to the trees, it must be dark inside, April surmised. But at least it would be cool.

She took some photographs and was about to head back down the hill when her phone rang. It was Maddalena. She sounded stressed.

'I'm in the hospital,' she said. 'Milo Conti has been here. He came right to the door of Papa's room, but luckily Elissa was still here and she told him to get out. He went away this time, but I don't think we can stop him coming back. Anyone can walk into this part of the hospital. I don't know what to do!'

'Is Enzo well enough to come home?'

'I don't know.'

'If it's safe for him to come back to the villa, we could look after him here, at least until after the broadcast. We could get a room ready this evening and pick him up in the morning.'

'I'll find out if it's possible. Are you okay, April? What are you doing?'

'I'm at the stables. Giuseppa told me about the stable hand who died in the earthquake. Do you remember him?'

'Vaguely. I know he was a brilliant horseman. My grandfather thought the world of him.'

'Do you know his name?'

'I did... Oh, I can't remember. But if you divert into the graveyard on the way back down to the villa you can find out. He's buried there. My grandparents decided to put him in the family cemetery in case anyone ever turned up looking for him. His grave's at the back, behind the main monument. It's probably a bit overgrown, but if you persevere, you'll find him.'

When they'd finished the call, April followed the path down to the graveyard. She opened the gate and stepped across the gulley.

The cemetery was green and gloomy. Nothing grew there; the ground was covered with pine needles and cones and someone had placed an animal skull, a sheep or a deer's, on the top of the gatepost.

April approached the grand family vault. She glanced at the list of those Borgatas interred inside. Oval ceramic plaques showed the faces of the more recent additions. There was Patrick, a bushy-browed, good-looking man wearing the same cowboy hat he'd been wearing in the family photograph. Below him was Alia Oliveri, Enzo's first wife; so like her daughter that the image could have been taken from a photograph of Maddalena.

Treading carefully, April walked around the vault. Beyond was an area where the shrubs and trees of the woodland had intruded. The ground was thick with leaf and pine debris. There were several graves in this area, belonging to people who were not Borgatas, but who had lived and worked at the Villa Alba. The first headstone was the oldest, dating back to 1794 and belonging to someone whose name April couldn't make out. A couple were buried beside this, and a little further back, where the ground was less stony, was another grave. There was no headstone. Perhaps there had once been a wooden cross, or some other kind of temporary marker. Perhaps the intention had been to install a proper headstone at some point, but like the car that was never taken to the workshop, and the portrait that had never been restored, no Borgata had ever got round to organising it.

There was a stone, an ordinary stone of the kind that anyone could have picked up in the villa grounds and placed on the grave. April leaned down, and picked it up, and dusted off the sand and dirt and plant matter that encrusted it. With her fingertips, she made out the first letters of the name, scratched onto its surface. J A C...

'No!' she whispered. 'It can't be!'

J A C K H A R...

Jack Harding.

63

IRENE

June 1967

It's a hot day. I take Turi out early and we ride up into the mountains, following a track I've taken before. We go further than I meant to go. But it's all right. A canteen of water is hooked to the saddle, and I've packed half a ciabatta loaf, stuffed with cheese and tomatoes. I know the places now where Turi can find a drink, and where we can stop and rest.

I love riding these highlands. I love the quality of the air, and the light; the silence. Mewling birds circle high overhead. I drop the reins and lean back in the saddle. Turi walks on, his hooves clopping on the dry ground, and his shoulders moving beneath me. We spend all day in the mountains, he and I, and I think of you, Jack, and of us, and what could have been.

It is well into the afternoon as we head back, Turi and I, walking slowly and steadily downhill. I am tired, but it's that pleasant tiredness that follows physical exertion. The sun is beginning its downward journey but it has a way to go yet, and the light is still lovely. Turi walks, and I rock in the saddle; relaxed, hungry, looking forward to getting back and settling him before I go into the villa and shower. I plan to divert into the kitchen on the way through and see if there's any food going begging.

I see a figure, on the track, a long way distant. It's a man, I can tell, and he casts a long shadow. It's unusual to see someone on foot, alone, up here, especially at this time of day. I'm not afraid, why would I be? I hold the reins loose as we walk towards the man, who approaches us. Turi is loping along, half asleep, ears twitching at flies. I lean forward and rub the base of his neck. He shivers where I touch him.

I can't say when, exactly, I recognise the man. It is not a conscious thing but at some point, I realise that I know who he is.

It is you, Jack.

It is you.

Turi must sense my shock, because he lifts his head, ears pricked forward and you look up at the exact same moment and see us; you see me and, oh!

'Jack!' I call. 'Jack!' but no sound comes from my lips. Have I died? Am I imagining this?

I climb off the horse. I drop the reins. I walk those last yards between us. I am stunned. I feel as if I must be dreaming. This cannot be real.

'Jack?' I whisper, holding out my hands.

'Irene!'

We stare into one another's eyes.

'You're here?' I ask. 'You're really here?'

'I'm here.'

Behind me, Turi, nickers. Instinctively I reach my hand backwards, to reassure him. I feel his breath on my fingers.

'Jack?' I ask again.

I don't know how we come together, how we embrace, only that in the next moment, we are holding one another so tightly, and I am laughing and crying all at once. We delight in one another. We step back and examine each other. You are still you; thinner, with a beard, and your skin is brown as a nut. You're too thin. You don't look healthy, but you are still you.

Oh my love.

We stand beside the horse. You press your face into his flank, feel his warmth. Smell him. We are both overcome with a kind of shyness.

'He's a beauty,' you say, meaning Turi.

'He's mine,' I tell you.

'You've done well for yourself, lass.'

I have.

'Do you have anything to drink?' you ask.

I unclip the canteen and give you the last of my water. You drink greedily even though only the dregs are left, and they must be warm and stale. I wish I had saved some food.

'Where have you been?' I ask. 'You are supposed to be dead!'

'But I'm not!'

You tell me how you were rescued from the river; how you nearly died of pneumonia; how it was months before you were well enough to come looking for me; how your breathing will never be right. I put my hand on your chest and feel how your lungs strain to draw breath in, and let it out.

'They told me you'd married an Italian,' you say. 'They said he was a tuna-fish salesman. I thought, how many tuna-fish salesmen can there be in this world? All I had to do was track down each one until I found you.'

You searched all of Italy, looking for me. You have been sleeping in barns and under olive trees.

And then you came to Sicily and, at last, you found me.

You found me.

Oh dear God, you found me.

64

April photographed the stone that marked Jack Harding's grave several times, then put it carefully back in its place, with a rotting paddle of prickly pear cactus over the top of it so that it would be easy to find. Then she headed back down towards the villa, calling Inspector Mazzotta as she went.

He didn't answer.

She stopped in the shade, and called her friend Roxie, back in England.

Roxie picked up; she always did.

'Hey, you, how are you getting on?'

'Good, I think. Only things are more complicated than I anticipated and I need your help, Rox, if that's okay.'

'What do you need me to do?'

'Have you got a pen and paper?'

'Of course.'

'I can't remember the date exactly, but some time early in November 1962, the London *Evening News* reported that a young man, Jack Harding, had jumped in to the River Thames to rescue a young boy who'd fallen in. He got the boy ashore, but was too cold and weak to get out himself. Some time later, a body was dragged out of the water downstream. The article made it sound as if it was Jack Harding's body that was recovered, but maybe it wasn't. Could you check it out for me, Rox, see if the body that was pulled out of the river was ever identified?'

'No problem.'

'Thank you! Will you let me know as soon as you've got anything?'

'Of course. Only it's getting late now. I might not be able to get hold of anyone until tomorrow.'

'Tomorrow's fine,' said April.

Tomorrow was Friday. The day before Milo Conti's live broadcast.

65

IRENE

We sit together, beneath the old olive tree. I feel light as a breath, and heavy as lead, all at the same time. Turi stands nearby, one foot resting, his head held low, eyes half-closed. You hold my hand, turn it over, examine it as if it is something wondrous. I'm not wearing my wedding ring; I always take it off before I ride, but there is a paler band of skin at the base of my fourth finger, where the ring goes. You touch the band with your finger. Even though I'm grubby from riding, my skin looks clean next to yours. You're so thin! And your nails are filthy; the cuticles cracked. The whites of your eyes are yellowed; your hair is long and matted.

'You need a bath,' I say.

'I need you,' you reply.

I kiss your mouth. You hold my head between your hands and kiss me back. You taste of all the miles you've travelled; the hardships you've endured. I don't care that your lips are dry and chapped. I don't care about your stale breath, nor the smell of your clothes, nor the dust that seems to have settled in the cracks and pores of your face and your fingers. I don't care about anything but that we are together again.

'Where are you staying?' I ask.

'Nowhere.'

I could take you down to the stables you could sleep in the barn. You could draw water from the pump to wash yourself, and I could bring you some food. But Quintu comes and goes at unpredictable times. It would be impossible for you to stay in the barn without him noticing and how could we explain your presence to him?

No. It would be too dangerous for you to come to the stables. We couldn't tell Quintu, and if we tried to sneak you in without telling him, and he found you, he might hurt you. He might even kill you.

But I can't leave you here. I can't let you sleep another night in the open.

'We'll go to Gibellina,' I say. I'm thinking of the woman who sold me the figs. If we can find her, I'm sure she'll tell us where Jack can stay. I will bring up some money in the morning.

* * *

I can't face dinner tonight.

I tell Donatella that I'm feeling unwell and that I need to rest. I come up to the bedroom and lay on the bed for about two seconds and then I realise that bed is the last place I need to be. I am full of energy. I pace around the room, like a tiger in a zoo. I look out of the window. I can't see the lights of Gibellina from here, but I know you are there, only a few miles away. I cannot tell you how that makes me feel.

Giuseppa comes into the bedroom carrying a tray: it contains a bowl of pasta and some cherry granita.

'You're flushed,' she says, putting the back of her wrist against my forehead. 'And you feel warm!'

'I'm fine,' I tell her.

'You don't look yourself. You've been overdoing it. It's not good for you, being out on that horse all day.'

'You sound like Donatella,' I tell her. She doesn't like to be compared to Donatella and I see the flicker of pain in her eyes. 'Sorry, Giuseppa,' I say. 'You don't really sound like her at all.'

She nods towards the tray. 'Try and eat a little, Irene, if you can.'

I thought I'd be too excited to eat but it turns out I am ravenous! I wolf the food down, Jack, but then I am at a loss. I don't want to do anything, if I can't do it with you.

Something is worrying me, Jack. Do you remember that a truck drove past as we were walking up to Gibellina? I didn't say a word about it to you, because I didn't want anything to cast a shadow over our reunion, but that was Quintu's truck. He was heading back to Gibellina after a day spent fixing things at the Villa Alba. He must have seen us through the dusty windscreen, you and me. We were not touching, there was nothing inappropriate in our stance, but still I wish he hadn't seen us. I don't like the thought of him knowing you exist.

I am thinking about Quintu, and you, trying to order my thoughts, when life becomes even more complicated. The bedroom door opens and Enzo comes in, with a flourish. Ta da! He's holding one of the fancy flower arrangements that you can buy from the florists' shops in Palermo.

'Surprise!' he says, coming across the room to me and planting a kiss on my forehead.

'You're supposed to be in Calabria!' I say. 'You're not supposed to be back for three days!' My tone is accusatory, rather than affectionate. We both hear it. I can't help myself. I simply cannot make myself act pleased that Enzo is unexpectedly home, not when I've been looking forward to a whole uninterrupted night, thinking about you.

'I finished my business early and came home to surprise you,' says Enzo, 'only to discover you're not feeling well. What's the matter, Irene? What can I do to make you feel better?'

'There's nothing you can do,' I say, backing away from him. 'You'd better not come too close in case it's catching.'

'My darling,' he says, 'if you're suffering, then I want to suffer too. We can be sick together.'

He tries to embrace me and I tense. I can't bear his touch. When his fingers connect with my skin I want to bat them away. 'Get away from me!' I want to cry. 'Leave me alone!'

His face is full of concern and kindness.

'Enzo, please,' I say, 'if you really want to help me, let me rest for a while.'

'Of course,' he says. 'You lie down. I'll sit here and watch over you.'

No, no, no!

Oh, dear God, what am I going to do?

He loves me, Jack. He has never been anything but considerate towards me. He has said many times that he would do anything to make me happy. And when I thought you were gone, I was grateful for that. I thought we could get by, together, despite everything; that his desire to make this marriage work would be enough to make it work.

But now you are here. You are not dead. You are the one I love, have always loved.

What am I going to do?

What are we going to do?

How can we get ourselves out of this mess?

66

April was engrossed in her work, when Maddalena came into the bedroom.

April did not look up from her screen.

'How did you get on?' she asked.

'The doctor said if Papa has a good night tonight, we can bring him home tomorrow morning.'

'That's great news.' Now April looked up. 'Do you think we could have a look around your father's room tonight, Maddi, before he comes back?'

'Sure,' Maddalena said. 'We'll get the keys from Giuseppa.'

* * *

While April was changing for dinner, Inspector Mazzotta called. She filled him in on what she'd discovered, explaining about the grave, Giuseppa's insinuation, and telling him to look again at the newspaper article in the case notes.

'I've asked a police friend of mine to confirm the identity of the man pulled out of the river,' she said. 'It might have been a case of mistaken identity.'

'Is Jack Harding a common name in the UK?'

'Not that common. It would be too much of a coincidence for someone with the exact same name as Irene's former fiancé to turn up here.'

'Okay.'

'Irene can't have told Enzo she was engaged before,' April said. 'He can't have had any idea who Jack Harding was.'

'Right,' said Inspector Mazzotta. In the background, April could hear videogame noises. Then raised voices, one complaining, the other laughing.

'You sound busy,' she said.

'Sorry. Kids.'

'It's no problem. But I also need to let you know that the family is bringing Enzo back here tomorrow morning. Conti's been trying to get into the hospital to see him.'

'Is the villa secure?'

'Pretty much. And nobody will know that he's here. There are only forty-eight more hours until the live programme.'

'Right!'

'One last thing, Inspector. I spoke to the Borgatas' housekeeper, Giuseppa, today about the events of the evening that Irene disappeared and she backed up Sam's version. So, it looks as if Daria got it wrong.'

'They might both be lying. Sam and the housekeeper.'

'Well, yes. I'll see if I can talk to Daria alone either this evening or some time tomorrow.'

'Okay,' said the inspector. 'Stay in touch.'

* * *

When April went downstairs for dinner that evening, the rest of the family, with the exception of Donatella, was already gathered in the dining room.

April took her place at the table, glancing from one face to the other. Everyone seemed tense.

'Has something happened?' she asked Sam, beside her.

'Conti,' he muttered. 'On the *Serata* programme tonight he said he has proof that Enzo was planning to murder Irene.'

'Did he say what proof?'

'No. But he said he had it on good authority that Irene was living in fear of her life. And,' he added, shooting a dirty look towards Daria, 'before my darling sister accuses me of feeding this crap to Conti, I didn't! I wouldn't have told Conti Irene was worried about Enzo hurting her because she wasn't! It's not true.'

April masked her own concerns with a smile. Truthfully, she felt less confident about Enzo's innocence now than she had done at any time before.

She reached for her water glass and took a sip.

'Conti said,' Sam continued, 'that he's going to reveal the "proof" tomorrow evening, and then he'll lay out the whole case against Enzo during the full programme on Saturday.'

'I heard people talking about us in Salgareale today,' said Daria. 'I heard them saying that if Enzo was guilty of murdering Irene, then we should leave the villa. They don't want us here any more.'

Maddalena shifted in her chair. Elissa looked up, wide-eyed.

'We need to be prepared for trouble, if Conti does have proof that—'

'How can he have proof?' Maddalena interrupted. 'My father never hurt Irene! He couldn't have! He *wouldn't* have!'

'They're talking about Alia too,' Elissa said quietly. 'Tonio told me. He said people are saying the Borgatas covered up the true reason why she died. They're saying Conti ought to be asking questions about her, next. They're convinced that we're guilty.'

67

IRENE

A few days later

I am in bed, facing the window, and the light wakes me, as it does every morning. And each morning, I forget for a moment that you are here, Jack. I forget that you are alive, and then I remember and my heart leaps with joy and I cannot wait to escape from the villa and make my way out to the mountains; to you.

Enzo comes into the room. He has brought me a cup of English breakfast tea, as he always does, placing it at my side of the bed like an offering. I can smell the rose that he's cut for me, fresh from the garden. Its scent is so strong, so distinctively perfumy, that I know it's one of the yellow ones with the milky interior and the outer edges of the petals streaked red, as if they've been dipped in blood. I'm not particularly fond of those flowers, but the smell is divine.

He leans over me, I feel the warmth of his exhaled breath, and my body reacts to the proximity of his; the little hairs on my arms and legs standing on end. Every atom of my being is begging him not to touch me.

It's not Enzo's fault. None of this is Enzo's fault. It makes me feel so bad. If he were a horrible man; if he beat me or were mean with money or if he were *unfaithful, then I wouldn't feel so wicked. But he's a good, kind man. He hasn't done anything wrong. He doesn't deserve to have a wife who is in love with someone else.*

He kisses my forehead. He's brushed his teeth already; his breath smells of peppermint.

'Thank you,' I murmur, 'for the tea.'

'It's my pleasure,' he says.

Please, I beg, please, please, please, don't get back into bed.

He goes round to the other side of the bed and climbs back in. He shuffles into the middle, turns towards me, puts his arms around me.

Part of me is thinking: Just let him do it. It'll be over in five minutes and he'll be happy. But the rest of me knows that if I lie beneath Enzo while he has his way with me, he'll know that something is different. Now that you're back, I won't be able to fake it. I might cry, or push him off, or feel bound to confess. One way or another, my deceit will be obvious.

And I can't do it. I can't have sex with my husband when my heart belongs to you. I can't!

Enzo, typically, blames himself for my reticence.

'We haven't spent much time together lately, have we?' he says. 'I've been neglecting you. I've been so tied up with my work.'

'It's important that you work,' I murmur.

'I was thinking we could maybe have a little holiday. Just you and me. Maybe go back to Donnalucata in July or August. You liked it there, didn't you?'

I did, but that was before I knew you were alive, Jack. It was when my heart was broken and I was grasping at anything that could divert my thoughts from my grief.

'There's that hotel where we ate one evening, with the balcony overlooking the sea,' Enzo says. 'You said you'd like to stay there one day, didn't you?'

'It's okay, Enzo,' I say, 'you don't need to spend your money on me. I'll be fine in a few days.'

'Let me spoil you,' he whispers into my hair. 'Let me do something nice for you. I've made enquiries about booking the bridal suite. I thought how wonderful it would be if you and I could have a second honeymoon.'

68

When they had finished eating, Sam went to watch the football in the television room, Elissabeta disappeared into the garden – probably to join Tonio. Daria wished everyone a good night and said she was returning to her cottage.

April and Maddalena started stacking the dishes and clearing the table, but Giuseppa came back as they were halfway through the task and shooed them away.

'You'll make a mess of it,' she said, 'and I won't be able to find anything in the morning.'

She immediately set to work, head down, bustling.

Maddalena and April exchanged glances.

'Giuseppa,' said Maddalena, 'please could you let me have the key to my father's room? April wants to have a look round to see if there's anything that might help with her investigation.'

'I don't see what there could possibly be.'

'A diary,' said Maddalena hopefully.

'There's no diary,' said Giuseppa. 'I'd know if there was a diary there, and there isn't.'

'Just let us have the key, please,' said Maddalena. 'We'll bring it back in a little while.'

Giuseppa frowned, but headed off towards the kitchen.

'She keeps the keys in a special cabinet on the wall,' said Maddi. 'Nobody else is allowed to touch it.'

The older woman returned a few minutes later with a glass fob in the shape of a horse's head with an old-fashioned mortice key attached to it. She passed it to Maddalena.

'Thank you,' said Maddalena. 'We'll return it to you in a little while.'

They set off together, Maddalena and April, making their way through the ancient house while the moon, waxing now, cast its pale light through the windows. An owl hooted distantly. Maddalena was carrying a half-empty bottle of wine leftover from dinner, grasping it by the neck.

'Dutch courage for when we go into the dressing room,' she said. 'It still feels...'

'What?'

'Full of Irene.'

When the evening was warm, like this, and the darkness of the night sky was visible through all the windows, it was easy to feel the history of the villa closing in; the breaths and footsteps of the generations of Borgatas who had lived and died here as they made their way to and from their rooms; to sleep, to wash, to pray, to make love. April could almost hear them, almost catch the words they were whispering, their laughter, their sadness; their knowing that they wouldn't be here forever, but that the villa would.

She tried to imagine how it would feel to belong to a place like this; to be part of a family with a long history. She could not.

They reached the top of the stairs. The landing was long and forbidding, moonlight falling through the windows.

Maddalena tucked the wine bottle under her elbow, put the key into the lock and opened the door into Enzo's room; the room he had once shared with Irene.

They stepped inside and Maddalena turned on the light. The air in this room felt old and dry; perhaps breaths that Irene had exhaled were still present; and hair that she had shed might still be caught amongst the furniture; fingerprints hidden amongst the patterns of the polished wood. If April inhaled deeply, she might catch a hint of Irene's perfume.

It was a large room, being on the corner, with a window on each outside wall; one facing out to the side of the villa, like the one in April's room, and the other overlooking the back terrace and the swimming pool. The furniture was grand and masculine; the pieces looked like heirlooms. The bed was a huge, antique piece of furniture, with heavy steads at the head and foot carved with fruit, flowers and cherubs. Behind it were two panels, each with a peacock-blue background, each beautifully painted.

On the dark chest of drawers was a leather binocular case. It was possible Enzo only used the binoculars to look at wildlife. But it was also possible that he used to watch his young wife climbing the hill to the stables at the top, catching brief glimpses of her as she moved between the trees.

Had Enzo known about Irene and Jack?

'It's so hot in here,' said Maddalena.

She unhooked the catch and opened the windows wide. The insects that had been batting against the glass came into the room.

'Giuseppa will kill me,' Maddalena said. She took a swig from the mouth of the wine bottle.

'What are we looking for?' she asked.

'I don't know.'

April looked around. On the chest of drawers, as well as the binoculars, was a group of framed photographs.

Most were snapshots of Maddalena as a child. There she was as a baby in her father's arms; as a chubby toddler pedalling a little tricycle, as a shy seven-year-old in a party dress with ribbons in her hair. Behind these was a photograph of a woman April recognised from the image she'd seen at the vault in the graveyard. Maddalena's mother, Alia.

She picked up a photograph of a group of people in work clothes standing in the sunshine outside a single-storey office block, beneath a sign that read *TonnoFelice* and bore a graphic of a leaping tuna, with a knife in one fin, a fork in the other, and a napkin round its neck with the Sicilian triskelion, the three-legged woman, in the centre. On closer inspection, April picked out Enzo in the middle of the group. Those must be his work colleagues.

Taking pride of place was a picture of Enzo and Irene.

It was the original of the photograph in the case notes pack. This image had far better definition. April could see perfectly well now that the couple were standing on the terrace of a trattoria; behind them were tables that looked as if they were laid for a celebration. Enzo was beaming into the camera. He looked so happy, happier than April ever remembered seeing him, that she found herself smiling back at him. His hair was slicked back, his tie neatly tied, his shoes polished. One arm was around his young wife.

She, Irene, was so alive, in the photograph, that she almost jumped out of it. She was standing stiffly, smiling but not interacting with her husband. Her head, and her body, were inclined away from his.

'Do you know where this was taken?' April asked Maddalena.

'A little seaside town called Donnalucata,' she replied. 'It was where Irene and Papa had their honeymoon, but that picture was taken on holiday, the summer before Irene disappeared.'

'And these?' April indicated three different pictures, all of Irene holding a rope attached to a headcollar being worn by a beautiful, fiery-eyed horse.

'That's Turi, the horse my grandfather bought for Irene.'

'And who's the man on the other side of the horse?'

'Quintu Baresi. He used to work for my grandparents.'

'Is he still alive?'

'He hasn't been alive for a long time. He lived in Gibellina. He was amongst those who died in the earthquake. He was so badly injured that his body was never identified.'

69

IRENE

July 1967

Enzo and I are in Donnalucata. It's beautiful. Sunlight sparkles off the sea; there's a little beach with sunbeds and umbrellas and Enzo has been buying me cocktails from the bar.

The hotel is divine; small and upmarket, about as removed from the Pimlico Hotel as it's possible to imagine. Where the Pimlico was all creaky stairs, sticky carpets and dripping taps, this one is marble and mirrors and flowers and light. There's a restaurant with tables on a terrace that juts out over the rocks so that we can hear the splashing of the sea as we eat. Last night a man came and played a violin; the music was so pretty it made me weep and Enzo, seeing my tears, took my hand and asked me what was wrong.

'Nothing's wrong,' I told him. 'I'm crying because I'm happy.' And he, of course, was moved by my words. He was pleased because he believed the hotel, and his bringing me here, were the source of my happiness and I did not spoil his pleasure by telling him he was wrong. I could not tell him that my every thought is consumed by concern for you, by wondering how you are, what you are doing, if you are well. I know that Maria Grazia, the fig woman, is looking

after you. I have paid her well and she is a good person, she has a kind heart. But your cough worries me; and your pallor. I worry about the filthy Thames water that got into your lungs, and the damage it has done. And I miss you. After so long without you, this new, unnecessary separation is almost unbearable. It is so difficult for me to be civil with Enzo when he is the one who has caused me so much heartache. And yet he's only acting out of love for me, which makes it worse.

We went for a walk after dinner, Enzo and I, through the hotel gardens. I was wearing my pale blue gown, and I know I looked good because having you near is making me beautiful. My skin is clear, my eyes are bright, even my hair seems more sun-kissed blonde, less English mouse since you found me. Enzo and I went onto the beach. I took off my sandals and carried them by the straps. The night was velvety and black; no moon; only bats darting above us, hiding the stars for the briefest instant. I went to the water's edge; let the tiny waves break over my feet, felt the sucking as the water withdrew.

It was lovely. Everything was perfect. Only I was with him.

And, Jack, I should have been with you.

70

Maddalena sat on the bed, smoothing the bedspread with her hand. The gauze curtains billowed in a breath of breeze. There was the faintest clinking as the glass droplets hanging from the chandelier touched one another.

April sat beside Maddalena.

'I was born on this bed,' Maddi said. 'And this is where my mother died.

I was here when she breathed her last breath.' She patted the place at the top of the bed, between the pillows. 'They swaddled me and lay me beside her so she could hear me breathing as she died.'

April had never been good at trotting out clichés during difficult conversations, but she knew she should say something helpful to her friend.

'I'm sure that was a comfort to her,' she said quietly.

'Maybe. If she even knew I was there.' She hesitated. 'Can I tell you something, April?'

'Of course.'

'For weeks now, ever since we first knew that Milo Conti was trying to dig up dirt about my father, I've been having these dreams... *nightmares,* about Irene.'

'What kind of nightmares?'

'She seeks me out. She won't leave me alone. Sometimes, in my sleep, I hear someone on the landing, or in the bathroom, and I get out of bed and go to see who it is and it's always her, standing there, bruised and battered like she was when they pulled her out of the stables after the earthquake. And her leg... her leg is crushed and bloody and she's holding onto the side of the door for support and she's saying, "Help me, Maddi, please, help me!" and I say, "What is it that you want me to do, Irene?" but she never answers.'

She sat up straight and ran her fingers through her hair.

'I feel stupid even telling you this...'

'Don't feel stupid.'

'I used to dream about her occasionally, but now... Now I can't get away from her. There's no respite. I'm afraid to sleep because she won't leave me alone.'

'Were you actually there,' April asked, 'when Irene was brought back from the stables after the earthquake? Did you see her?'

'Yes. I saw her.' Maddalena held the bottle to her lips, tipped it back and drank.

'Were her injuries very bad?' April asked.

Maddi nodded. She held the wine bottle up to the light and peered at it.

'They were horrific. Everyone thought she was going to die.'

She upended the bottle and shook it. A solitary, deep red drop fell from its mouth and made a pink stain on the bedcover.

'It's empty,' she said. 'I'll go and get another.'

April heard her footsteps receding along the landing, and then the tapping of her heels as she ran down the stairs and then there was silence.

Without Maddi, the atmosphere in the bedroom felt very different.

April had the sensation of being watched. If she turned her head quickly, she was almost certain that she would catch a glimpse of Irene observing her from the shadows. Or maybe it wasn't Irene who haunted this room. Perhaps it was Alia.

Perhaps it was them both.

Did they bring Irene back up to this room, she wondered, after the earthquake? Did they lay her in this bed? Did they nurse her external injuries, not realising half the extent of her suffering was because her love, her Jack, who had somehow, miraculously, come back from the dead, had been killed a second time, this time in front of her eyes?

April felt dizzy with the thought of all that Irene had endured. It was enough to drive a person insane, she thought, the losing of love, and the finding of it, and the losing again.

Maddelena returned with a new bottle in her hand. 'Mission accomplished,' she said.

They sat together on the floor with their backs against the wall and drank a few mouthfuls each, passing the bottle between them.

'Remember the séance we held at school?' Maddalena asked.

They had been fifteen years old, sitting cross-legged on the floor of the room they shared in the creaking old boarding house of St Hilary's school in Sussex. They had a home-made Ouija board, an upturned glass and a candle. The glass had moved, apparently of its own volition. They had been frightened out of their wits.

'Do you think it was Irene who came to us that night?' asked Maddalena.

'Nobody came,' said April.

'Something was there.'

'It was one of us, subconsciously manipulating the glass.'

'The temperature definitely dropped.'

'It was a draughty room.'

'And the smell of perfume...'

'I didn't smell anything.'

Maddalena nudged April with her arm.

'When did you get to be so cynical?'

'I'm not being cynical. I'm being pragmatic. There is no life after death. If there was, Cobain would have contacted me. He was a persistent bugger.'

Maddalena put her head on April's shoulder. 'Sorry,' she said.

'It's okay,' said April. 'Pass me the bottle.'

The wine was warm and it was not refreshing, rather, it made April thirstier.

She rested her head back against the wall.

'It's still so hot,' she said. 'How come it's so hot, Maddi? It must be almost midnight.'

'It's always hot here in summer. The heat gets trapped in the valley. You get used to it.'

April wiped her lips with the back of her hand, and passed the bottle back to Maddalena.

'Did you have a good look round,' Maddalena asked, 'while I was fetching the wine?'

'Not really. I felt like I was intruding.'

'You didn't go the dressing room where Irene used to sleep then?'

'Where is it?'

'On the other side of the bathroom.'

'Do you know why Irene moved in there, Maddi?'

Maddalena shook her head. 'I don't know why exactly. It might have been because of her leg. I'm pretty sure she started sleeping there after the earthquake.'

71

The door on the far side of the bathroom was locked, but the key was in the lock.

April turned it and stepped into the room beyond, pressing the switch on the wall.

An electric candelabra hanging from the ceiling in the centre of the room lit up. Several of the bulbs weren't working and those that remained flickered, dimmed and then brightened, seemingly at random. One whole wall was taken up with built-in wardrobes; the opposite one was covered in a fussy yellow wallpaper. At first April's eyes read the pattern as snakes, writhing in a giant, seething mass, but soon she realised it was only some kind of thick-stemmed vine, climbing through other vines, with snake-head-shaped leaves and feelers that resembled forked tongues.

This room had obviously been used by an invalid. A walking frame was at the foot of a single bed with a cover over the mattress. A wheel-chair was parked beside it.

Placed at an angle was a dressing table; with three oval mirrors in a fancy Gothic frame. The mirrors were age-spotted and tilted at angles that only reflected the yellow wallpaper. On the dressing table was a miniature screwdriver and a single tiny screw. The only other furniture in the narrow room was a small chest of drawers.

A doll sat on the dressing-table chair: a baby doll, with a staring face and faded blonde hair tied back in a bow. Someone had placed a tiny plastic hairbrush in the doll's hand and she was holding it up to her hair as if she were about to brush it.

'Is this how you remember it?' April asked Maddalena. Her voice came out very quiet, almost a whisper. She was thinking about the noises she'd heard from this room two nights before. She was wondering who had been in here and what they'd been doing.

'Yes.'

'It's been like this for thirty-five years?'

'Yes.'

'Even the doll?'

'I'd forgotten the doll,' said Maddalena. 'Her name is Bella. But yes, she was here. She was Irene's – a gift from Nonna Donatella. She was supposed to make Irene ovulate or something. Donatella wanted more grandchildren.'

She giggled. 'I'm sorry! I don't really think it's funny... it's *terrible!*'

'Poor Irene!'

April opened the wardrobe door. Inside, hanging neatly on hangers, were Irene Bortaga's clothes, her shoes lined up beneath them. The smell of mothballs was strong.

Irene's dresses were beautiful: well cut, well made, lined and tailored. As well as day dresses, there were party gowns and shoes to go with them; a white dress, the fabric of the dress sewn with hundreds of silver beads, long gloves folded over the hanger and beneath a pair of dancing shoes; a blue cocktail dress with a flouncy net petticoat; an apricot gown.

'Did you ever try these clothes on, Maddalena?' April asked.

'I wasn't allowed to touch them,' Maddalena said. 'Irene was very protective of them. She said it had taken her her whole life to have clothes as good as those in her wardrobe and I could "jolly well wait" for my good clothes too.'

'What about after she'd gone?'

Maddalena shook her head.

April closed the wardrobe door and at the exact same moment the light flickered.

She looked over her shoulder and saw the reflection of the doll staring at her from the dressing-table mirror.

Maddalena was opening the drawers in the chest. 'Underwear,' she said, 'bedlinen, swimming costume, swimming hat. Nothing interesting.'

April did not want to touch the doll, to move it, so that she could look in the dressing-table drawers. She knew what they would contain anyway: ancient cosmetics; dried-up lipsticks; face cream turned to a yellow wax. Someone, definitely Donatella, almost certainly Giuseppa, possibly Daria too, would have searched the drawers already. If there was anything of relevance in there, it would have been found, or destroyed.

What else could there be? A diary would be ideal, but Giuseppa had said no such thing existed, and surely it would be too serendipitous to find such a big clue now.

April looked around. Where in this room would she hide something, if she had something she wanted to hide?

Not the drawers, not the wardrobe, not under the bed. She turned a full circle.

Her eyes went back to the doll.

'We need to undress Bella,' she said. 'To see if anything is hidden in her clothes.'

'Okay.'

'Will you do it, Maddi? I don't want to touch her.'

With a sigh, Maddalena crossed the room. She lifted the doll carefully off the chair, and carried it across to the bed and laid it on its back, legs and arms sticking up at right angles. She climbed onto the bed herself, and sat, with her legs tucked beneath her. She took another drink from the mouth of the bottle of wine, put it on the floor and proceeded to take off the doll's clothes.

'There,' she said after a few minutes. 'She's naked.'

April took the doll and examined it.

There was a door in its back.

'There used to be a mechanism,' said Maddalena, 'so if you tipped her forward, she would say, "Mamma!" But it stopped working after I gave her a bath one time and Irene took the mechanism out. She said she didn't like the doll talking anyway, it gave her the creeps.'

She peered at the doll's back. 'There used to be a little screw to keep the door shut.'

'It's on the dressing table,' April said.

She prised opened the little door and slipped her hand into the cavity. Inside was a tiny velvet pouch which contained two rings.

'Those are Irene's,' Maddalena said. 'The wedding band and the engagement ring.'

'She must have left them here then,' April said. 'She can't have been wearing them when she went to Palermo that last day.'

Or someone else had taken them from her and brought them back here.

'I think there was something else hidden inside the doll,' April said.

'Why do you say that?'

'I heard someone moving about inside this room. And the screw had been removed but the rings were still there. So there must have been something else.'

'Nothing makes any sense,' said Maddi. She took another drink.

'It will do,' said April. 'We're just not seeing it yet.'

72

FRIDAY 15 AUGUST 2003

The day before Conti's exposé

April had returned to the police case notes after she and Maddalena left Irene's room. She'd been reading them by the light of the small lamp, and fallen asleep at the desk. When she woke, her head was pillowed by her arms. Her back was aching, her neck was stiff and she had a headache from the wine she'd consumed the night before.

'Idiot,' she told herself as she stumbled into the bathroom for a drink of water. She took a shower and then returned to the bedroom, wrapped in towels, and sat on the bed.

It was already Friday. If all went to plan, Maddalena would pick her father up from the hospital in Palermo this morning and bring him back to the villa.

But tomorrow evening, Milo Conti would broadcast his 'special' programme on the disappearance of Irene Borgata. April only had a matter of hours to construct a case proving that Enzo had nothing to do with whatever had become of his wife. Yet so far the only lead she had to follow was the disparity in the accounts of Sam and Daria about what exactly had happened on the evening that Irene disappeared and that might not even be relevant.

April sat quietly, putting her thoughts in order. Until yesterday, there had been no motive that April was aware of for Enzo to be jealous of Irene, but now it seemed highly likely that Irene had resumed her relationship with Jack Harding, right under the nose of her husband and his family.

That situation would have been unsustainable in the long term. Jack and Irene must have been making plans. Perhaps they were intending to run away for a second time; perhaps they had it all worked out – and then the earthquake struck.

Irene must have been devastated. She'd lost her lover, and her leg. She'd moved out of her husband's bedroom. She'd taken off her rings. She appeared to have given up on her marriage. She had nobody to confide in, no ally, as far as April was aware; a mother-in-law who was still hoping for more grandchildren – and who perhaps believed Irene's injuries might make her more inclined to lean into motherhood; no means of escaping from the gilded cage in which she found herself.

Bearing all this in mind, April thought it was perfectly feasible that, during the long drive back from Palermo on 23 May 1968, Irene and Enzo had argued. Perhaps she had told him everything; said that she would never love him as she had loved Jack. Perhaps she'd humiliated her husband, explained that their whole marriage had been a sham; that she had fallen into Enzo's arms from expediency because she did not want to go back to her parents' home in Yorkshire following what she believed had been the loss of her lover. And Enzo, although superficially the quietest, calmest man on the planet, even he would have a breaking point. Irene might have pushed him too far.

Then what? One ill-judged moment of blind temper resulting in one life cut short and the other ruined? The Borgatas had a capacity for violence. April had seen it herself, in gentle Maddalena, in that hostel in Bangkok. Maddi had described jealousy as the family's curse.

April pulled off the towel that had been wrapped around her hair, and shook it out.

What if it was Enzo? she wondered.

What if he did kill Irene?
What then?

* * *

April dressed, collected her towel and swimming costume from the balcony, and headed down through the house, into the kitchen. Elissabeta was standing beside the coffee machine, listening to pop music on the radio. She was wearing a pair of shorts pyjamas that showed off her pale legs and a bulge of tummy, beneath a brightly coloured kimono. She had a glass in one hand, and as April approached she swallowed the tablets that had been in the palm of the other, washing them down with water. Then she hitched the shorts down a little, which hid the top of her thighs but revealed more of her belly.

'Hi,' she said.

'Hello.'

The coffee machine whistled and juddered.

Without her make-up and with her hair half flattened and half sticking up from the way she'd slept on it, Elissabeta looked a mess. She had a love bite at the base of her neck. April glanced at the counter. Two coffee cups. Okay, so Tonio was upstairs, in Elissa's bed. That was brave. Or maybe it happened regularly. Maybe Elissa was an expert at sneaking her boyfriend in and out without her grandmother noticing.

'I was going to go for a swim,' April said. 'I thought I'd make myself an espresso first.'

'I'll make you one,' Elissa said quickly.

April hopped up onto a stool by the breakfast bar and waited while Elissa pottered about the kitchen, the soles of her slippers slapping on the tiles, her kimono billowing behind her.

'Where's Giuseppa?' April asked.

'She's taken a tray up to Nonna Donatella.'

Elissa put a cup beneath one of the coffee machine's spouts and flipped the lever. The dark brown liquid spurted out in gasps. The smell was bitter and burnt and intoxicating.

She put the cup on a saucer and passed it to April.

'Sugar?'

'No, thanks.'

Elissa was fidgeting, anxious to get back to Tonio.

'I'll get out of your way,' said April. 'Thanks for the coffee. I'll see you later.'

73

IRENE

When Enzo and I arrive back from our little holiday, I can't wait to be back with the horses. I tell my husband I need to check on Turi and he sighs and says, 'Can't we just...?' and I turn before he finishes the question and come running up the hill, in my sandals and shorts, no time to change, hoping I might be able to fit in a ride up to Gibellina, to find you.

But I don't need to saddle up. As I come into the stable yard, I see that you are here already, standing with Patrick and Quintu. And I have a moment's panic, my love, I think, Oh, God! What's Jack doing here? but Patrick is smiling. When he sees me approaching, he takes off his hat and waves.

'Irene! Come over here! Come and meet our new stable hand, Jack Harding.'

I walk forward, feeling as if my legs might give way beneath me.

'Hello,' I say, holding out my hand. 'I'm Irene Borgata.'

My mouth is dry as dust.

'Pleased to meet you, Signora Borgata,' you say, taking hold of my hand. I feel dizzy at your touch.

You look better, Jack, than you did before. Maria Grazia has clearly been looking after you. You've put on some weight and your complexion is brighter. Your beard has been trimmed and your hair cut and you're wearing different clothes. You hold my hand for a moment longer than you should and I'm sure Patrick must notice.

'I hear that you're an accomplished horsewoman,' you say.

'I ride a little.'

Patrick is watching me, looking to see if I approve of you, and Quintu, standing back a little, is watching too and I have to concentrate to stop my arms from throwing themselves around you. Behind you, James is tied to one of the rings. He raises his head and whinnies a greeting to me. I go to him and embrace him, hold onto his mane.

'Jack's from England,' Patrick explains to my back. 'I met his old boss, Bill Marrs, in America a few years back. Bill's given Jack a fantastic reference and he's agreed to join our little band as stable hand.'

'That's fabulous,' I say.

You cough. Your cough still sounds terrible.

'Have you seen a doctor about that?' I ask.

You shake your head.

'We could ask Daria if she could recommend something to help you,' says Patrick. 'Daria's my daughter,' he tells you. 'She works in a pharmacy.'

You cough again.

'I really think you ought to see a doctor,' I say.

And then I notice Quintu's expression. His eyes are flicking from you to me. He saw us together at the side of the road. He knows something is going on between us but he doesn't know what.

'Jack is going to move into the cottage,' Patrick says. 'That'll be a great relief. You know how worried I've been about the horses being up here at night without anyone nearby to keep an eye on them.'

'That's excellent news,' I say.

Quintu turns to one side, and spits. Only I observe his reaction. We're going to have to be careful of him, Jack. We're going to need to watch our every step.

That's the bad news, but the good news is that you're going to be here, living here, sleeping just a few hundred yards from where I sleep; waking up to the same sunrise, the same sky. When I look out of my window each morning, I'll almost be able to see you. When I walk up the hill, I'm going to know that you're there, in the stables or the barn, or out in the paddocks, or exercising one of the horses. We'll be able to see one another every day. Every single day. And when Enzo is away on his business trips...

Enzo.

What am I doing? What am I thinking?

Here I am, planning ways I can deceive my dear husband to be with the man I love. What kind of woman am I?

What is going to become of me?

Somewhere down the line there'll be a price to pay for my deceit. Already I can feel it in my bones.

74

Sam was swimming lengths when April arrived at the pool. Troy was lying in the shade, panting and watching him.

April changed, and then slipped into the cold water, thinking she would never tire of enjoying a morning swim if she were fortunate enough ever to live in a place like this. She swam a sedate breaststroke on the other side of the pool from Sam, and when he at last surfaced, having completed the target of however many lengths he'd set for himself, she responded to his cheery salute with a wave. He pulled the lilo, shaped like a crocodile, into the pool, climbed onto it, and paddled alongside April. She was conscious of holding her chin out of the water like one of the matriarchs she and Maddalena used to see swimming with their hair tucked inside flowery swimming caps at the beach outside Enzo's holiday house.

'How are you this beautiful morning?' Sam asked.

'Good, thank you.'

'How's the sleuthing going?'

'Also good. I'm getting a pretty comprehensive picture of what life was like in the villa while Irene was here.'

'Ah,' said Sam. Then he said, 'We all liked her, you know. I thought she was really attractive. She *was* really attractive. But she wasn't a flirt or a tease. She was respectful of her elders, didn't flaunt herself – well, occasionally, but only to wind up Donatella. But sometimes she'd be here, by the pool, sitting on a lounger, wearing a bikini and those cat's-eye sunglasses that she always wore, and I couldn't get out of the pool for hours.'

April wondered if he meant what she thought he must mean.

'Because of my erection,' he added helpfully.

'Thank you for clarifying,' said April.

'I was a young teenager.'

'I'm not judging.'

She reached the end of the pool, turned neatly, and began to swim the other way. Sam paddled furiously to turn the crocodile and catch up with her again.

'What about Daria?' April asked. 'Did she like Irene?'

'Hmm,' said Sam. 'The jury's out on that one.'

'Did Daria and Enzo get along?'

'Oh, she's always been fine with Enzo because Enzo never did anything wrong. Enzo is Signor Never-Puts-A-Foot-Out-Of-Place.'

'But you did?'

'I've been in a spot of bother once or twice in my life. Gambling mainly. It sometimes gets a bit out of hand.'

'Okay,' said April.

'You've probably heard my darling sister make reference to it already.'

'Do *you* want to tell me about it?'

'Do you want to know?'

'It might be useful.'

Sam sighed. 'It started when I was a kid. I was doing the Borgata thing and working my way through the ranks at the tuna company, hating every minute. I'd reached the dizzy heights of the accounts department, which gave me easy access to petty cash. Cash that I put on the horses. Won some, lost more. When Enzo realised what was going on, he tried to make things right, but by then I was out of control. My parents got involved; I was packed off to rehab and then I came back here for a while and helped look after the gardens. After I met my future wife, Valeria, Papa set us up with an apartment in Siracusa and a wine shop.'

April wondered if a wine shop was a good idea for someone with a predisposition towards addiction, but didn't comment.

Sam was still talking.

'That was all great, for a while. Valeria and I got married, we had little Elissabeta and we were happy. Only then a new bookmaker's shop opened literally next door to the wine shop. What are the odds of that happening? He, the bookmaker, was a genial chap – they always are to start with. We became friends. I started gambling. He cut me some slack when I started losing; I chased the losses; he turned out not to be such a nice chap after all. He threatened my family. We lost the apartment.'

'Wow,' said April quietly.

'And the wine shop. Everything, actually. I can understand why Valeria was miffed.'

April leaned back against the pool wall, turning her face up to the sun.

'That's the pattern of my life,' Sam said, 'moving out, messing up, coming back to live at home. My father, Patrick, used to make light of it. He was a good man. But Donatella doesn't even bother to pretend that she likes me.'

'Why come here, then?'

'I don't have a choice. I'm broke. And Valeria's got a new man friend who Elissa doesn't like, so she doesn't have a choice either. This villa is like Hotel California. Three middle-aged siblings, all of us living back at home with our mother. It's pathetic really.'

'There are worse places to be stuck with one's family,' said April.

'You're right. I shouldn't complain.'

'What about the horses, Sam?'

'What about them?'

'Did you used to help out at the stables?'

'No. I like betting on horses, I'm not so keen on dealing with them close-up. None of us siblings were. They're big animals. Big feet; big teeth. Unpredictable. My father bred some good horses, you know. He loved them. He really loved them.'

'And Irene loved them too?'

'Yep. She was the daughter Patrick always wanted. I used to go to the stables sometimes just to hang around with her. She used to put up with me trailing after her, at least, until the English stable hand came along.'

'What happened then?'

'The energy changed.'

Sam was silent for a moment, then he said, 'I dare say someone or other will already have told you that Irene and the stable hand were close.'

April nodded.

'I'm not saying there was anything untoward going on... I mean, maybe there was. I don't know. I was possessive of Irene, I practically stalked her and I never saw anything I shouldn't have seen. Quintu didn't like the Englishman, but my father was really happy; the happiest I'd ever seen him during that time. Right up to the earthquake. That was the beginning of the end. After that everything went wrong.'

75

IRENE

Autumn 1967

Jack, Jack, Jack.

I thought I was alive before you came, but I wasn't living, I was sleep-walking.

And you, you're almost back to your old self, although you are still under-weight and when you start to cough, I fear that you will never stop. I never, in my whole life, saw anyone so wracked with a bad chest as you.

'Has it been like this all this time?' I ask and you say that it has.

Still, your strength is building, and your stamina.

Some days you don't cough at all. You say the dry, Sicilian air helps you. I thank God for the beautiful air.

Yesterday, we rode the horses into the mountains and stopped by the shep-herd's hut, to let them drink and rest, and you and I, we lay together in the sun, and afterwards there was grit in my hair and my shoulders and back were burned raw.

'What on earth were you doing?' Enzo asked when he saw my back, later — it was blistered and peeling, and I could only sleep on my stomach for the pain. I

told him I had been sunbathing by the pool, and fallen asleep. It was a stupid lie, easy to disprove if he'd asked anyone else. Fortunately, he didn't question me further, although he must have had his doubts. I hadn't realised that the sun is so much stronger in the mountains, so much more dangerous. I only had my shirt off for a short while, but it was enough. We should have been more careful, you and I. We are too giddy with our own happiness. We don't think about anything else.

And now we're here, in the cottage that is your home. We play at being man and wife, as we played before, in the hotel, only this time our game is even more intense because the stakes are so high. You try to tune in the radio – it's almost impossible to get a signal here on the side of the mountain. I cut some bread and cheese for us to eat when we have had enough of making love. I sit cross-legged on the couch beside you. I am wearing your shirt, you are wearing shorts. We interrupt our meal to kiss; you put your hands on each side of my head so your fingers tangle in my hair, and you pull me to you. You look older than you used to: less boy, more man. The beard suits you. You look like an explorer.

Oh, Jack. I can't get enough of you. I want to climb into your pocket so that I can go everywhere with you. Every moment I'm not with you feels like a moment wasted. We need to be calm, we need to rest; to let the passion settle so that we can think and make a plan. But it's impossible to be rational when all my heart wants, with every beat, is for the two of us to be together, mouth on mouth, body on body; you inside me, making me come.

76

Maddalena was already finishing her breakfast when April arrived in the courtyard.

'I called the hospital,' Maddalena said. 'Papa had a good night. The doctor has to see him before they'll discharge him so I'm going to leave now, to make sure I'm with him, just in case Cunty turns up.'

'I'm surprised it's taken you this long to come up with that nickname.'

'Doesn't work in Italian,' said Maddalena cheerfully. 'By the way, I spoke to Donatella this morning and she has agreed to talk to you. She said you can go up at 10 a.m. She wants you to bring Elissa with you, though, as I won't be around and she finds it difficult to understand you. And Giuseppa will be there too. Donatella doesn't like to talk to strangers without Giuseppa present.'

'It's only a few questions; not the Spanish Inquisition.'

'My grandmother says you can never be too careful,' said Maddalena. 'She likes to have her back well covered.'

* * *

Donatella Borgata had a separate apartment on the first floor of the Villa Alba accessed via a lift constructed in a corner of the second hallway.

The apartment was as elegant and dilapidated as the rest of the villa but darker and more cluttered. Heavy drapes hung at the windows to keep out the light and the heat; every inch of the walls was covered with religious iconography; there was even an altar to one side of the living room with statuettes and framed pictures of the dead draped with rosary beads.

Giuseppa fussed as she ushered Elissa and April into Donatella's rooms.

'The only people usually allowed up here are Giuseppa and Uncle Enzo,' Elissa whispered to April. 'You should consider yourself honoured.'

They sat, as directed by Giuseppa, on chairs placed to one side of the window in the living room. Soon after, they heard the squeaking of the wheelchair and Giuseppa brought Donatella in. She parked the chair opposite Maddalena and Elissa and took a seat on the sofa to one side.

Donatella was dressed in a pink linen trouser suit and apricot silk blouse with her gnarled feet somehow squeezed into matching court shoes. Even the varnish on her nails had been changed to match. She was wearing a blonde wig, and a great deal of gold jewellery.

'You want to talk to me?' Donatella said to April.

'Yes, please. About Irene, Enzo's wife, the young woman who—'

'Yes, yes,' said Donatella, nodding so that her wig slid forwards and backwards, and then slipped a little to one side. 'I know who Irene is. Show her the picture, Elissa.'

'Which picture?'

'The photograph of Enzo and Irene arriving back here as husband and wife.'

Elissa got up and took a framed picture from the window-ledge. She passed it to April.

In the photograph, Irene was wearing a summer dress that flared at the waist and a straw hat fastened under her chin with a ribbon. Enzo stood beside her with his arms at his sides looking drunk with happiness. Daria, tall, thin and heavy-browed, was standing to one side, scowling. Little Maddalena was holding a box that contained a doll dressed as a flight attendant. She was a smaller version of her aunt, neither of them making the slightest effort to disguise their displeasure.

'Maddi doesn't look very happy,' April said.

Donatella gave a snort of disdain. 'She wasn't the only one. It was a shock to us all.'

'Didn't you know Enzo was bringing home a new wife?'

'He'd told us it was the bad weather that was keeping him in England. We didn't know he'd met a woman,' said Donatella. The last phrase was uttered with a heavy dose of sarcasm. Donatella clearly thought Irene had seduced her favourite son while he was alone and vulnerable in a foreign land.

Donatella then muttered almost to herself for a few minutes.

'What did she say?' April asked.

'That it would have been better if Enzo had brought Irene to Sicily before they married. It would have given the family time to talk him out of it,' Elissa explained. 'Donatella says she could see from the start that they should never have married. They weren't suited.'

'Could you ask her what she means by that?'

Elissa did as she'd been asked.

'It was obvious to anyone who saw them together. Enzo was a good man, a humble man. She, Irene, was a handful.'

'Did Donatella talk to Irene when she arrived? Did she try to befriend her? Help her?'

'Irene spoke no Italian, Donatella spoke no English. And besides, my grandmother was busy. My grandfather spent all his time with his horses, which meant it was entirely up to Donatella to help Enzo with the business as well as managing the household and family affairs.'

Donatella was suddenly overwhelmed by a bout of deep coughing.

Giuseppa leapt up and took hold of her hand, rubbing her hunched back and speaking to the old woman in low, reassuring tones.

'Would you fetch her some water, Elissa?'

Elissabeta disappeared into the apartment and returned with a glass of water and a straw. Donatella's breathing was horribly laboured.

'Perhaps we should stop,' said April.

'Would you like to finish there, Nonna?' Elissa asked.

Donatella shook her head. The wig slithered onto the floor. Giuseppa twitched, but didn't move to replace it. Donatella resumed her ranting.

'All Irene cared about was her bloody horse. She should have been looking after her husband, helping her mother-in-law, being a good wife, but no. She was up at the crack of dawn every morning to go riding. It was like she was obsessed.'

April had a sense of the depth of Donatella's anger. Irene's behaviour still rankled all these years later.

'I never heard anything so stupid,' she said, 'as a woman spending all day in the saddle, in the heat. I told Enzo. I said, "You want to stop your wife from carrying on like that or she's going to fall off and kill herself," but he said it was Irene's life and she was a grown woman and she could do what she liked. I think he was afraid to sit down and talk to her. He was afraid of what she might say.'

Donatella sniffed loudly. 'My opinion, not that anyone listened to me, was that Irene should have a baby to take her mind off the horses. Babies do make some women happy, you know.'

She put up a hand and realised the wig was no longer on her head. She had a brief, tetchy exchange with Giuseppa, who picked it up, dusted it off, and replaced it, and then nodded at April to let her know she could continue with her questions.

'I'll be as quick as I can,' said April. 'Does Donatella have any theories about what became of Irene on the day she disappeared?'

Donatella sniffed. Then she said: 'I don't have any theories. But I wouldn't have blamed Enzo if he had killed her! Nobody would've blamed him. They'd have said at last he'd stood up for himself and grown a pair.'

'Nonna!' said Elissa, her cheeks flushing deep red. 'You can't say that! You can't say it's okay for a husband to kill his wife just because she didn't behave like he wanted her to!'

'I didn't say it was "okay", I said nobody would have blamed him if he had!'

'Jesus!' Elissa muttered, dropping her head into her hands.

Donatella glowered at her granddaughter. 'Two things, young lady! Firstly, don't you ever, *ever* blaspheme in my villa and secondly, don't judge me! It was a different world back then! Everything was different! You don't understand!'

'I understand the moral difference between right and wrong!'

Donatella was wracked by another violent coughing fit.

Giuseppa jumped up. She looked across to Elissa and April. 'That's enough now. You can see the state she's in. Go away. Let me settle her! Let her rest!'

77

IRENE

I walk back down from the stables, through the dappled patches of dark and shade, love-sated. Happy. Enzo has been away all week and Patrick went to Siracusa yesterday to look at a horse and you and I have had our freedom, my darling. We have worked together in the stables; we've eaten together; we have snoozed together on a blanket in the shade of the trees. We have sat on the paddock gate, our feet tucked beneath the crossbar, our faces shadowed by our hats, side by side, talking.

I have neglected Maddalena. I feel bad about this. If Donatella would let her come up to the stables, then we could have some fun with her, but Donatella remains adamant that Maddi stay in the villa. I've tried to spend a little time with her each day. The poor child has no friends; nobody lives nearby. Sam used to play with her, but he's a teenager now, he doesn't want to be kicking a football round with his niece, or letting her swim between his legs in the pool. He gets on his bike and goes off to meet his friend. They take their guns to go 'hunting' in the mountains. He never seems to shoot anything. I'm sure it's deliberate, this lack of kills, he has a gentle heart, that boy.

There's Daria. She is willing to read with Maddalena, but Maddi has a great deal of energy. She likes to be doing something and Daria only enjoys quiet activities.

I fear that while I am with you, Jack, Maddi spends most of her time alone in the dressing room at the Villa Alba, playing with Bella-doll, making up stories about her in her head.

Apart from my guilt about Maddalena, guilt compounded by Alia's reproachful glare from the photograph every evening, the only stain on our happiness has been Quintu, who lurks, watching me, and you. Us. I hate how he creeps up on us, soft-footed. Several times I've only known he was close because Turi has become anxious. Quintu is not even supposed to be at the stables any more, so why does it feel as if he's always there? I'm sure he's hoping that you will put a foot wrong, so that he can go to Patrick, telling tales. He's jealous of you, Jack. He knows that you are physically weaker than him but he sees how you are so much better with the horses. Patrick was right to remove him from horse duties. You have the patience of a saint and the horses are reassured by your confidence and Quintu cannot bear the fact that you are superior to him in every single way.

I'm thinking about this when I reach the end of the path. The swimming pool looks so inviting, even though autumn is definitely in the air now. There is gold amongst the green of the leaves on the trees in the garden. I decide to run upstairs and find my costume; there's time for a swim before dinner. But then I go in through the French windows and there is Donatella, perched on the edge of a chair, and with her is a man I recognise: the doctor from Salgareale.

'Good afternoon, Doctor,' I say. I glance towards Donatella, who is looking shifty. 'Is everyone all right?'

'The doctor dropped by with Patrick's heart medicine,' says Donatella. 'He's in no rush. He has time to see you.'

'But I'm perfectly well.'

Donatella gives an awkward little half-smile and glances at the doctor. I feel a rush of rage.

'It makes sense to give you a quick examination, while I'm here, to check everything's working as it should,' says the doctor. 'Think of it as the human equivalent of a car being serviced.'

'I'm not a car,' I say, 'and I don't need to be serviced.'

I walk out of the living room with my head held high, but when I reach the hallway, I start to run. I run up the stairs, into our bedroom, and I push the door shut behind me and lock it. I am gasping with anger and frustration.

'Irene?'

Maddalena appears from the dressing room. She is holding Bella-doll in her arms. It's too much!

'Put that thing down,' I tell her.

'What?'

'Put it down! That awful, ugly thing! I don't like to see you with it. I don't want you to play with it any more. I'm going to burn it!'

'You can't!' Maddalena cries, holding onto the doll all the more tightly. 'She's mine and I'm not going to let you hurt her!'

'For God's sake!'

I grab the doll by one of its stupid baby arms and snatch it out of Maddalena's embrace. I throw it onto the floor. It lands face down, balanced on its hands and feet, making a triangle shape.

'Mamma!' it says bleakly. 'Mamma!'

* * *

When Enzo returns, I know what's going to happen. Donatella will tell tales on me. He'll say that I hurt his mother's feelings and embarrassed her in front of the doctor. He'll take her side and he'll refuse to see how her obsession with my body and my womb offends and distresses me and he'll say: 'Irene, Irene, calm down! You're overreacting... again!

Because of this, I'll put another brick in the wall that I'm building between me and Enzo. Several bricks. A whole new wall. And I'll try not to think about the fact that while Enzo is guilty of insensitivity towards me, and disloyalty, always taking his mother's side, I am guilty of worse.

I could not have let the doctor examine me earlier, no matter what, because less than an hour before I'd been in the cottage, making love with Jack.

78

'I'm sorry about my grandmother,' said Elissa as she and April walked back down the staircase.

'You don't have to apologise for her,' said April.

'But what she said was terrible and *she* won't say sorry.'

'I know she won't. That doesn't make it your fault.'

'She only says those things because she's old and doesn't know any better.'

April didn't answer this. She had never believed that age was an excuse for bigotry.

Listening to Donatella had hardened her resolve against the family.

If one of them, Enzo, Donatella, Sam or Daria, *was* responsible for doing harm to Irene, then she would follow due process and make sure they faced the consequences of their actions, never mind how other-worldly they were, or that they lived in this old villa as if it were an island, separate from the rest of the world, or that they sometimes pretended, at least to themselves, that the rules of the law didn't apply to them.

Not Elissa. Elissa was the most 'normal' one of the family.

'All of this kind of makes me glad that I won't be here much longer,' Elissa said. 'I'm moving to Naples at the end of next week.'

'Oh?'

'I've got a friend who's in a flat share and one of the guys is moving out so there's going to be a room free. Papa doesn't know yet. I'll tell him tonight, probably.'

'What about Tonio?'

'I haven't told him yet either.'

They had walked through the downstairs of the villa and emerged, blinking, into the courtyard.

'See you later,' said Elissa and she disappeared into the kitchen.

April continued into the garden. She was strolling amongst the trees when her phone rang. It was Roxie.

'I've got some information for you,' she said, 'about your Jack Harding.'

'Tell me!'

'I called the London *Evening News* and it turns out they still have an old-fashioned cuttings library. The archivist could not have been more helpful.'

'And...?'

'She found the cutting from November 1962, about the child slipping into the river near London Bridge and Jack Harding jumping in to save him. Before he jumped into the river, Jack took off his coat and there was a wage packet from the Pimlico Hotel in the pocket, which is how they knew who he was. You were right, it does say *a* body was later pulled from the water downstream. There was a more comprehensive article in the later edition of the newspaper, which says: "The body of a young man fitting the description of Jack Harding was pulled from the river downstream later that evening." So, yeah, everyone believed Jack had drowned. I guess the police would have gone to the Pimlico Hotel to let them know and to see if they could find an address for Jack's family amongst his belongings.'

'Didn't anyone identify the body?'

'Jack was from Yorkshire, the weather was bloody terrible and it was the run-up to Christmas. There must have been some delay before they managed to get a family member to London to ID the corpse and reveal that it wasn't Jack.'

And for all that time, Irene would be believing him dead.

'But if the body belonged to some other poor soul who happened to have fallen into the Thames that same afternoon, where was Jack Harding?'

'I'm working on that one, but I guess he could have been picked up by a boat or fished out at the next bridge and taken by road to somewhere outside London. He might have been unconscious or had amnesia. Who knows?'

'Thanks, Roxie. That's fantastic. Really helpful.'

'There's one more thing...'

'Yes?'

'You've got the *Evening News* archivist to thank for this little nugget too. She did a search under the name Jack Harding, and came up with this from the small ads – Lost and Found section. You ready? I'll read it to you:

Lost

Irene Marilyn Weatherbury, last known address: The Pimlico Hotel, Victoria, London. Please contact PO Box: 4180 with any information. Jack Harding.

That was published on 14 March 1963, and was the first of eighteen identical notices. So by mid-March Jack was recovered and back in London, but Irene was gone.'

'They must have just missed one another,' said April. She sat down on the bed and gazed at the window. 'It took him another four years to track her down to Sicily.'

'Four years,' said Roxie.

'But he never gave up. He never stopped looking.'

79

IRENE

December 1967

I come out of the cottage, my hair damp from the shower, wearing your sweater over my shirt, and Quintu is there, standing at the foot of the steps that lead up to the stable yard. He is leaning against the rock from which the steps have been hewn. A length of orange twine hangs from the pocket of his trousers like a rodent's tail.

Quintu doesn't say anything. He looks me up and down slowly. His gaze is blatant and rude. He is chewing gum. His jaw rotates lazily. I wonder how long he's been there.

A few feet to the right of his shoulder is the cottage's exterior wall. The little bathroom window is open a few inches, to let out the steam from the shower. The glass is patterned, but I can see the shape of the basin; the colours of the towels that you and I hung on the rack. If Quintu was standing here while we were showering, he will have seen enough. Too much.

'Scusàtimi,' I say, Excuse me, thinking my only option is to be brazen.

He doesn't move. He stands there with his arms folded across his chest.

And then you come out of the cottage behind me. You have my scarf in your hand. *Your hair is damp and messy like mine. We both smell of the cherry essence with which Giuseppa scents the toiletries she makes.*

'You forgot this,' you say, playfully lassoing me with the scarf, and then you see Quintu.

And we both know, in the same instant, that we have been careless. We are in trouble.

80

Some time later, April wandered into the kitchen and found Elissa cooking pasta.

'Hi,' she said. 'Is Giuseppa still up with Donatella?'

'She's worried about Nonna's cough,' said Elissa. 'The doctor's here. They're in the apartment with Nonna now.'

She fished a piece of penne out of the pan and tasted it. 'Mmm, *perfetto*! Will you have some?'

'Please.'

They dished up the lunch and then took their bowls outside, to the courtyard table. Troy came padding over, wagging his tail at half mast.

'He's trying to look as if he's never fed,' said Elissa, 'aren't you, Troy? You're making those sad, puppy-dog eyes that say, "Nobody ever gives me anything. I'm so starving!" but you're hardly wasting away, boy, are you?'

The dog put his chin on April's thigh and sighed deeply. She gave him some pasta.

'This is delicious, Elissa. Honestly, you should be a chef. You could open your own restaurant in Naples.'

Elissa stared into her bowl, moving the sauce around the pasta. 'Maybe.'

'Did you talk to Tonio yet?'

'Not yet. I don't know where he is. He's not answering his phone.'

'It's the sort of conversation you'd be better off having face to face anyway.'

Troy suddenly stood up and pricked his ears. He tipped his head to one side. The hackles on his shoulders were raised.

'Did you hear something?' April asked him.

She listened. She could hear voices; many voices.

Troy growled.

April put her bowl down on the table feeling dread, like a weight in her stomach. She stood up, picked up her phone.

'Wait here, Elissa, I'm going to look.'

She went through the front of the villa and down the drive. The closer she came to the gates, the louder the voices. She could pick out what they were chanting now:

'Justice for Irene!'

'Justice for Alia!'

April walked slowly forward, through the dappled shade cast by the trees. Troy was behind her, so close she could feel his breath on the back of her legs.

'Tell the truth, Enzo Borgata!' a woman's voice called.

'Tell us how you murdered your wives!'

April kept to the shade, creeping forward past a blue Mercedes with a 'Doctor On Call' badge until she could see through the gates. A small crowd had gathered. They were probably mostly from Salgareale, April guessed, members of the extended Oliveri family and their friends.

April couldn't be sure how many people were assembled; no more than twenty, but that was enough to bang on the roof of Maddalena's jeep when she returned; enough to hurl abuse at Enzo.

No doubt Conti was out there too, or at least his camera operator, waiting to get footage of it all ready for the big exposé tomorrow night.

She took her phone out of her pocket, called Maddalena.

'Hello?'

A man answered. His voice was weak but familiar, it reminded April of her childhood and of the happiest summers of her life.

'Enzo, hi, how good to hear your voice! It's me, April.'

'Hello, April, how nice to hear you too, my dear. How are you?'

'I'm good. Is Maddi driving?'

'Yes. We're about fifteen minutes from the villa.'

'Enzo, tell Maddi not to come to the main entrance. Tell her to drive in at the top, down the old horse-riding track.'

'Why?'

'There's a blockage at the bottom of the road,' April said. 'You can't get in that way. We'll meet you at the stables. Have you got that?'

'Yes, yes. Come in through the top entrance.'

'That's right. We'll see you there shortly.'

81

IRENE

Quintu hasn't said a word. He watches me. He's biding his time.

And meanwhile the preparations for Christmas are taking place at the Villa Alba and Enzo is being particularly attentive to me and Donatella is feeding me up – I suspect the doctor said I was more likely to conceive if I was a little heavier. I used to adore the marzipan fruits that are delivered in boxes from the Caramella sweet shop in Salgareale, but you can have too much of a good thing and I have become sick of the cloying feeling of sugar and almond paste in my mouth.

I'm sitting here at the kitchen table, making Christmas tree decorations with Maddalena who is excited about the forthcoming celebrations.

She is a bright, funny little thing and we have an affectionate, teasing relationship.

'Look, Irene!' she says, holding up a dried persimmon studded with cloves.

'That's beautiful,' I tell her. 'You're so clever with your hands!'

She smiles shyly; delighted by the praise.

I'm trying to relax, but I can't help imagining the devastation that will be wrought on this family, on this child, if Quintu tells Enzo about Jack and me. What will we do? How will we defend ourselves? Will we try to brazen it out? Lie? Say that Quintu is mistaken? Malicious? Attacking us out of spite?

No, we have to act first. We have to take the initiative. We can't live in constant fear of him and what he might do; or say; and to whom. We must think of a way to get Quintu off our backs for good.

We could leave, of course, but I can't bring myself to consider that option. How could I desert Maddalena? In any case, we couldn't go now, in the winter time, not when you are still so physically frail. The walk across the mountains would take too long. The weather is too severe. We wouldn't be able to ask for help, because once word was out, everyone would know who we were. For the time being, our only option is to stay put, at least until your health and the weather improves, or we come up with a viable plan.

82

April returned to the courtyard. Giuseppa and the doctor were there now, with Elissa, all three of them appeared stressed.

'What's happening?' asked the doctor. 'What's all that noise?'

'There's a crowd at the gates,' said April. 'Conti's rent-a-mob.'

'What do they want?'

'To cause trouble.'

'They're saying Uncle Enzo killed both his wives,' said Elissa.

She looked anxiously from one face to the other. Giuseppa noticed her distress, put an arm around the girl, and hugged her. It was the first time April had witnessed the housekeeper showing any affection to anyone. She turned to the doctor.

'Enzo's on his way back from hospital,' she said. 'His daughter's taking him directly to the cottage at the top end of the estate. Would you mind coming to check him over when he arrives?'

'It's no problem,' said the doctor. 'I don't particularly like the idea of running the gauntlet past an angry crowd anyway.'

* * *

April and the doctor walked up the hill, reaching the stables at the same time as Maddalena's jeep pulled into the yard.

Through the dusty windscreen, Enzo smiled at April.

It had been almost three decades since she had last seen her best friend's father and she was taken aback by the depth of affection she still felt for him. His hair had receded and was silver where, the last time she'd seen him, it had been black, but he still had the same serious gaze, the same dark brows, dark eyes and the long nose that was so like Daria's.

The memory of dozens of small kindnesses assaulted her, little emotional bubbles popping. Enzo had always had time for her. He had always listened to her, paid attention to her, made her feel that what she had to say was important. He had never teased her or made light of her problems, or appeared bored by her.

He'd never told her, as her mother did, frequently, that she was selfish, pathetic, useless.

He'd never criticised her appearance or her clothes; never made her feel that her worth as a human being was relative to other people's opinion of her.

When she was sixteen and in love with a boy who was involved with someone else, Enzo had sat up all night with her, telling her that she was valuable; precious; that she was too wonderful to be somebody's 'bit on the side'; that she should be their all, or their nothing. He told her that it was up to her to make the rules about herself, and how she was to be treated; and what she would tolerate, and what she would not and her responsibility to make those rules clear to any person with whom she intended to have any kind of relationship.

'You are valuable,' he'd told her. 'You're incredibly special. Don't give yourself away to anyone who doesn't see that.'

He had always encouraged her to follow her dream of joining the police, even though her mother had thought it was a ridiculous aspiration for a teenage girl.

The memory of these, and myriad other ways in which Enzo had helped April and supported her through her painful teenage years, came back to her.

The frail old man in the car raised his hand and waved.

She lifted her own arm in response.

Oh, please, she begged him silently, *please be innocent, Enzo.*

The car door opened. Distantly, from the front of the villa down below, came the sound of angry voices chanting: '*Justice for Irene! Justice for Alia!*'

'Hello, April,' said Enzo.

'Hi,' she replied with a smile.

83

IRENE

December 1967

Christmas is coming. My fourth in Sicily. The candles are burning in the windows and along the streets of Salgareale, and a fire has been lit in a brazier outside the church to keep the baby Jesus warm. The hilltop towns look especially pretty at this time of year: hundreds of lights twinkling through the darkness; smoke curling from the chimney pots. The tops of the mountains are sprinkled with snow. It looks as if they're wearing white shawls.

Enzo and I took Maddalena to the town of Custonaci, to see the presepe vivente, a live nativity scene arranged inside a cave. We spent the night together in a hotel, like a proper little family.

I did not want to leave you, but I had to go, for Maddalena's sake. It has become our tradition to make a pilgrimage like this each mid-December and she looks forward to it very much. Enzo believes Maddalena will soon be too old to appreciate the gentle magic of the people and animals acting out the story of Christ's birth. I think he's wrong. Maddi tries to act grown up, she pretends she's sophisticated, but she's still a child. She comes into our room and plays with that hideous doll, and I hear her narrating the game out loud, she speaking her own 'mother' role and also giving a voice to the 'daughter', Bella-doll. It makes me sad to hear her, poor motherless child. I'm all she has and, at present, I'm neither use nor ornament to my stepdaughter. My mind is too occupied with other concerns.

I am worried sick, Jack, and I know you are too. It's so difficult for us to have time alone now that the horses are brought in from the cold, and we are exercising them together, you, me, Patrick. Quintu sometimes comes too, as a safety precaution, so that nobody is out riding on their own on the mountains in this inclement weather. I tried to slip into the barn where you were stacking the hay this afternoon but Patrick called me to help him. He was trying to put on Turi's blanket. Turi was playing up, as he does when he senses tension in me. He pushed me against the stable wall and I have bruises on my shoulder, but that doesn't matter. What matters is that Quintu is blackmailing us.

Quintu came to you, while you were mucking out the stables, barrowing the dung and soiled bedding to the heap at the far end of the paddock, your breath clouding in the air, your fingers stiff from clutching the handles of the wheelbarrow. Every now and then you had to stop, to rest, because you were struggling to draw enough air into your lungs. You know that Quintu notices these pauses. You know that he assesses them, calculating your weaknesses.

He came to you while you were leaning on the pitchfork, head low, breathing slowly to reduce the constriction in your airways. You knew he was there, but you did not acknowledge him. You say it is best not to engage with him. But this time, he came to you.

He told you that his wife is pregnant. He wants the best for her and for their child. They are living in a draughty little house in Gibellina. He wants to install some mod cons. He needs money. The easiest way for him to get money is to demand it from us. Otherwise, he will tell the Borgatas about you and me, my love. That is the deal.

I find it rather sweet that Quintu felt the need to justify his extortion by explaining his domestic situation to you. As if the fact that he's doing this for his family somehow makes it acceptable.

In a way, I suppose it does. We all do what we can to protect the ones we love.

You give Quintu what money you have.

'It's not enough,' he tells you.

'I don't have any more,' you say.

'You might not, but she does.'

I don't. I don't need money because I never go shopping on my own. If I ask for something, Enzo buys it for me, or orders it. If we go into Palermo for the day, he gives me some cash to spend in the same way he treats Maddalena. When you were living in Gibellina, I had to steal the money we needed to pay Maria Grazia from Enzo's wallet. I spent the whole time worrying that he would notice and blame his daughter.

The bottom line is, we don't have any cash.

You explain this to Quintu.

'Something else then,' he says. 'Something valuable. Something I can sell.'

You report back to me. I tell you I'll think of something.

84

Maddalena found the key to Daria's cottage beneath a terracotta pot containing a leggy lavender plant.

She opened the door and went inside. April followed, with Enzo holding onto her arm. The doctor brought up the rear.

The interior of the cottage was tiny; it reminded April of a doll's house. It was also spartan; the walls crudely plastered and whitewashed; the furniture basic, chairs and a small settee covered with crocheted throws. The floor was plainly tiled; most of the space occupied by a kitchen-cum-diner-cum-living room.

Enzo sat on the couch and Maddalena filled glasses with bottled water from the fridge while the doctor checked Enzo over. He remained in good humour, although his skin was waxy and he looked terribly tired.

'Would you like something to eat, Papa?' Maddalena asked. 'Or something warm to drink? Do you need a pillow? Or a cushion for your back?'

'I'm fine,' Enzo said. 'Really, my love, you must stop worrying about me.' He turned to the doctor. 'Am I going to live?'

'I can't promise for ever, but the next few days are looking promising.'

She checked her watch.

'I really need to get back to the surgery.'

'I could give you a lift,' said Maddalena, 'and we'll drop your car back to you later, after the protesters have gone.'

'If that's okay with you?'

'You'll be all right with Papa for a short while, won't you, April?'

'Yes,' said April. 'Of course, I will.'

She hadn't intended to ask Enzo about Irene, not straight away, but by the time she'd gone to open the gate for Maddalena and then closed it behind her, Enzo had fallen asleep on the couch so there was no opportunity.

April had seen Enzo sleeping before, on the beach at the Marina, where they used to holiday, but that had been the healthy, restorative sleep of someone who was relaxing after months of hard work. This was different. This was a weak body gasping at its rest as if Enzo's troubled heart was struggling to find the strength to beat.

Enzo was lying on his side, like a child, with one hand under his chin. The other hand, beside it, looked small, the fingers curled inwards. April saw, with a pang, that he was still wearing his wedding ring; the one that matched the ring she'd found hidden inside the doll in Irene's room.

She picked up a cotton throw from a basket on the floor and gently covered him over. She examined his face, saw how the skin draped more softly over the bones these days, how the eyes and lips were surrounded by lines and how the stubble on his chin was silver now. When she was young and vulnerable, he had looked after her. The urge to reciprocate now was strong.

April went to stand by the window. All she could see were the strong vertical lines of the trunks of pine trees, growing upwards, competing with one another for the best of the sunlight, and the leaf-litter on the ground. She half listened to the quiet sound of Enzo's snoring but in her mind she had gone back to the days of Jack and Irene.

They would have hidden themselves away in this cottage, she thought. This is where they would have come to make love.

Perhaps, when Patrick was snoozing in the barn, or had gone back down to the villa for his lunch, they came in here to talk, to fill in the gaps in their histories, those four years when they should have been together, but were apart.

Irene would have told Jack about Donatella and Maddalena, and the doll. They would have cried and laughed and held one another's hands, and touched each other's cheeks in wonderment.

You're here, my darling, you're really here.

And they, smelling of hay and horses, dust in their hair, must have undressed and put their bodies together.

April wrapped her arms about herself, feeling a pang of longing that could never be requited, because her man, her Cobain, was gone.

How long did they have, Jack and Irene, before the earthquake separated them again she wondered? Weeks? Months? She didn't know.

'Justice for Irene!' the voices chanted, way down below, outside the villa. *'Justice for Alia!'*

Irene would have stood here, April thought, exactly where I'm standing now, her bare feet on these red floor tiles. Perhaps she was wearing one of Jack's shirts, holding a glass of water, knowing she should go back to the villa, reluctant to leave. And he, Jack, would have been right here with her. She closed her eyes and imagined his presence. She felt Irene so strongly in the villa, but she had little sense of Jack; it was easier to feel him here.

As she stood there, quietly, Enzo's soft snoring behind her, April realised that the story about Turi behaving oddly during the day that preceded the earthquake, and Irene coming up to the stables to check on him, must have been a lie.

Irene had been here already, in the cottage, with her lover when the earthquake struck.

That would be how they spent time together. Irene would sneak up to the cottage under the cover of darkness while Enzo was away on business trips. As long as she was careful to be back before anyone else was up, it would have been easy for her. For them.

It was an awful betrayal of Enzo though and Giuseppa had said he was at the villa on the night of the earthquake. Surely Irene wouldn't be so brazen, or reckless, as to slip away to come to her lover while her husband slept in the marital bed, beside her?

85

IRENE

Last night, I went into the dressing room alone and I laid out all the jewellery that Enzo has given me to decide which piece to sacrifice to pay off Quintu. Most of it used to belong to Alia. I know what I'm doing is wrong; terribly wrong. I am using another woman's belongings to buy my way out of a situation brought about by my own selfishness.

Alia was faithful, loyal and true.

I am the opposite. I am now adding theft to the list of ways I have wronged the Borgatas.

I took ages deciding which piece to give you to give to Quintu, weighing up the pros and cons, not for me, but for Enzo and Maddalena. I even tried to imagine what Alia would tell me to do. In the end, I settled on the ruby brooch that Donatella gave to Alia. I've hardly ever worn it, no more than two or three times since I came to Sicily. I know Maddalena doesn't like it. I don't believe she will miss it when she is older and the remaining jewellery is passed to her. For the time being, nobody will notice it is gone.

I take the brooch up to the stables, in its box, wrapped in a piece of rag. I pass it to you, so that you can slip it to Quintu, to buy his silence.

'You must tell him that this is all he's getting,' I say. 'If you don't make that clear, he'll keep asking for more.'

We are standing in Turi's loose box, in the corner, with the horse between us and the door. I have always been happy here, listening to Turi blowing air out through his nostrils, hearing him paw at his bedding. What we are doing now is corrupting this perfect place.

You take off your gloves, remove the rag, and open the lid of the little box. The brooch is nestling in a bed of oyster-coloured silk. The name and address of the jeweller's in Salgareale, where Donatella purchased the brooch, is printed on the silk.

I don't know what the brooch is worth. Maybe nothing; maybe tens of thousands of lire, maybe many millions. It would have been better for you to have taken the piece into Palermo, to have it valued. Then we could have sold it at the optimum price and given Quintu some, or all, of the money. But there is no straightforward way for you to get to Palermo, we don't have time to think of a plan and, even if we did, Quintu wants to be paid now.

There are no words for how guilty I feel.

The brooch is not to my taste or style, but it belonged to Maddalena's mother and, by rights, it should go to Maddi. It is not mine to give away; especially not to protect a secret that has the potential to cause so much pain to my stepdaughter. I am torn.

I can't balance things in my mind. I can't come to terms with the fact that our love, Jack, a love so indisputably good and inevitable, is the cause of this ugliness. It's not right. It's not how things should be. I wish I could see a clear way forward for us, but I can't. Right now, everything seems to be getting worse, not better.

'We'll be alright,' you say. 'We'll leave together when the winter is over.'

And I don't reply because all I can think of is the damage that would do to Maddalena.

86

What if, April thought, Irene hadn't come up here on the night of 14 January 1968 to sleep with Jack? What if she'd come up here because that was the night that they'd chosen to run away? Irene might have stashed a suitcase in the cottage. She might have lain awake until she was certain Enzo was sleeping deeply, and then crept out of the villa and made her way, through the dark, up to the cottage. She and Jack must have had some kind of transport ready. Or maybe they were planning to steal one of the Borgatas' cars.

She stood by the window and rested her head on the side of the frame. Her brain had blanked out the chanting of the protesters and the sounds of Enzo sleeping. She was imagining Jack creeping out of the cottage in the early hours and going to meet Irene so she didn't have to climb that steep path in the dark on her own. She imagined the two of them coming into the cottage to collect their belongings. They would have been anxious, but also exhilarated. Thrilled.

And then the earthquake came. Perhaps they were loading up whatever vehicle they were planning on taking when the ground began to shake beneath their feet.

Would those two young people from Yorkshire have realised that they were experiencing a catastrophic tremor? Would they have known what to do? Did it cross their minds that this might be the perfect opportunity for them to slip away, because everyone's attention, for the foreseeable future, would be focussed on the natural disaster?

Perhaps it did, but no matter. Irene would never have left without making sure the horses were safe first, especially her beloved Turi.

April felt as if she could open the curtain that separated past from present. She could see Irene and Jack, all thoughts of their own futures forgotten as they scrambled to the stables and attempted to soothe the terrified animals, to lead them out into the safety of the paddock. It would have been dark and cold and, to Jack and Irene, the night must have felt apocalyptic, yet still they risked everything to save the horses. They were in the stable together doing what? Trying to calm a rearing stallion? Pressed against the wall to avoid his flailing hooves, his great, muscular legs, when the wall, already weakened by the tremor, gave way and collapsed, killing Jack; trapping Irene?

April covered her face with her hands.

'Oh, Irene,' she whispered. 'I'm so sorry.'

87

IRENE

New Year's Eve, 1967

Everyone is together in the Villa Alba for the end-of-year celebrations. Giuseppa has been preparing for this since Christmas and the results of her labours, dishes of the same incredible food she produces every New Year's Eve, are spread on the table in the dining room. The centrepiece is an enormous cassata, covered in pink and green icing and decorated with candied fruit and nuts. Giuseppa is flushed and breathless, batting away the thanks and praise heaped upon her; all she really wants is to see the family enjoying eating what she's made. Sam is wolfing down everything she puts in front of him. She watches him with such pleasure. He eats like a horse, that boy, but never puts on any weight. Poor Enzo only has to look at food for his belly to grow another ounce of fat.

It's not only the family who is here, but friends of the Borgatas, and business acquaintances. These people come every year, wealthy men and their beautiful wives. They arrive in big cars; some of them have drivers who are now in the kitchen, drinking cider.

The villa's main rooms are a swirl of laughter and colour. Patrick is playing his fiddle in the living room and the furniture has been pulled back to make a dance floor. The Sicilians are having a marvellous time doing their version of a traditional Irish jig. Quintu is here with his wife. She is a tiny, pretty Sicilian woman, her belly already swollen with pregnancy. Quintu is protective of her, and proud. She is wearing a new dress. I wonder if it was paid for with the money Quintu received when he sold the ruby brooch.

I'm watching you, Jack, of course. This is the first time you've set foot inside the Villa Alba. The prospect of you being here, within these walls, both thrills and terrifies me.

For the briefest moment, I take my eyes from you and look, instead, at Enzo. He is dancing with Maddalena. She looks so sweet tonight; she's wearing a Mary Quant-style dress with long sleeves, a contrasting collar and cuffs and a cute skirt that bounces as she spins. This is the last New Year when she'll still be a little girl; the last year, I suspect, that she'll dance with her papa with unselfconscious joy. Enzo tips a pretend hat to me. I sip my champagne. Sam comes to stand beside me. He has a bottle in one hand with which he keeps refilling the glass he holds in the other. Donatella would be furious if she saw him. She's so hard on that boy. His friend is hovering nearby.

'Hi,' says Sam, swaying.

'Take it easy, Sam,' I say.

'I'm not a kid, you know.'

'I know.' I nudge him and nod towards a teenage girl. She's thirteen or fourteen, giggly, wearing braces. 'That girl keeps watching you,' I say. 'You should ask her to dance.'

'Not interested.'

'No? She's pretty.'

'If I talk to her, I'll have to marry her.'

'No, you won't.'

'I will.'

'What are you on about?'

'Her father is El Capo. The big boss.'

'Big boss of what?'

Sam rolls his eyes. 'What do you think?'

I know some of these people are Mafiosi. I have known since before I came to Sicily that the Borgatas mix with dangerous men and women. Enzo told me. He said they have no choice but to be 'good neighbours' in order to stay on the right side of the clan. On occasions, Enzo said, Donatella dishes out fake contracts, so the Mafia can launder money through the tuna business. He told me that such complicity disgusts him; that he will have none of it when he takes over the reins in a year or two.

I have seen these people before, at parties, and when they came to the Villa Alba for meetings. It's obvious now I think about it, but until now I hadn't consciously realised the significance of those visits.

'Which one is the girl's father?' I ask Sam.

'That one.' He nods in the direction of a short, bespectacled, bull-necked man with a tuft of black hair on his head. He is a man with dead eyes. A bully. A creep.

The man is talking to Quintu. As I watch, he puts an arm around Quintu's shoulder, pulls him closer, and kisses the side of his face.

88

Enzo was still sleeping. April was restless. She went out of the cottage and up to the yard. The heat was stifling. She walked to the derelict end of the stables where the wall had collapsed. The sun was cutting over the top of the mountain, shining down its yellow beams.

She found a patch of shade, took her phone out of her pocket, and called Inspector Mazzotta.

He answered at once.

'I heard you've got some trouble down at the villa,' he said.

'Protesters, yes. They're standing by the gates calling for justice. They've been here for hours.'

'Is everyone okay?'

'Enzo is out of harm's way. We're hoping the mob will go away soon.'

'Conti's doing his broadcast from down there this evening. He'll want an audience and they'll be vying to get their faces on TV. I'll come down with a few uniformed officers and we'll make sure everyone disperses after that.'

'Thanks. Will we have a chance to talk later?' April asked. 'I have a lot to tell you.'

'Can't you tell me now?'

'It's a long story.'

'Make it short.'

'Okay. Well... The main thing is...' April looked down at the cottage. 'I think Irene was planning on running away with the stable hand, her old fiancé. If I'm right, and they were intending to leave on the night of the earthquake, then Irene might have left a note for Enzo. He might well have known about their relationship.'

'So now you have a motive for Enzo murdering Irene. To stop her leaving him.'

'Except she wasn't going to leave him any more, at least not with Jack, because Jack was dead.'

'Right.' The inspector was silent for a moment, then he said, 'If you're right, Enzo might well have been angry and humiliated by Irene's betrayal. He might still have been driven to hurt her.'

'I need to talk to him. Only he's in a bad way, health-wise. I'll have to tread carefully.'

'Good luck,' said the inspector. There was another pause, then he said, 'Perhaps, after Conti's broadcast, we could go and grab something to eat in Salgareale. We could have a proper talk.'

'That would be great.'

They finished the call and April went back into the cottage.

Enzo was sitting up on the couch, looking dazed.

April perched beside him. 'How are you feeling?'

'I've been worse.'

She took his hand and held it between hers hoping that she might intuit, somehow, if Enzo was guilty or innocent. It was almost, but not quite, impossible for her to believe that this was a hand that could have killed.

89

IRENE

5 January 1968

'We have to get out of here,' you say under your breath. You're not looking at me. We are working together in the stables, mucking out. The bleachy smell of horse piss is making my eyes water. I'm wrapped in layers of clothes and my breath is clouding in the cold, but beneath the jumpers and scarf and coat I'm sweating.

Turi is tied up by the door, pulling hay from his feed net. He has a habit of tossing it onto his head, between his ears, and wearing it like a hairpiece. Patrick and Quintu are in the next-door loose box.

I fork dirty bedding and clumps of manure into the wheelbarrow.

'Is Quintu putting pressure on again?' I ask.

You nod. The transistor radio is balanced on the little wall outside. The music is masking our words yet you are twitchy. I've never seen you like this before.

'Is he demanding we steal something else?'

'I told him he wasn't getting anything else from us and then he pulled out a pistol. He was waving it around. He's fucking proud of it.'

I know Quintu has a gun. I've seen the game he shoots; I've eaten some of it. I hadn't worried about it until now.

'What are you saying?' I ask. 'That he'll shoot one of us if we don't do as he demands?'

'He wasn't directly threatening us.'

'What then?'

Your eyes flick towards Turi.

Turi turns to look at me, with his hay toupée sitting at a jaunty angle.

'No!' I cry! 'No! No! No!'

Patrick appears at the stable door. He pushes Turi aside. 'What's the matter, Irene?'

My father-in-law is looking straight at me. The bastard, Quintu, stands behind him, watching over his left shoulder. Quintu is chewing gum and the collar of his donkey jacket is pulled up around his neck. He's smirking.

Turi gives me an affectionate nudge with his nose. I put my hand to his cheek, feel the warmth of him beneath my palm.

'I dropped the barrow on my foot,' I say, my eyes fixed on Quintu's. 'That's all.'

90

Because Enzo was stuck in Daria's cottage until the crowd outside the villa gates dispersed, Sam, Maddalena and April watched *Serata* on the television set there.

Daria had put a couple of wooden chairs outside the door, and she and her brother, Enzo, sat side by side, waiting for the air to cool and listening to the rustling of the evening breeze in the tops of the trees.

Inside, Sam, directed by Maddalena, spent the best part of half an hour moving the aerial on top of the set from one place to another in order to get a picture. When he finally found one, it was grainy and distorted.

They had the volume turned low so as not to distress Enzo.

'Now,' said the presenter cheerfully, 'we're going live to Milo Conti outside a multi-million euro villa on the outskirts of the town of Salgareale, *Enzo Borgata's luxury hideaway*! Hi, Milo! Can you tell us what we've got to look forward to this evening?'

There was Conti, outside the villa gates, surrounded by people holding placards. They cheered as the feed cut to them and, at almost the exact same time, the group gathered in the cottage heard a distant cheer from the bottom of the hill.

'Ciau!' Conti boomed, holding the microphone as if it were a trophy.

'This evening, ladies and gentlemen, I'm going to show you a crucial piece of evidence pertaining to the mysterious disappearance of the young and beautiful Irene Borgata, thirty-five years ago. If any of our viewers are still in any doubt about the guilt of Enzo Borgata, this evidence will convince them.'

'The fuck it will,' muttered Sam.

'Sam...' Maddalena reproved gently.

'And also,' Conti continued, 'we'll be asking an important question.'

'What question is that?' prompted the presenter.

'The question is: was the death of Enzo Borgata's first wife, Alia Oliveri, really due to natural causes? Or was he responsible for her death, too?'

91

IRENE

Night-time, 7 January 1968

We haven't had any time alone together to talk, Jack, since you told me about the gun. But tonight, for one night only, Enzo is away. We have agreed to meet at the cottage at midnight, but at quarter to twelve, as I am preparing to leave the villa, Maddalena appears at the bedroom door, barefoot. She looks like a wraith.

I was half into my coat. Now I pretend I was taking it off, rather than putting it on.

'What's the matter?' I ask, trying to smother my impatience. She coughs, bright red spots of colour on her cheeks, her eyes glittery. I soften. 'Oh, darling Maddi, do you feel poorly?'

She nods. I bend down so that our eyes are level, push aside strands of sweat-soaked hair and put my wrist to her forehead. She's burning up. 'Ouch!' I say, waving my hand in the air, pretending to be scalded.

She doesn't smile.

'I'm scared,' she whispers.

I become serious. 'Why are you scared, honey?'

'Because the Befana came into my room.'

The Befana is the Christmas witch. Since I came here I've observed how Maddalena is half thrilled, half petrified by the old hag. Really, she's too old for this kind of nonsense, but she acts young for her age. I'm sure it's because she doesn't mix with other children.

'What did the Befana want?' I ask.

'She said she had come to take me to Mamma.'

'The Befana is not real,' I say.

'But she was there,' Maddi insists. 'She says Mamma is in the cemetery. She says she's looking for me.'

I shudder. I have run up the path in the dark past the cemetery many times now. Each time, it feels as if someone is amongst those dark trees, watching me. I have been afraid that if I look over the gate, I might see Alia, hollow-eyed and ghostly, staring back at me. How strange that my nightmares and Maddalena's are so similar. It is a sign of how close we are now.

'Listen, Maddi,' I say, 'when people's temperatures are as high as yours is now, they often see things that aren't there. It's called "hallucinating". It's quite normal. I promise you that nobody came into your room.'

She's trying not to cry, bless her soul. She doesn't argue with me but I can see she's not convinced.

'Come on,' I say, 'you get into my bed. You can sleep in your papa's space tonight and if you are frightened again, you only have to nudge me and I'll wake up and we'll deal with whatever it is together. Okay?'

She nods stoically.

'Only no snoring like your papa, okay?'

She grins feebly and climbs into the bed, sweating and shivering, and I lie beside her, stroking her forehead. Eventually she drifts into a restless sleep.

I know that you're waiting for me, Jack. I can feel your concern manifesting itself from the top of the path but what can I do? I can't leave Maddalena like this. I can't risk coming to you and she waking and finding herself alone.

92

While they waited for the cameras to return to Conti, April went outside, to sit with Daria and Enzo.

Enzo had fallen asleep in his chair. Daria had placed a pillow to one side of his head, and was watching him, wafting away insects.

'Do you know what it is, this evidence that Conti is boasting about?' Daria asked quietly.

'No,' April replied.

'What if it really is irrefutable?'

'If Enzo is innocent, then it cannot be irrefutable.'

'Have you found any evidence that proves my brother didn't hurt Irene?'

'Without an alibi, it's almost impossible to prove that someone didn't do something.'

Daria sighed. 'You should hear what people are saying in Salgareale. They say the Borgata family has been sheltering a murderer for all these years.' She glanced at her brother with pity. 'It's difficult for Franco, who owns the pharmacy, having me working there. I have a feeling I'll end up resigning so I don't have to put him in the position of having to let me go.'

There was a roar from the crowd at the gates.

'Conti's back on!' Sam called.

'You go,' said Daria. 'I'll stay here with Enzo.'

April went back inside and watched the TV from behind the couch where Maddalena and Sam sat side by side. Conti had roused his crowd of supporters to a new energy. They were baying for Enzo's blood.

Conti went through his rigmarole again. He counted on his fingers the 'evidence' he had amassed against Enzo. He railed against the police for their inactivity.

Then he produced a folded piece of paper and held it up to the camera.

'This,' he said, '*this* is what is going to convict Enzo Borgata. It's a note written by his wife, Irene, and hidden in her bedroom shortly before she died. It's a message to the future that she wrote at a time when she feared – yes! *feared* – for her life. Tomorrow, I'm going to return to the Villa Alba, and I urge all lovers of justice, men, women and children, to join me when I reveal the words Irene wrote, and let's see what happens. Let's see if Enzo Borgata will finally admit to his heinous crimes!'

93

IRENE

1.10 a.m., 8 January 1968

*Maddalena tosses and turns in the bed behind me. The fire flickers in the hearth.
I pace the room, sick with worry: I'm worried about my stepdaughter, about
Quintu, about Turi, about us.*

*After Enzo left for Sardinia this morning, I crept into his office. He keeps the
key to his desk beneath the papier mâché ashtray that Maddalena made for him.
I took the key and opened the locked drawer. Inside was the roll of notes he uses
to pay contractors. I took a third of the money, about 500,000 lire, and replaced
the rest. Enzo might not notice for a while, and if he does... Oh, God, if he does, I
shall have to think of some story to tell him.*

*The cash is in my coat pocket. I was supposed to bring it to you to give to
Quintu. How am I to get it to you now?*

On the bed, Maddalena talks in her sleep.

'Mamma!' she whimpers. 'Don't cry. Please don't cry!'

*She has never called me 'Mamma'. How strange that she dreams of Alia;
the woman she didn't know; the mother who died in that same bed where
Maddi now lies. Alia had a fever then. Maddi has one now. What goes around*

comes around. Thieves never prosper. My mother's threats rattle around in my head.

I walk from one end of the room to another. I touch Maddalena's cheek. Her temperature is still high. I wonder if I should alert Donatella, or call for the doctor. Giuseppa said it was best to let the fever do its job and wait it out, but is she right? How hot is too hot? The responsibility is overwhelming.

The sudden noise, a clattering, scares me half to death, but although my heart's racing, I realise it is you, outside, throwing pebbles at the window. I open it and come out onto the balcony. It's freezing.

'Did Enzo return?' you call softly.

'No!'

And you are already climbing up, using the holes in the villa's old walls as footholds. You reach the top, take hold of me, press me against the window, kiss me.

How cold it is. How my teeth chatter. There is no pleasure in this, only fear.

We go into the room. I'm holding my finger to my lips. 'Shh, Maddi is here...'

You glance at my stepdaughter, then back at me. I go to my coat, hanging on the hook on the back of the door, take the money from the pocket, but before I can do anything with it, you take hold of my shoulders and turn me to face you.

'Listen, I have some good news. I was speaking with the farrier today. His brother owns a fishing boat. If we can make it to Messina, he will take us to the Italian mainland.'

'You told the farrier about us?'

'No, of course not. I said I had a friend who needed a favour.'

You're bright-eyed, buzzing. I am full of concern for Maddalena. I can't switch it off simply to share your excitement.

'Even if we make it to Italy, we'll be stuck there,' I say. 'I don't have a passport of my own.'

'We'll make up some story; give false names; say that you were robbed. Or we'll buy a stolen passport.'

'Jack! We'll get ourselves arrested.'

'We won't.'

'It's too dangerous.'

'It's the only way.'

'Irene?'

It's Maddalena. She's sitting up in bed. 'Why is he here?'

I press the cash I stole from Enzo into your palm. 'Go!'

You pull back the curtain and leave the way you came in. I close the window behind you, go to the bed and sit beside the child, hold her in my arms. 'There now,' I say, 'everything's all right. Shall I bring you some water?'

Maddi snuggles against me.

'Why was Jack here?' she asks again.

'He wasn't,' I say, wicked stepmother that I am. 'It was a fever dream, darling.'

'No, it wasn't a dream. He was here.'

'Why would he be here, in this room at this time of night? Of course he wasn't here, you silly thing?'

I rock her gently and begin to hum 'My Bonnie Lies Over the Ocean'.

She closes her eyes. Sorry, I think. Sorry, sorry, sorry, for lying to you darling girl, my sweet, lovely Maddalena.

94

Inspector Luca Mazzotta arrived at the villa just after 8.30 p.m. He did not drive a flash car, but a dusty old Fiat Tipo. He leaned across to open the passenger-side door for April, who was waiting for him at the gates.

'So the Enzo Borgata Misappreciation Society has dispersed,' said the inspector as he turned the car round. They drove downhill, heading towards Salgareale via a road that April hadn't travelled before.

'For now.'

'There'll be more of them tomorrow. Those who saw the programme tonight will be wanting to get in on the action. There's nothing like a spot of group sanctimony to make people feel better about their own behaviour.'

'It's depressing,' said April.

'It's human nature.'

Ahead was a bridge that crossed the ravine, its base devoid of water, but full of boulders that had been washed down the mountain. April imagined what the spot must be like in spring when the snowmelt swelled the river.

The ravine would have been comprehensively searched at the time of Irene's disappearance. The locals would have known where to look. If she'd been in the river, they'd have found her.

'I don't suppose you've seen any of Conti's big "reveal" programmes, have you?' asked Inspector Mazzotta.

'No.'

'It all gets pretty emotive. Conti knows how to manipulate a crowd.'

'Do you think it might turn nasty?'

'Possibly. Conflict makes good television.'

'It's horrible.'

'It's the root of all drama.'

They had crossed the bridge now and both fell silent as the inspector drove the car around a series of hairpin bends as the road climbed back uphill. Shortly afterwards, the town came into view.

'Here we are,' said the inspector. 'Welcome to Salgareale.'

It was a quirky little place with cobbled streets, cream and buff-coloured buildings with plants tumbling from ornate iron balconies, ornamental architectural touches everywhere. Lights were lit in many of the windows.

The inspector parked the car at the far edge of the town, on a rocky ledge jutting out from the side of the hill. The moonlit view was bleak and beautiful.

April slipped her jacket over her shoulders and followed the inspector back into the town, eventually arriving at a small square. A church at the far end had a simple but architecturally pleasing and beautifully illuminated façade and steps leading up to its doors. Four tall palm trees grew, one in each corner of the square. In between the trees were tables and chairs, a restaurant on either side, one advertising itself as a pizzeria, the other a trattoria. Lights were strung between the street lamps and were wrapped around the lower parts of the tree trunks. Waiters moved in and out of the restaurants, carrying trays, bottles, jugs. And there was a buzz to the place; the chattering of dozens of voices, laughter, a child saying, 'Watch me, Papa! Watch me!'

Both restaurants were busy, but the inspector walked towards the pizzeria. He and April were greeted warmly by the waiter at the door, and they were shown to an outdoor table covered with a red checked table-cloth held down by a stumpy candle in a jar. The inspector asked April if she'd prefer red or white wine. She chose white, and he ordered a bottle of Alcamo. 'It's made locally,' he said. 'The grapevines are cultivated on the slopes of the mountains around us.'

'This evening, I feel like I'm on holiday, Inspector,' said April.

'Please, call me Luca.'

'Luca. And I'm April.'

The waiter returned with a bottle of wine, a bucket full of ice and a corkscrew bottle-opener. He opened the bottle and poured the wine.

April picked up her glass by its stem and held it up to the light, then she drank.

'Good?' the inspector asked.

'Delicious.' She drank some more.

'You look tired.'

'Oh, I'm okay. It's just frustrating. I feel as if I've failed my friend, Maddalena.'

'Failed how?'

'I haven't been able to find any conclusive evidence to suggest that Enzo Borgata didn't harm Irene. If anything, every fact I've unearthed has only strengthened the case against him.'

'Hmm,' said the inspector. 'Choose a pizza and then we'll talk.'

'I'll have a Margherita please.'

April relaxed back into her chair. She pushed off her sandals and rested the soles of her feet against the wooden brace of the table. They ordered and then the inspector said, 'Okay. Now, tell me what you've found out.'

April took a deep breath and she recounted the story of Jack, Irene, and Enzo. She started with Irene believing Jack drowned in the Thames, and finished when the stable wall collapsed during the earthquake on the same night, she believed, that Irene and Jack had planned to leave.

'It must have been horrific for both Enzo and Irene,' April said. 'Irene must have been in awful emotional and physical pain and even if she had the energy to propagate the lie about why she was up at the stables in the early hours, I don't see how Enzo could have believed it.'

'You think she told him the truth?'

'She'd just watched her lover die literally beside her. She'd have had to be incredibly strong to hide her grief from her husband.'

April took another drink of wine. 'Maddalena says her father won't talk about the events of 1968, he won't even answer the most basic questions. But I'm certain that he knew about Jack and Irene. He knew that she didn't love him and that she'd been trying to leave. And if that's true, then imagine what the time between the earthquake and Irene's disappearance must have been like, for the pair of them.'

'Hmm,' said Luca. He was swirling his wine around the bowl of the glass.

'"Hmm," what?' asked April.

'I've been thinking about the disparity between the witness statements of Daria and Sam.'

April was mildly disorientated. 'What does that have to do with Enzo and Irene?'

'Nothing. But I told you right from the start that I didn't like the fact that the statements didn't match.'

'I spoke to Giuseppa and she confirmed that Sam's version was correct.'

'I know that's what she said,' said Luca, 'but still it was bugging me. So, I came into Salgareale earlier, called into the pharmacy, and invited Daria Borgata to come and have a coffee with me and a chat.'

'Oh,' said April. 'Right. And what did she say?'

95

IRENE

10 January 1968

Maddalena is better today. She's sitting in the bedroom, playing with Bella-doll.

I'm half listening to her, half concentrating on what I'm doing, which is looking through my possessions; working out what I should take if we leave. You say we need to be ready to move quickly when the right moment comes; when you feel well enough to face the long trip, and the weather has improved. I'm still torn. I want to be free of Quintu. I want Turi to be safe. I want to be with you.

But I don't want to leave Maddalena. I don't want to hurt her. I don't know what will become of Enzo if I leave him. I can't bear the thought of the pain my desertion will cause.

I'm afraid to go. But then I see Quintu's face; I see the cruelty in his eyes, and I am also afraid to stay. We were stupid to play into his hands. We should never have given him the chance to have any kind of hold over us. I wish I could turn back time and do things differently. I wish I could go back to London, to the day the boy fell in the river, and I would go to him and put my arms round him and stop him falling and then none of this would have happened.

But it has happened.

And I can't go back.

You say that we must leave at night. You consider taking Patrick's old van, or one of the cars, but that would be dangerous. It would also be stealing, I say. We have stolen too much from the Borgatas as it is.

Better to go on foot, you say, following the agricultural tracks; avoiding the roads. We can rest in the shepherds' shelters and divert into the larger towns, where we won't stick out so much. You say we have enough nous, between the two of us, to keep out of trouble but I am afraid. You barely speak any Italian and people tell me I still have a strong English accent. It will be difficult for us not to draw attention to ourselves. I think of Quintu at the party. I think of the Mafia boss kissing his cheek. I think of all the links and connections and loyalties that these old families have established. I imagine them spread about the land-scape like a net.

I hear Patrick and Donatella talking. I see the newspapers that Patrick leaves lying around. I know there have been car bombings in Palermo and that the trials of Mafiosi involved in the heroin trade are taking place. Tensions are running high. I don't think you realise, Jack, how pervasive the Cosa Nostra is, in this part of the world. I don't think you have any idea of the dangers we'll be facing.

And besides all these worries, there are practical concerns, and moral ones too.

I feel so awful about what I'm about to do to Enzo. I have to keep reminding myself that I tried to be a good wife to him. I did my best. Everything I did was done in good faith. I never set out to hurt him. I never intended to cause him pain. The series of events that led us to this point were not my responsibility. They were out of my control.

Even as I'm thinking of my husband, I hear footsteps on the stairs and then they approach along the landing, and Enzo comes into the room.

'Hello, Papa,' says Maddalena.

'Go and find Giuseppa, Maddi,' says Enzo.

'Oh, but I'm playing, look—'

'Go!' says Enzo. He holds the door open for his daughter. She picks up the doll and slopes away, turning on the landing to pull a rude face at her father's back. Normally this would amuse me, but today Enzo's demeanour is alarming me.

'Is everything all right?' I ask him.

'No,' he replies, 'no, it's not!' and he pulls the door shut behind him.

96

Before Luca could elaborate on his meeting with Daria, the pizzas were delivered to their table and the no-discussing-business-while-eating rule came into play. April was grateful for the opportunity to concentrate on the food. The pizza crusts were thin and crispy, the topping scalding hot, salty, sweet and oily. They finished the wine and ordered another bottle. April was enjoying herself. It was good to be out in this lovely little town, eating good food, in the company of a colleague. It was a relief to be away from the Borgata family.

'So,' she said as their plates were cleared away, 'tell me, what happened with Daria.'

Luca had already taken off his jacket. Now he rolled up his shirt-sleeves. He rested his bare forearms on the tabletop and played with a beer mat, flipping it from the side of the table and catching it.

'She's an odd one, isn't she?' he said, 'but she strikes me as an honest person. What do you think?'

'I'd agree with that. Her heart's in the right place.'

'So... We went to a café close to the pharmacy where she works. I asked her to go through the events of the night that Irene disappeared again, as she remembered them. I didn't prompt her. I didn't remind her of what she'd said when she was first questioned. She talked. She gave the exact same version she'd given before.' He tapped the beer mat against the edge of the table. 'She repeated that she and Enzo passed Sam coming in as they were going out again in her car to fetch Irene. She said he was pushing his bicycle and crying. They didn't stop to ask what was wrong because they were in a hurry. And things escalated so swiftly after that that she forgot about it. But she was adamant that's what happened.'

April leaned her chin on her knuckles, listening intently.

'If Daria's recollections are correct,' the inspector continued, 'Sam saw something, or heard something, or did something the evening that Irene disappeared that troubled him deeply. But he didn't say anything about it to anyone at the time, nor afterwards. And to keep what happened secret, he lied about the time he got back to the villa.'

'When I spoke to Sam, he was adamant that he hadn't gone anywhere near the ruins of Gibellina on the evening of Irene's disappearance,' said April.

'You think he was protesting too much?'

'Perhaps.'

'What if he and his friend *were* near Gibellina? What if they were there with their shotguns at dusk and then saw something moving in the distance, something that they thought was a – oh, I don't know, a wild boar or something?'

April sat up straight, an awful picture forming in her mind.

'Maybe Irene did get out of the car, and fell, or was crawling along the ground. To the boys, in the fading light, it would have been easy to mistake her for an animal. They would never in a million years have expected Irene to be out there, on that stretch of road, on her own.'

They both stared at one another, each, mentally, putting the pieces of this new story together, and finding that they fitted.

'So, one of them shot her. And then realised they'd shot a human being. What would they have done next?'

'Panicked? Run away? Gone to Sam's friend's uncle for help?'

'We need the name of the friend,' said Luca. 'Can you find out?'

'Of course. And if this theory is right, if Sam accidentally shot Irene, it would explain a lot about the way he's turned out,' April said quietly. 'Perhaps he's sabotaging his own life because he's crippled by guilt.'

'Where does the housekeeper come into this?' Luca asked. 'Why would she lie too?'

'Giuseppa? I don't know. But... did you see Conti on TV tonight?'

'Yes.'

'That letter he was boasting about, the cry for help allegedly written by Irene. It might have been Giuseppa who gave it to him. She has the key to Irene's old room. She would have known about Irene's secret hiding places, about her secrets.'

'But why would she want to make things worse for Enzo?'

'I've no idea,' said April. 'Not one clue.'

They finished their drinks and after a while, they stopped talking about the Borgata family, and the possibility that Irene had been accidentally shot by her teenaged brother-in-law, and they talked instead about themselves.

Luca told April about his daughters, Greta who was nine and wanted to be an actor and Georgia who was eleven and was into astronomy. He explained how his marriage had been rocky for some time before the current separation.

'What does your wife do?'

'She runs a boutique in Palermo. It involves her going to lots of fashion shows and trade fairs and suchlike.'

'That sounds fun.'

'It would be more fun if she wasn't co-parenting with a grumpy bastard who often has to work late himself.' Luca sighed and gazed around the piazza. The square was becoming busier as the night wore on. Teenagers were gathering, sitting on the walls and the steps outside the church, smoking and texting on their phones, sharing earbuds to listen to music. Old couples walked arm in arm, taking the air, and there were beautifully dressed women with little dogs on leads, and men in open-necked shirts, smoking. It was hard for April to reconcile the peaceful atmosphere in Salgareale now, with the anger of the protestors who had turned up at the villa before.

As she considered this paradox, a man set up a portable keyboard on an upturned orange box beside one of the palm trees. He accompanied himself as he sang a song about unrequited love.

'Would you like to take a little walk?' Luca asked April.

'That would be nice.'

They went through the piazza, climbing the steps to the doors of the church, so they could gaze back over the valley. If April were to look to her right, she thought she might be able to spot the distant lights of the Villa Alba.

It was a beautiful evening. The sky was deep and black, and filled with stars that seemed to shine brighter than they did back home; as if the warm Sicilian night air was less dense, or maybe it was simply that April was seeing more clearly now.

The anxiety caused by knowing what tomorrow would bring; not knowing how they were going to handle it, or deal with it, only served to make this time in this town more precious.

They bought ice creams from a gelato vendor; April chose apricot, Luca had lemon. She thought she spotted Elissa and Tonio sitting on a wall on the far side of the piazza; she thought, *So what if it is them? Why shouldn't they enjoy their time together?*

The clock in the church tower struck midnight. The piazza was still busy but Luca had to drive back to Palermo. He would need to be up early for work in the morning.

'Come on, Cinderella,' he said. 'It's time to go home.'

They turned and the backs of their hands touched.

'Sorry,' April murmured.

They walked back towards the place where Luca had left his car, and he rested his hand very lightly on the small of her back. It was easy and comfortable; their steps were aligned, there was none of the awkwardness April would have expected and she didn't feel guilty about betraying Cobain by being out with another man, she imagined him saying, 'About bloody time.' As they reached the corner that turned into the car park, Luca stopped and April felt something pass between them: an erotic charge like an electric current. If she'd had less to drink, she might have been appalled. As it was, she accepted the sensation as a natural progression of the evening and she did not resist when Luca Mazzotta held her face between his hands and leaned towards her.

She did not hold back when they kissed.

97

IRENE

'What's wrong?' I ask Enzo.

'Did you take money out of my desk?'

I hesitate for a moment: should I deny stealing the cash? But then I realise that lying will only make things worse because if it wasn't me, Enzo will start questioning the rest of the household.

'Yes,' I say. 'I took it.'

'Why?'

I am silent.

'I don't get it!' Enzo said. 'I don't understand why you would take money out of my desk, when all you have to do is ask me, Irene, and you know I'll give it to you, willingly, no matter how much it is you want.'

'You weren't here for me to ask you,' I say quietly. 'You were away on business.'

This is sly and mean, but I can't help myself.

'You needed the money so urgently that you couldn't wait twenty-four hours for me to come home?'

I stare at the floor. I know what his next question will be.

'What was it for?' he asks.

Reassurance. A few days' grace.

'I can't tell you.'

'Why can't you tell me?"

'I just can't.'

There is an awfully long silence.

'We always said,' says Enzo, 'that there'd be no secrets between us.'

'One day,' I said, 'you will understand.'

'I don't understand why it's so difficult for you to be honest with me now.'

There's nothing I can say to this.

Enzo frowns. He is hurt.

I feel like the worst woman in the world.

* * *

Two days later I'm with Maddalena, sitting at the table in the kitchen, when Patrick comes through the door, bringing with him a blast of cold air.

I look up and there he stands, an imposing figure from this angle, in his canvas trousers and his bulky jacket, the leather hat. The beard he wears in winter is thick and bushy, ginger-grey.

'Hello, Granddad!' says Maddalena cheerfully. 'Irene's teaching me how to draw ponies!'

Patrick ignores her. He's staring at me.

'What's going on, Irene?' he asks. His tone is friendly, but I am immediately defensive.

'Nothing.'

'You haven't been up to the stables for days.'

'Maddi has been unwell. I've been looking after her.'

'Turi is pining for you.'

I try not to react to this. I have to stay away from Turi. The more attention I pay to him, the more likely Quintu is to hurt him.

Silence. The sound of water splashing in the sink; Giuseppa humming to herself as she kneads the dough for the day's bread. Maddalena looks from her grandfather's face to mine and back again.

'Enzo's acting weird too,' says Patrick.

'I hadn't noticed.'

'He's hardly come out of his office since he got back from his trip.'

'He's busy,' I say.

'Have you two had a falling out?'

'Not at all.'

Patrick leans down a little. 'Something's wrong, Irene. I can help you. I will help you. Tell me what it is.'

'It's nothing,' I say again, more brightly. 'Everything is fine.'

98

SATURDAY 16 AUGUST 2003

The day of Milo Conti's exposé

April was woken by voices on the landing outside her room. Giuseppa and Maddalena, whispering. They were discussing whether or not to wake Enzo.

'He needs his rest,' said Giuseppa.

'I need to reassure myself he's all right,' Maddalena said. 'He can always go back to sleep again if he wants to.'

Giuseppa mumbled something and April heard a tapping on the door down the corridor, and then muted voices as the two women went into Enzo's bedroom.

April propped herself up on her elbows. Her phone pinged. It was a message from Luca.

Could you find out the name of the friend Sam was shooting with asap?

Okay, April thought, I can do that.

But first, she needed to talk with Enzo.

A little later, she walked along the corridor. The door to Enzo's room was ajar. She knocked. 'Enzo, it's April. May I come in?'

'Please do,' he replied.

He was propped up in the bed with pillows behind him. On the bedside table was a tray with a cup of some kind of weak tea, and the remains of a brioche, a boiled egg, and an orange.

'I see that Giuseppa's looking after you,' April said.

'Yes.' He reached for her hand. 'Everyone is looking after me. Thank you for coming here to support Maddi.'

'I've done my best, Enzo,' April said, 'but I've reached a dead end. I can't do anything more unless you talk to me.'

He was silent.

'I know you don't like talking about Irene,' said April, 'but tell me what happened on the night she disappeared. Just tell me the truth. Please.'

Enzo closed his eyes and said, as if narrating a poem he'd learned as a child: 'We were driving back from Palermo. The car broke down just beyond the ruins of Gibellina. I left Irene in the car while I walked back here, to the villa, to summon help. By the time Daria and I returned, Irene was gone.'

'Did you and Irene argue that day?'

'No.'

'Can you remember what you talked about?'

'Inconsequential matters. Nothing important.'

'Were things all right between you and Irene?'

'All right?'

'Were you happy? Was she?'

Enzo removed his hand from hers; reached for his cup.

'Enzo...'

'I won't talk about my marriage,' he said.

'I know that the stable hand...'

'No,' said Enzo. April could see that the very question had caused him pain. She waited a moment. His breathing had become more laboured; he would not look her in the eye.

She tried a different tack.

'Are you telling me everything, or are you trying to protect someone? Your brother perhaps?' she asked gently.

'Sam has nothing to do with this. I'm tired, April. It's as simple as that. I've had thirty-five years of people whispering about me behind my back, and pointing fingers. Thirty-five years is enough. It's too much. And in that time the only useful thing I've learned is that most of the time, it's best to say nothing at all.'

'I'm not going to give up,' April said. She looked at her watch. 'It's quarter to ten. The Conti show goes out at eight. That's ten hours to get you off the hook, Enzo. Ten hours and I'm going to use them well.'

99

IRENE

Mid-afternoon, 14 January 1968

I'm in the living room with Maddalena. We are doing a jigsaw puzzle; a 500-piecer. It's a picture of Lady and the Tramp eating their spaghetti dinner. The fire is crackling in the grate and every now and then I feed another log into the flames. Then I hear a commotion coming from the courtyard, raised voices.

Quintu's voice.

Enzo's.

'Wait here, Maddi,' I say.

I slip out of the room, closing the door behind me.

I go through the villa and stand at the window, looking out into the courtyard. Enzo is on one side of the table, Quintu on the other. Between them, on the table, is something, it looks like a small box. Enzo is pointing to it, jabbing with his finger. Quintu's body language is shifty. He scratches his head, shifts his weight from foot to foot, holds his hands out and turns both the palms upwards in that Sicilian way of saying: 'Don't ask me! I don't have the answer.'

My breath clouds the glass.

What is it? What is it that they are arguing over?

Enzo's voice is high-pitched, angry.

There's a movement beside me. It's Giuseppa. Her black hair is pulled back from her face and tied in a tight bun. She's carrying arms full of sheets and pillowcases, freshly ironed.

'Do you know what the problem is?' I ask her.

'The jeweller from Salgareale was here,' she says.

'Why?'

'Because a piece of jewellery had come into his shop that he recognised.'

My heart tumbles in my chest. 'Do you know what it was?'

'A ruby brooch that Donatella bought for Alia.'

My mouth is dry as dust.

'What does this have to do with Quintu?'

'It was Quintu who took it into the shop to sell.'

The idiot. The stupid, careless, thoughtless fool!

'He must have stolen it,' says Giuseppa. She shakes her head and carries on up the stairs with the laundry. 'Enzo there is threatening to call his business associates,' she loads these last two words with emphasis, and I know she means the Mafia. 'They don't look kindly on stealing from one's employers.'

Oh God! I don't want Quintu to be punished by those wicked men! I don't want this situation to be any worse than it already is. And what has he said to Enzo? What is he saying now? What if he tells the truth? What if he tells Enzo that I gave the brooch to Jack to give to him?

What if he tells him why?

Even as I'm thinking these things, Quintu points to the villa. I back away from the window. Everything is falling apart.

Everything is going wrong.

I don't want to leave Maddalena, but I think I must. I can't see any other way out of this mess, than to run away from it.

We can't put off leaving any longer, you and I, Jack. We need to get out of here now.

100

April looked for Sam but couldn't find him. Instead, she climbed up to Daria's cottage, thinking Daria would be the next best person to ask about Sam's friend. Daria was outside, tending to her little garden.

'Hi,' she said, straightening when she saw April. 'I was just...' she indicated the soil she'd been prodding ineffectually with her trowel '... trying to tidy it up a bit.'

'It looks like hard work.'

'The soil's too dry. I don't know why I'm bothering. It's something to do while we wait for the family to be torn to shreds.'

'You think that's what's going to happen?'

'I don't see how we can ever recover if Enzo is declared a wife-murderer.'

April perched against the low wall.

'I heard you met my colleague, the inspector, yesterday,' she said.

'He came to the pharmacy. Franco wasn't best pleased.'

'He's asked me to find out the name of Sam's friend, the one he went shooting with. Do you remember?'

'It was Pietro someone-or-other. Oh, what was his surname?'

Daria stared into the middle distance and then she clicked her fingers.

'Esposito,' she said. 'His uncle was an Esposito too.'

April thanked Daria. She took the phone out of her pocket, but there was no coverage.

'You'll need to go up to the stable yard,' said Daria.

They walked up together. April stood in the sunshine and texted the new information to Luca.

He replied almost at once.

Thanks. Will check if uncle Esposito still alive. Meanwhile could you try to find out why the housekeeper is lying for Sam. Is he blackmailing her maybe?'

April replied with a thumbs-up.

Daria was standing in the centre of the yard, looking around.

'It's so quiet,' she said. 'I remember when this was a busy yard; horses and people coming and going all the time. All the neighing and clip-clopping. The horses were beautiful and Patrick treated them like royalty.'

'You never rode yourself?'

'When I was small my father tried to teach me. But I had no confidence.' She looked about her. 'It seems a shame to have all these stables standing empty for so long.'

'Was your father was never tempted to replace the horses he sold after Irene left?'

'The ones he'd bred had been his life's work. Once he'd found new homes for them, he had no appetite for starting again.' Daria paused, then continued. 'He was never the same after Irene left. He'd lost his joie de vivre. It was as if he'd lost more than a daughter-in-law. Like something of himself had gone, along with her.'

* * *

Down at the villa, a three-wheeled truck was parked by the gate and Giuseppa was deep in conversation with an older man wearing blue overalls over a baggy blue shirt, and a flat cap. He'd delivered a bottle of propane gas for the cooker.

While Giuseppa was occupied, April took the opportunity to go into the kitchen. She went to the little cabinet where Giuseppa kept her most important things, opened the door and looked inside. The keys were hung neatly on hooks. Beyond were Giuseppa's purse, a box of tablets and a half-empty bottle of something that was almost certainly home-made honey liqueur, a jar of moisturising lotion and hairclips. Further back were various papers, invoices and recipes, and at the very back, tucked away, was an ancient prayer book. April glanced over her shoulder; there was no sign of Giuseppa or anyone else. She took out the prayer book and flicked through pages made of the thinnest paper. She found a small white envelope.

There was no writing on the envelope, nothing to say what it was, or what it contained.

It was not sealed. April opened it and took out the photograph inside.

It was a small square photograph, black and white, pin sharp.

It showed a young woman, a very young woman, barely a teenager, in a hospital bed. A nun was standing beside the bed, and in the nun's arms was a swaddled baby. April took the photograph closer to the window so she could see more clearly. She didn't recognise the young woman who had just given birth, but she recognised the wan, dazed expression, she'd seen it on newly delivered women several times. She turned the photograph over. On its back were written the words: *14 September 1952.*

April looked at the front of the picture again.

She texted Luca.

Could you please check to see if Giuseppa, the Borgatas' housekeeper, had a baby in 1952, in a convent, or some kind of maternity hospital run by nuns? Sorry, but that's all the info I have.

101

IRENE

Late afternoon, 14 January 1968

I need to talk to you. I need to tell you what's been going on. Enzo has sacked Quintu; sent him packing off the premises; told him never to darken the doorstep of the Villa Alba again. Quintu has left, but he'll be back. He'll be back with his gun to get his revenge on you and me. He'll blame us for his humiliation.

As he was leaving, he looked towards the villa, and he saw me watching from the window. I've never, in my whole life, seen anyone look at me with such hatred.

He wanted me to know that this was not over.

* * *

It's Daria's birthday; how could I have forgotten? I did not get her a present; fortunately, Enzo had brought a book on wildflowers back from his most recent trip which we can give to her. Maddalena and I wrapped it together. It is a shame there are no flowers at this time of year to press between the pages.

Maddalena has made a card: a picture of two rabbits, each holding a gift-wrapped carrot.

'Will you draw a rabbit for me?' I ask her, sliding the palm of my hand along her silky hair, feeling the shape of her head beneath. I want to make the most of her, so that I can remember her when we are apart. In certain moods, I fantasise about you and I taking her with us. I imagine the good times we could have together in England. I see us in some modest house, me teaching Maddalena to make fairy cakes and flapjack. I'd take her to the fair at Bridlington. We could go to the pictures together; go shopping; paddle in the sea; eat candyfloss; be friends.

This will never happen.

Once we are gone, I will never see Maddalena again. She will be lost to me forever.

'Will you draw a rabbit for me?' I ask again.

'Maybe,' she says.

Oh Maddi, Maddi! You always play hard to get!

A little later and we are dressing for a celebratory dinner. Enzo stands in front of the wardrobe, adjusting his bow tie, while I sit on the dressing-table stool, fastening the tops of my stockings to the suspenders. Enzo is watching me via the reflection. He likes to watch me dress. When we were first married I used to put on a little show for him, a reverse striptease. Since you came, it makes my flesh crawl to feel his gaze slipping over my bare skin. Normally I go into the dressing room, where he can't see me. This evening I am acting out of character because he is. It is as if we have been playing one game, and now we are playing another, and neither of us is sure of the rules.

He has hardly said a word to me all day. He knows I took the money from his desk. He knows that Quintu sold the stolen brooch to the jeweller. He is trying to work out how the two things are connected.

I stand up, go to my wardrobe, take out the apricot satin dress on its hanger; slip it over my head. Enzo watches my every move in the mirror.

'Will you do me up?' I ask, crossing to him, standing with my back to him, my hands holding my hair up out of the way.

He pulls up the zip as gently as ever. We're so close I can feel his exhaled breath on the back of my neck. He must smell my perfume.

Then I hear a gasping noise. A sob. I turn to him. 'Enzo?'

His hands are covering his face. He is weeping. And though I don't love him like I love you, I still care for him. I can't pretend all the kindnesses he has done for me, and that I soaked up, never happened.

'What is it?' I ask him, not quite able to bring myself to hug him.

'What are you playing at, Irene?' he asks. 'What's going on?'

'Nothing!' I say. 'Nothing is going on.'

'You're lying!'

'No! No, I'm not!'

He cries: 'Oh, I wish I could believe you!'

102

Giuseppa came into the kitchen; the gas bottle man was behind her, cleaning his hands on a piece of rag. April, who had replaced the prayer book, took a cup from the shelf.

'I was about to make coffee,' she said to Giuseppa, who was eyeing her suspiciously.

'Wait outside,' said Giuseppa. 'I'll bring it to you.'

April did not argue.

She found Maddalena on the back terrace, pacing. Troy was watching anxiously, his chin between his paws.

'You okay?' April asked.

Maddalena shook her head. 'The waiting around is going to kill me.'

'Do you fancy taking me up the mountain again?'

'What for?'

'I'd like to test out a theory that Inspector Mazzotta and I came up with last night.'

* * *

Half an hour later, April and Maddalena were in Maddalena's jeep, back on the track leading up towards the Cretto di Burri.

The temperature was touching thirty-eight degrees and in the midday sun, the light reflecting from the stones on the road was blinding.

The colours of the landscape were grey, buff and ivory; parched, bone colours. The plants at the sides of the road were baked; dead. The sky was halfway between grey and blue but washed out with heat. Everything shimmered. April slid her sunglasses from her forehead to cover her eyes, shifted her position so that the sweat on her back wouldn't stain her shirt.

Maddalena parked the jeep in the same place as before and they both got out. Troy, who had come along for the ride, jumped out too, and started following the trail, nose to the ground. April looked around her.

'Do you remember the search for Irene, Maddi?'

'Yes.'

'Were there a lot of people involved?'

'About a hundred, I'd say. Local volunteers and employees of the tuna company, friends of my grandfather's; all sorts.'

'How did they conduct the search?'

'They were organised into groups. Each group was allocated an area. At first, people still thought Irene might have tried to make her own way home, and fallen. They hoped she might still be alive. So, they started from where the car had been found and fanned out from there.'

'But nothing was found?'

'Nothing at all that was Irene, or that had belonged to her. They spent a long time in the ruins of Gibellina town, and of course things *were* found there... shoes and hairclips and lipstick tubes. But these were items other women had lost or left behind.'

They walked towards the Cretto di Burri. April tried to imagine a town like Salgareale, where the concrete swathe now lay, baking beneath the sun.

'Did you join in the search, Maddalena?'

'I wasn't allowed, but I remember standing in the garden at the villa and all I could hear were voices echoing through the valley calling: "Irene! Irene! Irene!"'

They walked on.

'Did your family have much to do with the people of Gibellina?'

'Not really. It was easier and quicker to go to Salgareale if we needed anything. Irene used to come to the hairdresser's here and she was friendly with a woman called Maria Grazia. There was a mechanic who specialised in Alfa Romeos who looked after Papa's car. And Quintu, the handyman, lived up here, of course, after he got married.'

Troy was rolling in a patch of dust, all four legs in the air.

'So, why are we up here?' Maddalena asked. 'What is this theory that you want to test?'

'Luca and I—'

'Oh, you're on first-name terms now?' Maddi said, teasingly.

'He and I wondered,' said April, 'if hunters might have been up here on the night that Irene disappeared. Dusk is the best time for shooting game, isn't it? What if one of the hunters saw a movement over here, where Enzo's car was parked, and shot at it? What if Irene was accidentally shot?'

'When you say "hunters", are you talking about Uncle Sam and his friend?'

'Possibly. Daria said Sam was upset when he came back to the villa. Sam's statement contradicts her but...'

'He might have been trying to hide the truth.'

April nodded. Maddalena considered for a few minutes. Then she sighed deeply and said, 'Okay. I agree. The scenario you described is feasible. But if you're right, and the two boys accidentally shot Irene, what happened next? Shooting her wouldn't make her disappear.'

'We think they'd have gone to Sam's friend's uncle for help. Luca is hoping to speak to him today.'

'You think she might have died and he disposed of her body, somehow?'

'Yes.'

Maddalena gave a small, sad sigh. 'Dear God,' she murmured.

Troy righted himself, and shook vigorously, from his nose to the tip of his tail. Then he picked up a stick and came wagging up to the women. He dropped the stick, flopped down on the ground and lay at Maddalena's feet, panting.

'The thing is,' said Maddalena, 'we can come up with all these theories about what *might* have happened to Irene. She might have been eaten by wolves, or been accidentally shot by hunters, or snatched by looters, or fallen into the ravine. But with no proof, it makes no difference when it comes to Conti and my father. Conti can say whatever he wants to say and people will feel vindicated in the fact that they always believed Papa was guilty of doing away with his second – and possibly his first wife too. After today, Conti will milk the publicity generated by this case for a few weeks and then he'll move on and he'll forget about us. But the people here won't forget. Even after Papa is dead, he'll be remembered as the man who murdered his wife. People will point to the villa, and they'll say: "That's where he used to live, the wife-killer.'"

'If Sam's friend's uncle confirms what we think...'

'It'll still be too late,' said Maddalena. 'Conti's juggernaut is already rolling. A new witness isn't going to be enough to stop it now. And anyway, I think Papa would rather take the blame himself than sacrifice his younger brother. Either way it's a no-win for the family.'

They walked back to the jeep. The sun was right above them, and there was no shade. It was like walking through a furnace. Maddi poured some water into a bowl for Troy and he lapped it up greedily, spattering dark patches into the dust. She drank from the bottle herself before offering it to April. April's phone pinged: a message from Luca.

Giuseppą Russo gave birth to baby boy, 14 September 1952, at the convent of Santa Maria in Siracusa. She was 15. Child given into the custody of his father, Patrick Borgata & Patrick's wife, Donatella.

103

IRENE

Evening, 14 January 1968

Here we are, the whole family, gathered in the drawing room at the Villa Alba to celebrate Daria's birthday. The men are in their suits, the women in evening dress. Enzo's face is blotchy, his eyes swollen from crying. He keeps his head down, no eye contact, barely says a word to anyone. I stand close to him, being attentive. I hate to see him like this, knowing it is my behaviour that has brought him to it.

Patrick produces the champagne he'd put on ice and everyone tries to be happy for Daria's sake, but our hearts aren't in it. No matter that we are inside a beautiful villa, lit with chandeliers and decorated with horribly expensive out-of-season flowers, lilies, roses and freesias, fires burning in every grate. The atmosphere is all wrong. I know what's causing my discomfort, and Enzo's. I'm pretty sure I know what's wrong with the others too.

Daria dislikes being the centre of attention so birthdays are a particular ordeal for her. Maddalena is sulking because she's been scolded by her grandmother for pretending to be Nancy Sinatra – 'that vulgar woman' is how Donatella describes her. Sam, sensitive as ever to everyone else's discomfort, is sneaking drinks of forbidden alcohol and is becoming verbose and funny but it won't be long before his good-humour turns to introspection. Patrick and Enzo have fallen out over the sacking of Quintu – Patrick thinks Enzo acted too hastily and besides it should be up to him to do the hiring and firing. Donatella is cross with Maddi, annoyed with Daria because Daria's not enjoying herself, and furious with me for not keeping Alia's precious, ugly, heirloom safe.

Me? I wish I were anywhere else but here.

We go into the dining room, and take our places around the enormous table all laid just so with the silver and the best crockery, candles lit, napkins folded. Giuseppa serves fish. The atmosphere is deadly. Sam makes a few ill-advised jokes, slurring his words. Daria nudges him to make him shut up. Donatella attempts to engage Enzo by asking questions about the tuna-processing business. Could there be a less appropriate topic for a birthday dinner conversation? I'm anxious and tetchy. I'm thinking of you, my love, up in the cottage alone, waiting for me, wondering what's going on. I told you to make sure the door was locked tonight and to stay away from the windows. I'm worried about Quintu coming back in a vengeful mood, with his gun.

I'm so worried about Turi.

'Irene?' Maddi is looking at me in a way that means she's just asked me a question that I didn't hear.

'What is it, love?'

'I said, will you take me into Palermo to buy some records?'

There is a record player in the villa. The choice of music available is limited to opera and the singer Umberto Bindi. Maddalena wants to buy American pop music.

Donatella doesn't approve of pop music. Obviously.

'Yes,' I say, 'sure.'

She smiles. 'Thank you,' and I wonder, for the hundredth time, how I'm going to find the strength to leave her behind.

104

A couple of men with mopeds were standing by the villa gates, laughing together. They had cameras with enormous lenses hung around their necks. Maddalena pulled the jeep up beside them and leaned out of the window.

'Who are you?' she asked. 'And what are you doing here?'

'We're snappers,' said the older of the two. 'Paparazzi. Sent here to pick up some shots of the action this evening.'

'You're vultures,' said Maddi. 'Carrion crows. You're pathetic! You make me sick!'

The men exchanged glances and the younger, massively overweight and wearing a Grateful Dead T-shirt, raised his camera as if to take a picture.

'Oh, fuck off,' said Maddi.

She opened the gates with the remote, and drove the car through, parking round the corner, out of sight of the photographers at the gate.

'Bastards,' she muttered.

'There might be others around,' April said. In the woodland, a pigeon took flight, its wings cracking like gunshot. She shielded her eyes with her hand. Was somebody out there?

They went through the villa, following Troy. Elissa was reading on one of the loungers beside the pool. She'd been swimming.

'April thinks there might be paparazzi watching us,' Maddalena said. 'It might be a good idea if you cover up.'

'What?' Elissa grabbed her towel and held it over her body. She looked frantically about.

They're already inside our heads, thought April. *Even if there's nobody there, we feel as if we're under siege.*

* * *

April left Maddalena and Elissa together and went to find Giuseppa. She was in the kitchen, preparing vegetables, her fingers deftly separating spinach leaves from their stalks.

Normally April would have been more circumspect, but time was slipping by and she couldn't afford to tread carefully any longer.

'I need to tell you something, Giuseppa,' she said.

'Go on, then.'

'I know that you're Sam's mother.'

Giuseppa's neck flushed a deep red, but she continued what she was doing, turning over spinach leaves in the water, picking out the clean ones.

'You were very young to have a baby,' April continued.

'I don't talk about that time.'

'Wouldn't you like to? Don't you ever wish you could tell someone what it felt like to be you?'

'The past doesn't matter.'

'I think it does.'

Giuseppa took another handful of spinach. April waited, but the older woman wasn't going to offer up any information unprompted.

'Patrick was the father, wasn't he?'

The slightest nod of affirmation.

'These days, Giuseppa, what he did to you would be regarded as abuse.'

Silence.

'Did he and Donatella come to some arrangement with your family? They'd bring up the child as their own, you could stay here to be close to him. Scandal averted for both families?'

Another nod. Giuseppa closed her eyes and murmured something silently, a prayer perhaps. April had the strongest urge to put her arm around the older woman, but she knew such intimacy would be anathema to Giuseppa.

'It doesn't seem very fair to you,' April said. 'You had no opportunity to build a new relationship or life away from the villa if you wanted to stay close to your son.'

'It was a small price to pay.'

It was your whole life, thought April.

'My family didn't want anything to do with me,' Giuseppa said. 'It was only thanks to the generosity of Donatella that I still had a roof over my head.'

'You were fifteen,' April said quietly. 'There should have been no shame on your part.'

Giuseppa wiped her eyes with the back of her wrist. She picked up a spinach stalk, then laid it down again.

'Does Sam know what you know?' she asked.

'I haven't told anyone else.'

'Thank you.'

'You don't need to thank me, Giueseppa, but I really need you to be honest with me from now on. Will you help me? Please?'

Giuseppa did not move. She was barely breathing.

April continued: 'Now I know that Sam is your son, I understand why you've been doing the things you've been doing.'

Silence.

'I know that you lied to the police about what happened on the night Irene disappeared to provide an alibi for Sam. I believe that what really happened was that Sam came home that night in terrible distress and told you he and his friend had shot Irene. Is that right?'

'They didn't know who had been shot; only that it was a woman.'

'Okay.'

'It was an accident,' Giuseppa whispered. 'Sam was beside himself.'

'I'm sure he was. Did he know if the woman was badly hurt?'

'When they realised what they'd done, the boys ran to Pietro's uncle. He told them to go home. He said he'd deal with it.'

'Deal with it how?'

'He'd go back to Gibellina and find the injured party and... and do whatever was best for her.'

'Okay.'

'He told the boys not to say a word to anyone, to pretend it had never happened.'

'But Sam told you?'

Giuiseppa nodded.

'And you guessed that it was Irene who'd been shot?'

'I knew she was up there, on her own. I put two and two together. I didn't know what to do – oh, the timing was dreadful! We had all the guests here that night, all the important businesspeople... I went and fetched Patrick, and explained the situation to him. He told Sam that Pietro's uncle was right. That he must forget it, that if he didn't think about it, it would become no more significant than a dream.'

'Patrick knew about this too?'

'Yes.'

Giuseppa was breathing heavily. She had gone very pale.

'Talking about things, going over them, it keeps them alive,' she said. 'If you put something away, if you close the door and you don't mention it, don't think about it, then eventually it withers. It stops troubling you.'

'But you are still troubled,' said April.

'God forgive me,' Giuseppa whispered, 'and Patrick too. We were only trying to do the best by our son.'

'Sit down, Giuseppa,' April said. 'Would you like some water?'

'No.'

'Did Donatella know about this?'

'She never knew. It would have given her the ammunition she needed to have Sam sent away.'

'Right. Okay. Now tell me, why did you burn the car seat?'

'You know about that?'

'I saw you.'

'Oh. Well, I thought Irene might have crawled back to the car. I didn't know if they, the forensics people, could tell the difference between blood from a leg injury and blood from a gunshot wound. Can they?'

'Not after all this time, no. There's one more thing, Giuseppa. I need you to tell me about the note that was hidden inside the doll. The one you gave to Signor Conti. The one that he claims is the "proof" that Enzo killed Irene. Why did Irene write it and why did she hide it inside the doll? How did you know about it? And what does it say?'

105

IRENE

Late evening,14 January 1968

Daria has taken Sam to bed, and Giuseppa has gone up with Maddi. Patrick and Donatella have retired. Only Enzo and I remain downstairs. Giuseppa is clearing the table, clattering dishes.

'Come into the living room for a nightcap,' my husband says.

'If you don't mind, Enzo, I'd rather go straight to bed.' I touch my fingers to my temples. 'I can feel a headache coming on.'

'We need to talk.'

'I'm tired of talking,' I say.

Enzo looks exhausted. 'And I'm tired of your lies, Irene. Stop now. Tell me the truth.'

Giuseppa is concentrating very hard on loading up her trolley.

Enzo and I go into the living room. He crosses to the sideboard, where the liqueurs are kept in their fancy glass decanters, and he pours himself a drink. He doesn't offer me one. I open my mouth to ask for a limoncello, and then close it. I don't want to sound flippant. I don't know how much Enzo knows or suspects. I don't want my mind to be muzzy with alcohol.

'Quintu told me some things about you, Irene,' he says.

'He's never liked me,' I say. 'He's always been jealous of my friendship with Patrick. Whatever he said, he was trying to hurt us both, that's all.'

'He told me you're seeing the stable hand, Jack. He says you two are...' he struggles over the word '...lovers.'

I feel sick to my stomach. My knees are weak. I can't deny it outright. I can't deny us. I cannot pretend our love does not exist.

'Quintu was lashing out. He was trying to get back at you for firing him,' I say.

'He said you gave him the ruby brooch to buy his silence.'

'He would say that, wouldn't he?'

Enzo puts down his glass. He takes an orange from the fruit bowl. He picks up the paring knife and sticks the pointed end into the skin. I clasp my hands together to stop them from shaking. I'm trying to stay composed.

'Furthermore,' Enzo continues, 'Quintu said that Jack gave him half a million lire the day before yesterday. That's the same amount that was missing from my desk; the same amount that you admitted you took, although you wouldn't tell me why.'

He slices into the orange peel, twisting the fruit in his hand. There's a sharp smell of citrus.

'Too much of a coincidence to be a coincidence, don't you think?' Enzo asks. The tone of his voice is odd. He sounds cold and Enzo is not a cold man. He does not usually talk in this sarcastic way.

I don't know what to do, or say. I don't know how I can make this better. I wonder if I should tell him the truth; admit everything.

'Let's talk tomorrow,' I say.

Enzo turns to me, the knife in his hand. There's something in his eyes I haven't seen before.

'I want to talk now! I want you to look me in the eye and tell me that you love me. I want you to tell me that you haven't been unfaithful. I want you to convince me that you are my loyal wife, and that we are still strong, and that we will be together forever.'

He stops. He breathes. It is the fast, shallow breathing of a man whose veins are flooded with adrenaline; a man who is a hair's breadth from losing control. My mind runs through a thousand permutations. I could make up some convoluted story. I could twist myself in knots trying to talk my way out of this one. I could tell the truth, and see what happens. Or I could lie, and make everything okay.

The silence draws itself out painfully slowly.

'I can't tell you what you want to hear,' I say.

Enzo groans.

'I'm sorry,' I say. 'I never set out to betray you, Enzo! None of this was premeditated! But it's true, I have been seeing Jack. It's nothing to do with you! He and you are separate. He doesn't replace you, he has always been there in my heart alongside you. I thought he was dead, but he wasn't. I loved him first. I can't help myself. I've loved him for years; long before I met you.'

He wanted the truth, and I gave him the truth, and it was the cruellest thing I have ever done.

106

'How did you know that Irene had hidden the note inside the doll?' Giuseppa asked April.

'Detective work. And a couple of lucky guesses.'

'She hated that doll,' said Giuseppa.

'Tell me about the note.'

'The note. Oh, yes.' Giuseppa touched her fingers to her forehead. 'It was the evening before the earthquake. Daria's birthday; the same day that Enzo and Quintu fought.'

'Why did they fight?'

'Quintu had been stealing. When Enzo confronted him, Quintu told him some home truths about Irene. And Enzo was in a bleak mood afterwards; not like himself at all.'

'What happened?'

'They were alone in the living room,' Giuseppa continued, 'Irene and Enzo, after dinner. I was clearing away in the dining room. The doors were ajar. If they'd stopped to think about it, they'd have realised that I could hear them, but they didn't stop to think. I'm like the furniture. The Borgatas don't notice me. They forget that I'm there.'

'Were they arguing?'

'Not arguing exactly. Enzo pushed Irene and she admitted that she was in love with Jack, the stable hand. She was trying to explain to Enzo, trying to reason with him, but he was devastated. He was broken. He was like a bird that's been shot, that's falling to the ground, flapping one wing, going round in circles. He said he wanted the truth, but when she gave it him, he couldn't handle it at all.'

'How did it end?' April asked.

'Badly.'

107

IRENE

We're standing here, both of us, face to face. Enzo is so wound up that I can literally see the vein in his forehead throbbing and his eyes bulging. My skin is flecked with his spittle. He's holding the paring knife in his hand; it's inches from my face.

'Have you slept with him?' he asks, and I could say 'No,' because we haven't spent a night together here, which is what Enzo means, but to deny our intimacy would be another deception.

'Yes,' I say quietly.

And things get worse.

I've never seen Enzo like this before. Never. Always, before, when he's looked at me, it has been with affection. Now his expression is one of rage borne of a terrible hurt. I'm trying not to let him see that I'm scared but the knife is so close that I can see the white pith of the orange caught on its blade.

'I don't understand, Irene!' he cries. 'When we met, in London, you told me that you wanted the life I offered you. You said that you wanted to spend your life with me. You behaved as if you cared for me!'

'I did care for you.'

But that was because I thought you were dead, Jack. I can't explain all this to him now; it will make it sound as if I used him — maybe I did! I didn't mean to! And it doesn't matter. It's not important any more.

'I was scrupulously honest with you,' Enzo continues. 'I gave you everything I had! I've never lied to you! All I've ever done is loved you!'

'I know what you've done for me, Enzo.'

'I love you!' he cries.

'I know you do, but we were never meant to be together!' I respond. 'I was supposed to be with Jack. You and I, our meeting, our relationship, none of it should have happened. It was an unlucky twist of fate.'

'Unlucky?'

'I thought I had lost Jack, but I hadn't. If he hadn't come back, I would, of course, have stayed faithful to you.'

'That's all I was to you? Second best? A substitute for your real love?'

He brings the knife closer, so close that the blade is touching the skin of my cheek. His eyes are blazing and he's baring his teeth. I cry and back away and, in a flash, he turns and he slashes the portrait, my portrait, the one he had painted for my birthday. He attacks it so viciously, raising his arm and slamming the knife into the canvas, that I almost feel the wounds myself.

It is as if I am witnessing my own murder.

108

'I only ever saw Enzo lose his temper once, and that was it,' said Giuseppa. 'He didn't want to hurt Irene. He loved her. But he needed to show her how badly he was hurt.'

'What did he do?'

'He attacked Irene's portrait. The one he'd had done of her, as a gift. Irene cried out and I came running into the room to make sure she was alright and I saw him.'

Giuseppa raised her own arm and made a stabbing motion, acting out Enzo's rage.

'And when his anger was spent, Enzo threw the knife into the fire and collapsed on one of the sofas. I put my arms around Irene. She was cowering, holding onto me like a child. I didn't know what to do because I felt responsible for Enzo too. "Enzo," I said, "are you all right? Shall I fetch your mother?" and he said, "No, thank you, Giuseppa. Look after Irene. Leave me be." So I took Irene upstairs and made up the bed in the dressing room behind their bedroom. I thought she'd feel better if she could lock the door between them.'

'How was she?'

'She was in shock, I think. She kept asking me if I'd seen what Enzo had been like, how violently he'd attacked the portrait, and I told her that

I had seen, yes. "What if he'd done that to me?" she asked and I said: "Well, you were lucky that he didn't." She said: "I didn't think Enzo was capable of that kind of behaviour. I didn't know he had it in him to be so angry." I told her that the Borgatas all had it in them. That it was their family trait. She was upset. Really upset. That was when she wrote the note. She made me stay while she wrote it, had me help her with the Italian. She said: "If anything happens to me, Giuseppa, you're to show this to the police, okay?" She wanted to put it somewhere safe so I suggested she hid it inside the doll. I brought the tiny screwdriver up from downstairs and we opened the compartment in the doll's back and we put the note inside.'

'And it's been there ever since?'

'Yes.'

'Why didn't you give it to the police, Giuseppa, after Irene disappeared?'

Giuseppa was silent. She looked at her hands.

'I mean, that was the whole point of the note, wasn't it? To inform the police about Enzo if any harm were to come to Irene?'

Giuseppa didn't say anything.

'Oh, I see,' said April. 'You believed that Sam had shot Irene. You are a decent woman. You didn't want Enzo to be blamed for something he hadn't done.'

Giuseppa nodded.

'So why now? Why did you decide to give it to Conti now?'

'He came to see me,' she said.

'Conti came here?'

'No, no, he was waiting outside the church. He'd been given a copy of the paperwork from the police's original investigation. He'd noticed that Sam and Daria's witness statements didn't match. He asked me which of them was telling the truth. He was going to investigate that line of enquiry, exactly as you did.'

'So you had to put him off Sam's scent.'

'God forgive me, I thought Enzo was going to die last week, after the heart attack. We all did. So I gave Conti Irene's note because I thought, if Enzo's dead, it won't matter. It won't hurt him and it will put an end to the speculation about what happened to Irene Borgata once and for all. If I didn't close the case, Conti would keep trying to get to the bottom of it. He'd keep on pestering us and looking under stones and pointing his cameras at us. He wouldn't stop until he'd destroyed Sam, and that would destroy Elissa and it would destroy me too.'

'Okay,' said April quietly. 'I can understand why you did what you did. What does the note say, Giuseppa?'

The old woman took a deep breath.

'It says: "My name is Irene Borgata, née Weatherbury, and I am of sound mind. If you are reading this, it means my husband, Enzo, has killed me."'

109

IRENE

Giuseppa stays in the dressing room with me until I've calmed down and only when she's reassured herself that I'm not going to do anything 'silly' does she leave. I lock the door that connects with the bathroom behind her. I tell her I'm going to go straight to bed, but I don't. I sit on the single bed in that room, with my hands between my knees, my hair hanging over my face. Eventually Enzo comes up. He comes into the bathroom – I see the line of light beneath the door. I hear the soles of his slippers slapping on the bathroom floor tiles. Then he knocks on the connecting door.

'Irene?'

'I'm tired, Enzo,' I say.

'We need to talk.'

'Not tonight.'

'I'm sorry,' he says.

'We can talk tomorrow.'

'I want you to know that I'm truly sorry. I don't know what came over me.'

That's a stupid thing to say. We both know what came over him. I am too exhausted to argue.

'All right, you've apologised,' I say.

A silence. Then he says: 'Jack will have to go. You know that, don't you. He can't stay here. I can't have you betraying me right under my nose. I can't pretend it's not happening, not now you've told me.'

I don't respond.

'I'll speak to Patrick. I'll tell him to let Jack go in the morning. I'll ask him to make sure Jack leaves Sicily.'

I don't say a word.

'Things are going to be difficult between us for a while,' Enzo says, 'but we'll get over it.'

We won't.

'I know this, what's happened, is my fault. I drove you to be unfaithful, didn't I Irene? I've been away too often on business. And I talk too much about tuna, I know it doesn't interest you. I won't do that any more. We'll find some mutual interests. Maybe take up a hobby together. Ballroom dancing, perhaps? Or bird-watching. We'll make a new start.'

He waits for me to respond, but I can't. I sit on the bed with my hands between my knees. Tears run down my face.

'I love you,' Enzo says. 'I love you so much. I know you don't feel the same, right now, but you will do, one day. I have enough love for both of us. I'll wait, Irene. I won't put pressure on you. I'll wait for the day when you feel the same about me.'

Stop it, I beg silently. Stop pleading. It won't make any difference.

'I've had an idea,' Enzo says. 'I thought perhaps we might arrange another holiday. You, me and Maddi. We could catch the ferry from Trapani to Cagliari; stay in that hotel I told you about, the one with the incredible seafood chef.' A pause. 'What do you think, Irene? Do you like that idea?'

'I can't think about it now.'

'Are you crying?'

'No.'

'Oh my love! I'm sorry. I'm so sorry.'

'Enzo, don't apologise. Please don't. I can't bear it.'

There's a long silence.

'But you will consider it?' he asks at last. 'The holiday? We can talk about it properly tomorrow.'

Please, I'm thinking, please, please, please go to bed, Enzo. Stop talking to me. Leave me be.

'It will be very simple for us to get back on track,' Enzo says. 'We'll go away and have a little holiday. And then we'll come back, and everything will go back to how it was before Jack came. And he'll be gone, and we won't let him come between us again.'

'Right,' I say.

'You promise me, Irene, that you'll think about the holiday?'

'If you let me sleep,' I say.

'And maybe my mother is right. Maybe the best thing would be for us to have a baby together. A little brother or sister for Maddalena.'

'Maybe,' I say.

'Really?'

'Yes.'

'Oh, my darling, if we had a baby, I just know everything would be perfect.'

'Right,' I say. 'Let's talk tomorrow.'

I will say anything, literally anything, to make him stop talking; to make him leave me alone.

110

April took herself outside for some air; to give herself space to think. She felt overwhelmed. This was the worst possible scenario. Enzo was about to be accused of murder by his wife from beyond the grave even though it was more likely that Sam was responsible for ending her life. The Borgata family was going to be devastated. The only way to avoid catastrophe would be to stop Conti broadcasting his exposé from outside the villa, but April could not think how this could be done. If she were to try to explain about Sam and the gun, it would merely add more fuel to the speculative fire.

Given Enzo's frail health, the only realistic thing to do was to hunker down, stay in the villa, let the storm blow through. Only it wouldn't. Once Enzo was accused, and given the nature of Irene's note, the Sicilian police would almost certainly reopen their investigation. The implications for the whole family were far-reaching.

April didn't know what to do.

She called Luca, but Luca wasn't answering his phone. She called her friend, Roxie, hoping that she might have some advice, but Roxie didn't answer either. She paced around the villa. And the hands on the clock in the courtyard kept turning, and the sun was beginning its downward trajectory in the sky. The morning had turned to afternoon and the afternoon was sliding towards evening and she only had a little time left before Milo Conti would 'prove' that Enzo Borgata had killed his wife.

She went outside, walked around the side of the house, alongside the wall, until she was close enough to the gate to climb on top of a wheelbarrow and look over. The road beyond was busy now as people arrived to secure a good spot in readiness for the start of the programme. Cars and motorcycles were parked along the verge, stretching back down towards the bridge. Closer was a large outside-broadcast news van with satellite dishes on top, and another with a huge mast rising up from the middle of its roof.

A woman was selling T-shirts with Conti's face in the middle and he pointing a finger in the manner of the 'Your country needs you' poster. The caption read: *Justice for Irene.*

A stack of placards had also been prepared and lay in a heap to one side ready for distribution amongst the bystanders when Conti arrived. There was even a pizza van and another selling cold drinks. The 'spontaneous' protest had been very well organised.

April's phone rang.

It was Luca.

'I've just left Pietro Esposito's uncle,' he said.

April heard him unlock the car door and climb in.

'Did he talk?'

'Eventually. He confirmed what we thought. Sam and Pietro couldn't find anything to shoot that evening so had drifted back towards Gibellina.'

April could hear Luca settling into the car, securing the seat belt, winding down the window.

From the other side of the villa wall, laughter rang out.

'They were climbing amongst the ruins,' Luca said. 'It was growing dark. They'd been winding one another up, talking about ghosts and curses. They were spooked and jumpy. And then they heard something, they saw something moving, some kind of creature, and they shot at it, both of them. Immediately they heard a cry, a human voice. A woman screamed: "You've shot me!"'

'Irene?'

'They didn't go to find out. They were afraid, not only were they trespassing, but they feared they'd mortally wounded someone. They ran back to their bikes and cycled to Pietro's uncle's house. He told them to go to their respective homes and to keep quiet; not to say a word to anyone about what had happened.'

'Luca, please tell me! Was it Irene? Had they killed her?'

'I'm getting to it!' said Luca. 'The uncle took his truck up to Gibellina, and just outside the town he was waved down by a man, a derelict. He told the uncle that he and his wife had been trying to find shelter for the night. They'd gone into the ruins of Gibellina hoping to find a safe place, knowing, like the boys, they shouldn't have been there. It was the wife who'd been shot.'

'Not Irene?'

'No. She'd been hit in the arm and chest; flesh wounds but both the woman and the man were terrified, fearing they might be dealing with Mafiosi. They'd hidden until they were certain they were alone, and then they came out onto the road to try to find help. Pietro's uncle put them in his van and took them to the hospital in Palermo. I got someone to check, and yes, the hospital did admit a woman with gunshot wounds that night. The story checks out.'

April closed her eyes and pressed her forehead against the wall.

'It wasn't Irene?'

'No, it wasn't Irene. Sam didn't shoot Irene. Somebody probably ought to tell the poor sod, he's been living under the illusion that he killed his sister-in-law since he was fifteen.'

111

IRENE

Night-time, 14–15 January 1968

I don't sleep. I can't. I need to warn you about what's happened. I'm not just worried about what Quintu might do to you, I'm also worried about Enzo. You need to get away from here. We need to get away.

I can't get out of the dressing room without going through Enzo's bedroom so I have to wait until I hear him snoring. I am dressed, ready for outdoors. When, at last, I hear the familiar sound of his sleeping, I unlock the door and I creep into the bathroom. I look into the main bedroom. I can see the shape of Enzo on the bed. He is lying on his back, mouth open. I sneak through the room, heart pounding; open the door carefully, squeeze through, and run downstairs.

I daren't stop to find a torch. In the hallway, I pull on a coat and put on a pair of boots. I go outside. The air is icy.

I run up the steep path towards the stables as fast as I can and at last I reach the cottage and I try the door but it's locked. Of course it's locked, in case Quintu comes. I am panting. My lungs hurt. I look over my shoulder. I have the strongest feeling that we're being watched.

'Jack!' I call, breathless, too afraid to raise my voice. 'Jack!'

A light goes on inside the cottage. I see the shape of you, coming to the door.

'It's me!' I call. 'Jack, let me in!'

You open the door. You are squinting, your eyes not used to the light.

'Irene,' you say, the initial pleasure in your eyes immediately replaced with fear. 'What is it? What's happened?'

And I take a breath to begin to tell you everything that has transpired since we were last together, but I never say a word. Because at that very instant the ground lurches beneath my feet.

We both stumble. There's the sound of crashing from inside the cottage; crockery falling from the rack. There's a brief silence, trees sway as the tremor moves through the earth and then, from the stables, comes the sound of the horses, panicked, screaming.

'What was that?' I ask. We are both on our hands and knees, you inside the cottage, me outside.

'An earthquake, I think?'

I push myself up. 'The horses!'

You grab the torch that you keep by the door. 'Come on!'

* * *

Jack is seeing to James. I'm in Turi's stable. He's trembling, stamping, wild-eyed, terrified.

'Shhh,' I say, 'it's okay, boy, I know you're scared, but it's me, I'm here to help you. You know I won't let anything hurt you!'

I reach up for the headcollar but he backs away and swings round, knocking me with his rump. I fall against the corner, bumping my head. Pain shoots through my skull. Jack comes in, shining the beam of the torch at my head.

'You're bleeding.'

'I'm all right,' I tell him. 'Get Turi out!'

And Jack, he's so good with the horses, he takes hold of Turi's chinstrap calm as anything and he talks to him, leads him out of the stable and although I'm still slumped against the wall, I follow their progress through the yard via the clopping of Turi's hooves on the cobbles. When the sound stops, I know Turi's safely out in the paddock.

I'm holding my head in my hands. Blood is seeping through my fingers.

Something isn't right in this stable. It's the wall. The wall is sloping at an angle. As I try to push myself to my feet, I see mortar fall from between the stones at the top of the wall. There is an ominous creaking sound.

Jack stands at the door. He looks up. He sees the trickle of mortar.

'Irene,' he says, 'you have to move. You have to get up now.'

The wall groans. Mortar falls. One of the roof beams slips.

'Come on,' says Jack again. He puts the torch on the floor and he reaches his arms down to me, puts his hands in my armpits, is heaving me to my feet. The torchlight is directed at an odd angle. In its beam, I see someone behind him. Quintu.

112

A flock of starlings was murmurating above the roof of the villa.

The tiny shadows they cast fluttered over April. She felt light-headed and edgy.

She pressed her fingers to her temples. *All this effort,* she thought. *All these old secrets uncovered, and yet nothing has changed. Enzo is still the prime, the only suspect in the case of the disappearance of Irene Borgata.*

'There is one last thing,' said Luca, on the other end of the phone. 'There's one last lead. It's probably nothing, but Pietro's uncle told me that while he was driving up to Gibellina that night, to find the woman who'd been shot, he passed a truck coming the other way, which means it must have driven past the broken-down Alfa Romeo.'

'Okay.'

'Pietro's uncle recognised the truck. It belonged to a man called Quintu Beresi.'

'I'm pretty sure Quintu Beresi used to work here at the villa.'

'That's right. And the reason Pietro's uncle was surprised to see the truck was because—'

'Quintu had died in the earthquake, four months earlier!'

'At least he was *assumed* to have died.'

'What are you thinking, Luca?'

'That because Quintu was missing on the night of the earthquake, everyone believed he was one of the unidentified dead. But what if he wasn't? What if he wasn't dead at all?'

113

IRENE

It's as if it's happening in slow motion. Quintu raises his arm. He has the pistol in his hand. He is going to shoot Jack.

'Jack!' I scream, and he turns and he acts out of instinct; he barges into Quintu, in the same way that Turi barged into me. Quintu loses his balance and falls against the side wall of the stable. The wall moves, sways, like a drunken man. Mortar and dust fall on us like rain. Quintu puts his hands on the wall, trying to steady himself, but instead he unsteadies the structure. One of the top stones dislodges itself, and tumbles inwards. It bounces off Quintu's shoulder and he yelps in pain. The beams creak; laths crack and splinter, Quintu stumbles and falls to the floor. The wall sways; it is going to collapse. I reach out to Jack, he takes my hand.

'Quick!' he cries, and I try to move but Quintu has grabbed my ankle. I kick to free myself but when I turn I see his grimace, and I know he won't let go.

Behind him, the stones come tumbling down, bouncing on the cobbles of the stable floor.

114

At the same time as the sun slid down behind the mountains, and the sky, strung with massing cloud, turned red and gold, so artificial light lit up the front of the Villa Alba. A small army of technicians had rigged up the lights, and erected a stage at the side of the road. The audience was growing. There was an excited buzzing from beyond the boundary wall; people were looking out for Milo Conti.

'Is he here yet?'

'Someone said they saw him going into that campervan! That's where they do the make-up!'

'Did he say hello? Was he friendly?'

'He's even taller than he looks on the television. And so charismatic!'

At least, for now, the crowd sounded good-natured.

April checked her phone. She'd missed a call from Roxie, and Roxie hadn't left a message. She called her back, but the call went straight to voicemail.

The heat was oppressive. Clouds were blooming, growing, shifting, masking the moon and the stars.

The air was humid and heavy. Tiny black thunderflies speckled the skin of April's arms. When she looked up, she could see the artificial lights installed by the gates reflected on the undersides of the thunderous clouds overhead. A warm-up man was giving instructions to the crowd through a microphone.

'Make as much noise as you like when my arm is up, like this!'

The crowd bellowed and cheered.

'But when my arm is down, when Milo is speaking, I need you to be quiet as mice. Is that clear?'

April climbed onto the wheelbarrow and looked over the wall. She could see the people grouped around the stage. She checked the time on her phone. Ten to eight.

She should go back inside and be with Maddalena, and the others, but she also wanted to be here. That way, she thought, if Conti said anything that she knew to be factually wrong, she would challenge him!

April pulled herself up onto the top of the wall, and jumped down on the other side. She dusted herself off and made her way to the back of the assembled crowd. There were too many people, she thought, for them all to have come from Salgareale.

'Five minutes until we go live!'

The warm-up man put up his arm and the crowd roared their assent.

'Are we ready to discover the truth? Are we ready to have a mystery solved? Are we ready to embrace justice for Irene?'

Another roar.

At exactly eight o'clock, Milo Conti stepped onto the stage.

He was wearing a pale-coloured suit. The jacket had been cut wide at the shoulders and tapered down to the hips. His hair had been coiffed and his face made up. It might have looked all right on TV, but in the flesh, with the lights shining directly at him, his skin seemed orange and artificial.

He began by whipping the audience up, recapping past 'victories for justice', reminding his fans of his successes in ensuring certain criminals were finally forced to face up to their crimes.

'And tonight, we've come here, to stand outside this luxury villa in the heart of the countryside, to call on Enzo Borgata to give himself up to the police, and to confess, after thirty-five years, to the murder of his wife!'

He kept talking, spouting a rehearsed speech, going through the evidence already collated. He used video clips, relayed to the live audience via a screen, to show the reconstruction of what might have happened to Irene Borgata in her husband's Alfa Romeo on the night of her disappearance.

April dusted the thunderflies from her arms. She pulled her shirt from her skin, tried to get some air to her body.

'And now I can show you the ultimate proof that Irene was afraid of her husband,' said Conti. 'Proof that she was in fear of her life!'

He reached into his inside jacket pocket and, with a flourish, withdrew a piece of paper. Irene's note.

An image of it was blown up on the screen so that everyone could read it.

April zoned out and she thought about her friendship with Maddalena, and how close they used to be and how their relationship was growing stronger again now. She thought about how she had used the argument in the Bangkok hostel as an excuse to sever all ties with Maddi.

She shouldn't have done that. She should have tried to see things from Maddi's point of view. Okay, she'd been young then, and she hadn't realised how much Maddi had already lost but really, that was no excuse. The truth was, it had suited her to break off contact with Maddalena because April's life had been opening out in different ways. She, April, had behaved selfishly. She'd blamed the end of their friendship on Maddalena, when, really, it had been her choice.

She thought of Cobain, and how they'd always thought they'd have plenty of time to do the things they wanted to do, and that they would grow old together. But time had been taken from them, and they hadn't had the chance to see their plans through to fruition. It had been nobody's fault and there had been nothing anyone could have done to prevent it; it was just how it was.

She thought she wouldn't waste another minute when it came to friendship or love, or people. She would embrace every moment. She would be a better friend, a more considerate person. She would take down her barriers. She would reach out to the people who cared for her.

Above the clouds were huge and heavy, pressing down.

Conti was shouting, gesticulating. He was leaning over towards the audience, his face contorted into a mask of righteous indignation.

'That man, Enzo Borgata, that man who terrorised his young wife, who made her fear for her life to such an extent that she wrote a note of abject desperation, that man is inside this villa right now!'

The warm-up man's arm went up. The crowd roared their disapproval.

Conti turned to the camera and looked right into it.

'I call on you, Enzo Borgata, to admit to your crime. Own up, be a man about it. You've been hiding away like a dog these past thirty-five years. No more hiding, Enzo! Come out. Confess to what you've done!'

He turned back to the crowd, silent now.

'He won't come out,' he said. 'His sort never do. They...'

There was a commotion behind him. A small figure had appeared at the gates. They slid open.

And there was Enzo, walking slowly forward, with his head held high.

115

IRENE

Jack is gasping, he's crying. He's lifting the stones off my legs.

'Oh, God,' *he says.* 'Oh, Irene!'

And I, drifting in a soup of pain and nausea, watch as he tears off his shirt and makes a tourniquet for my thigh. He pulls it tight.

'Is it bad?' *I ask.*

'Yes,' *he says.* 'Yes, it's bad.'

'Am I going to die?'

'I don't know, Irene.'

'What about Quintu?'

'He's dead,' *says Jack.* 'He's gone.'

116

The crowd had fallen silent.

One of the crew was beaming the spotlight down on Enzo Borgata so that he looked like an angel, caught in a shaft of sunlight.

Enzo was dressed in his business suit and his shirt and his bow tie. His shoes were gleaming. He was leaning on a walking stick, but his shoulders were back and his posture was upright. He looked immaculate.

'Enzo!' April called, but he couldn't hear her, and the crowd was pressing closer together now, everyone trying to catch a glimpse of the infamous Enzo Borgata.

Conti, on the stage, had been momentarily dumbstruck by Enzo's appearance. Now he rallied. 'Well!' he said. 'What do you make of this, ladies and gentlemen? Milo Conti spoke and Enzo Borgata listened! He's come out to confess – what's that, Signor Borgata? – not to confess, but to give his side of the story!'

There was a huge flash overhead, and for a moment the whole world was brilliantly lit, then the flash disappeared.

'What was that?'

'What's happening?'

'Lightning!'

'Was it lightning?'

'I'm sure it was.'

'Where's the thunder, then?'

BOOM!

April had been expecting it but the noise still made her jump. She stepped back and felt a hand on her shoulder.

'It's okay,' said Luca's voice, 'it's me.'

She turned.

'I'm glad you could make it!' she said.

'It's good to see you too. Is that Enzo Borgata?'

'Yes.'

There was nothing April could do. She could not get through the crowd, all she could do was watch as her best friend's father laboriously climbed the flimsy steps at the side of the stage. April knew Maddalena and the others would be watching inside. She knew that when they saw what was happening outside, they would come out to try to save Enzo from his own misguided sense of duty, but for now he was there, alone, in the spotlight, taking hold of the hand Conti was extending to help him up the final step and onto the stage.

Conti was struggling to get back on script.

'Do you need a chair?' he asked Enzo, perhaps concerned that the man he was accusing of murder might collapse on the stage.

'I don't need a chair,' said Enzo.

'What is it you want to say to us, Enzo? Have you come out here tonight to tell the truth after thirty-five years of silence? Have you come to confess? Because you know what, you'll feel better when you do!'

The sidekick put his arm up, but the crowd didn't roar. They murmured uncomfortably. A woman close to April whispered: 'Look at him! He doesn't look at all well.'

Enzo reached for the microphone and Conti gave it to him.

'I've come out to speak to you,' Enzo began.

He was interrupted by another flash of lightning. A few big, fat spots of rain began to fall.

Luca was standing right behind April, one hand on her shoulder.

She counted in the way Enzo had taught her to count, to judge how many kilometres away the thunder was: one elephant, two elephants, three elephants... BOOM!

'I've come to tell you,' Enzo tried again.

'Tell us what, Enzo?' asked Conti. He was worried about the weather. 'What is it you want to tell us? Are you ready to confess?'

There was another commotion, this time on the other side of the stage.

Conti held the microphone to one side. 'What's going on?' he shouted.

'There's someone here! You need to speak to her!'

'Who?'

'Let her on stage!'

April was watching Enzo. She was watching him because she was worried about him and his fragile heart. She was watching him because it didn't seem as if anyone else was paying attention, but as she watched, Maddalena came running out from the villa, barefoot, and with her hair flying around her shoulders, she bounded up onto the stage and put her arms around her father. April relaxed a moment, then her eyes moved to the other side of the stage. Two women were climbing up the steps.

One, she recognised. She was tall, slim, about the same age as April. Her hair, dyed a bright shade of red, was tied back in a ponytail and she was wearing leggings, trainers, a long-sleeved T-shirt: Roxie Graden.

The other woman was smaller, slighter, older.

Her silver hair was neatly cut into a bob and her face was made up. She was wearing a midnight-blue linen midi-dress that showed off her youthful figure, and a good deal of silver jewellery. Her lipstick was bright red. Like Enzo, she had a walking stick.

The rain was coming down more heavily now, drops spattering on the stage. Enzo was staring at the older woman. She was staring at him.

'Excuse me, but who are you?' Conti asked. 'What are you doing here?'

The older woman reached for the microphone.

'My name is Irene Borgata,' she said in English. She leaned forward to look around Conti's stout frame. 'Hello, Enzo, my love,' she said. 'I'm sorry you've been put through all this bother.'

117

It was the biggest moment of Milo Conti's career, and for once he was lost for words. He stood back and watched as Irene and Enzo embraced. The paparazzi were going mad. The crowd, stunned at first into silence, started cheering and clapping. And Conti, finally regaining his composure, stepped forward and said: 'Well! What do you think of that, Ladies and Gentlemen! Surely that's our biggest success to date! Not only have we solved the mystery, but we've found the woman who's been missing for thirty-five years.'

'I wasn't missing, though, was I?' said Irene. 'I was just somewhere else.'

Conti stuck the microphone in front of Irene's face and said: 'I think you owe it to us to tell us your story, Mrs Borgata.'

'I don't owe you anything,' she replied. 'And it's raining. If you'll excuse us, Mr Conti, Enzo and I need to go inside. We have a lot to talk about. I'd be grateful if you'd stop going on about me being murdered, now you have all the proof you need that I wasn't, and turn your attention to some other poor bugger instead. Thank you.'

She and Enzo helped one another down the steps. The crowd parted for them as they went back through the gates and headed towards the villa. The thunder clapped overhead. Huge raindrops spattered down.

Umbrellas were opened. Some of the audience held placards over their heads to keep the rain off. Technicians scurried around the stage making sure the electrics were safe.

Luca and April were stuck at the back of the crowd. They didn't have an umbrella, or a coat between them. It was a good while later before they managed to make their way back inside the villa. The rest of the family, apart from Donatella, was in the conservatory. Sam offered to lend Luca some dry clothes. April ran upstairs to change. Then they came down and drank the coffee that Giuseppa gave them, and listened as Irene Borgata told them her story.

118

'We were in the stables,' Irene said, 'me and Jack, on the night of the earthquake. We got the horses out, as our priority, but then Quintu turned up. He would have shot us both, I'm certain of it, but the wall fell on him. He tried to take me with him. It was Jack as saved me.'

'But Jack died,' April said. 'I've seen his grave in the cemetery.'

'No,' said Irene. 'Quintu died. He was killed outright. I was trapped by the fallen wall. Jack escaped with scratches and cuts.'

April glanced to Enzo. He was looking at Irene with an expression that was a mixture of shock and disbelief.

'You mean, we didn't bury Jack Harding after the earthquake, we buried Quintu?'

'Yes.'

Maddalena, in particular, was struggling to come to terms with what she was hearing.

'You let us believe Jack Harding was dead,' she said to Irene, 'for all these years!'

Giuseppa shook her head and made the sign of the cross. 'That was a wicked thing to do.'

'How could you?' Daria asked. 'How could you be so deceitful!'

'Quintu had a wife! He had a baby!'

'I'm sorry,' Irene said. 'I'm sorry for all the lies I ever told, but this one in particular. All I can say is that to start with, I had no part in it.'

'You must have known!'

'I didn't. Not at first. I barely remember anything after the wall collapsed, only that Jack sat with me, amongst the fallen stones, holding me; cradling me. We were both covered in dust. He looked like a ghost. Quintu's body was next to me, under a heap of fallen wood and render and stone. His hand was still on my ankle. My mouth was dry and full of grit. Jack talked to me the whole time. I begged him to go away but he wouldn't leave me. He thought I was dying...' She paused. 'I'm not making excuses, but I want you to understand how it was; how desperate we were; how we thought it was the end of the road for us.'

She sighed. 'It felt like we were there for hours. Dawn was breaking. Then Patrick came. I was drifting in and out of consciousness. I remember hearing Patrick's voice. And then I don't remember anything until I woke up in the hospital in Palermo.'

'That's convenient,' Daria murmured.

'So whose idea was it to say that Jack was dead?'

'Jack told me it was Patrick's idea,' said Irene quietly. 'He said Patrick took charge. He had Jack swap his boots for Quintu's. Had him help lift the stones off Quintu's body and fetch a tarpaulin from the cottage. They wrapped the body together. Then he, Patrick, told Jack to take Quintu's truck and gun and disappear. He told him never to come to the villa again. He said if he saw him within a hundred yards of the villa, he'd shoot him himself.'

'Why would Patrick want to help Jack?' asked April.

'He respected him,' Enzo said quietly. 'He respected Jack because Jack loved the horses as he did.'

Irene put a hand, absent-mindedly, on the thigh of her prosthesis. She looked at the man she had married with tenderness.

'When I came round, in the hospital, you were there, Enzo.'

'I stayed with you round the clock.'

'Whenever I opened my eyes, there you were. Nobody could have had a more devoted husband than you. I know it now, and I knew it then. I can't tell you how sorry I am for all that I put you through.'

'You did what you had to do.'

He loved you, thought April. *He adored you. He still does.*

'I'm grateful to you too, Giuseppa, and you, Maddalena, and Daria,' Irene said. 'After they let me out of the hospital, and Enzo brought me back here, you were so kind to me. You used to change my dressings, Daria, and bathe the wounds. And Sam, you used to come and sit with me, and talk about football, making me laugh. And you, Maddi... You and your brilliant imagination kept me sane.'

Maddalena frowned.

'All those jigsaws we put together,' Irene said. 'All those books we read.'

Her eyes suddenly filled with tears. 'I couldn't have asked for anything more than what you gave me,' she said. 'You were wonderful. You showed me such kindness, all of you.' She fished a tissue from up her sleeve and dabbed at her eyes.

'So how did you do it?' April asked.

'The disappearing act? Oh Lord! Weeks went by and I never heard a thing from Jack. I used to sit by the window in the dressing room, looking out, not knowing when he'd come. One day, I was dozing, when a pebble came up through the window. There was a note wrapped around it. It was Jack. I wrote a reply and threw the pebble back into the trees. That was how we communicated. That was how we came up with our plan to stage a breakdown on the way back from Palermo. I made a small hole in the fuel line of the Alfa Romeo while Enzo was settling the bill in the restaurant where we'd had our lunch.'

'How did you know how to do that?'

'My Dad was a mechanical engineer and he'd taught me what to look for in broken-down cars. It was easy. I didn't know exactly where the Alfa Romeo would break down, but I knew it'd be somewhere on the Gibellina road. Jack was following us in Quintu's truck, at a distance. After you left me, Enzo, he picked me up. We drove to Messina, and from there we caught a boat to Italy. We bought some fake papers and made our way through Europe back to England.'

'Wow,' said Enzo quietly. 'And we were looking for you in the mountains.'

Maddalena shook her head, as if in disbelief. 'You did all that, Irene, and yet you never once gave a thought to the mess you were leaving behind, or how it would impact on us.'

'Oh, my darling Maddi, I knew that would be what you'd think. The truth is, there's not been a day, not an hour, not a single *minute* gone by when I haven't thought about you; when I haven't missed you, when I haven't regretted every moment of pain I caused you.'

119

A little later, Sam opened a bottle of wine, and it was shared out, but it didn't go far, so he opened another. Enzo was suddenly overwhelmed by fatigue. Maddalena took her father up to bed, using the torch on her phone to guide the way through the cavernous darkness of the villa's interior. When Irene stood up to help, Maddalena hissed at her to leave him alone.

Daria said that Irene could sleep in her old room. April invited Roxie to crash out with her. Daria didn't want to walk up the steep path to the cottage by the stables in the storm, so she went to find some blankets and pillows to make a bed downstairs on one of the sofas. Elissa and Tonio went up to bed together, and nobody said anything because they had more pressing matters on their minds, and lastly Luca said he'd better get back to Palermo.

'I'm sure it'd be okay with everyone if you'd like to stay here,' said April.

'I need to get back,' said Luca. 'I'm picking the girls up first thing.'

'Of course.'

'But if you're at a loose end over the weekend, April...'

'I'll be spending my time with Roxie.'

'Oh well,' said Luca. 'Another time, maybe.'

April found an umbrella he could borrow in the coat cupboard in the hallway.

'Thanks,' he said.

'Drive carefully.'

She stood at the door and watched him walk through the courtyard, rain falling all around. She waited until he had gone round the corner and was out of sight.

After that, April filled up her wine glass and Roxie's and they sat together in the conservatory, with Troy between them, listening to the rain pattering against the glass, and April said, 'How on earth did you manage to find Irene?'

'Well...' said Roxie, 'I thought, why don't I do a search for Irene Weatherbury, just on the off chance, and see what turns up? Straight away, I found her on the police database. She was living with her partner, Jack Harding, in a little town called Shapcott in Somerset, at least she was in November 1979 when they'd had a break-in, which is how their names and address ended up on the database. I thought I'd take a punt and drive down, see if they were still there. And they were.'

'It was as easy as that?'

'It was. I knocked on the door and Irene opened it and invited me in for a cup of tea. I could see it was a kind of relief when I told her why I'd come. She said she'd been waiting for thirty-five years for the truth to catch up with her. She was putting a brave face on it this evening, but she's had a hard time dealing with the feelings of guilt over what happened. She feels especially bad about abandoning Maddalena.' Roxie took a drink of wine. 'I don't think Maddalena will forgive her any time soon.'

'It's early days yet,' said April, 'but Maddalena has a good heart. They'll be okay, given enough time. Did Irene and Jack have children of their own?'

'Three strapping sons and now they've got two granddaughters too.'

'Are they married?'

'No. Irene believes she's still legally married to Enzo. She had no intention of committing bigamy, neither did she want to draw the attention of the Sicilian authorities to her whereabouts if she were to apply for a divorce.'

'So where's Jack now?'

'We all thought it best if he stayed behind in England. He's in good health. Volunteers up at the local horse rescue.'

120

Irene moved into a hotel in Palermo on the following day; she was worried about how Donatella would react when she found out her daughter-in-law was in the Villa Alba and thought it would be prudent to keep herself at arm's length. At Enzo's insistence Maddalena drove him into Palermo so that he and Irene could spend some time together. Maddi refused to join them. Enzo and Irene sat on a bench in the botanical gardens, and they talked, and they both felt better for it.

Afterwards, Enzo had a little more colour in his cheeks and a spring in his step. He asked Maddalena to talk to Irene, for his sake. Maddalena said she couldn't, not yet.

Irene met Sam and Daria for lunch. She showed them photographs of her family and told them about her life in Somerset, filled with horses. She said they must come and visit so that they could meet her boys.

Giuseppa explained the situation to Donatella; told her a curated version of Irene's story. She left out the part about Patrick being responsible for the fabrication of Jack's death. Donatella was furious. She cursed Irene and Jack and all the heartache they had caused. She made all kinds of threats against them. Giuseppa listened to her ranting, and, when her anger was spent, brought her a glass of Amaretto and together they watched the soap opera, *CentroVetrine*, on TV.

April had a private talk with Donatella. She told her that she knew the truth about Sam and that, while it was not her place to enlighten him, she believed it was essential for his future health and well-being that he was made aware of his true parentage. She pointed out that the truth always, *always*, no matter how deeply it has been buried, finds a way to the surface. She suggested that Donatella might sleep more soundly if she were to make things right in respect of Sam and Giuseppa. April explained this gently and tactfully, bearing in mind that it wasn't Donatella's fault that her husband had slept with a vulnerable employee young enough to be his daughter. She tried to make Donatella see things from Giuseppa's point of view; knowing how much it would mean to Giuseppa if she were able to acknowledge, in public, that Sam was her son, and Elissabeta her granddaughter. And also, Irene said, using tactics she'd learned during Hostage Negotiation training in her time with the police, if Donatella left it too late to tell the truth, it might not come out until after her death, and then how could she answer Sam and Elissabeta's questions? How could she tell them that everything she'd done, even if it was misguided, had been done through love?

Roxie and Irene returned to England at the end of the week. Jack was waiting to meet them at Heathrow. He had bought flowers for Irene. He was still handsome, according to Roxie; still a charmer.

'Don't go away and leave me again,' he said to Irene. 'I can't bear it when we're apart.'

'Don't be daft,' said Irene. 'It was only a few days.'

'A few days too many,' said Jack. 'I adore you.'

'He adores her,' Roxie told April on the telephone.

April was sitting on the beach. She was wearing a swimsuit and she had her arms around her knees. She was watching Luca swimming in water that was the purest turquoise colour she had ever seen. She had been in that water herself, but had come out to dry off in the last of the day's sunshine.

'Is everything okay with you?' Roxie asked.

'Yes,' said April. 'It's all good. Everything's changing at the Villa Alba. Now Sam understands why Donatella never cared for him, like she cared for her other children, he's come into his own. Donatella feels bad about the way she's treated him. She's decided to sell off what's left of the tuna business and she's going to give the money to Sam so he can convert the Villa Alba into a sanctuary for people with addictions.'

'Wow!'

'I know. The family is behind him all the way. It's like a light's been switched on in their lives.'

'I can't wait to hear about it. When are you coming home?'

'I'm going to stay in Sicily for another week or two, if you don't mind looking after the roses for a bit longer.'

'Not at all. The roses are fine. They send their love. How's it going with Luca?'

'Good. We're going to listen to a concert in an open-air theatre in Palermo this evening. And then we're going to have something to eat and then we're going back to Luca's place.'

'Are you meeting the children?'

'Not yet. It feels a bit early for that.'

Out in the sea, Luca swam through the sunlight that shimmered on the surface of the water. It danced and dazzled. It was difficult for April to pick out the shape of his head.

'You sound a bit sad.'

'I'm not sad, exactly,' said April. 'It's just…'

'What?'

'Cobain. Letting go of him. It's hard.'

'It's what he would have wanted.'

'I know,' said April. 'I know.'

EPILOGUE

Enzo steers the Alfa Romeo around a tight corner and over the narrow bridge that crosses the ravine. Now we are driving into the very last of the daylight.

We have reached a stretch of road with an upwards incline.

The engine coughs again. Little explosions are bursting from the exhaust.

'Come on,' Enzo says, both hands on the wheel, gripping tightly. 'Come on!'

But the upward slope is too much for the car. It spits and jumps and shudders to a halt.

Without the roar of the Spider's engine, the evening is silent. No cicadas, no birdsong, nothing.

Enzo climbs out of the car, opens the bonnet and peers into the engine, cursing as he burns his fingers on the cigarette lighter, whose flame he is using as a torch.

All around, as far as I can see, the landscape is desolate; not a single vehicle on the road, no shepherd, no boys on mopeds, nothing. We are alone with the sky and the hills, the rocks and those sparse old olive trees that survived the quake, their arms reaching out towards the fading light; Gibellina's ruins black and spiky against the sky.

'Can you see what's wrong, Enzo?' I ask.

'Hold on.'

Enzo comes back into the car and turns the key. Nothing happens.

The last tiny glowing piece of golden sun slides beneath the horizon and all that is left is a shimmering haze. The temperature drops. The colours of the wild landscape that surround us, already muted, fade and darken. Gibellina's remains become more sinister.

'What do we do now?' I ask.

'I'll walk back to the villa and come back for you in a different car.'

Enzo takes off his jacket and gently puts it around my shoulders.

'Nobody uses this road any more,' he says. 'You'll be okay. I'll be as quick as I can.'

He hesitates. He's waiting for me to say something but there's nothing I can say.

'Will you still be here,' he asks, 'when I get back?'

'Where else would I be?'

Another silence.

'Okay,' says Enzo but still he does not move. 'Irene, I—'

'Please, Enzo, just go.'

I watch my husband walk away. I watch until he disappears around the corner and then I pull his jacket tightly around my shoulders and I wait.

The wind whispers. From the heaps of rubble and the skeletal remains of the buildings in Gibellina comes a tapping noise, and the mournful song of air moving through pipes that had been underground, but are now exposed. From the other side of the town, a single gunshot rents the air and there's a scream. I can't tell if it was animal or human.

Silence settles again.

It seems an age until I hear the sound I've been waiting for: the sound of an engine. I turn to look over my shoulder, and I see the headlights of Quintu Baresi's truck bumping over the rocks as it heads towards me.

The truck pulls to a stop just behind the Alfa Romeo and the headlights are dimmed. The door opens and Jack Harding jumps out.

He comes to the side of the Alfa Romeo and looks down at me; smiles; holds out his hand.

'Come on, Irene,' he says. 'It's time we went home.'

ACKNOWLEDGMENTS

It is impossible for me to say a big enough 'thank you' to the Boldwood Books editorial team who have worked so hard to make this book the best it possibly can be. Sarah Ritherdon is a dream editor; she's patient, good-humoured, optimistic, generous and so supportive and I know how lucky I am to be working with her. Sue Smith went over and above the call of duty with the copy edits for this book, when it was still rough around the edges. Her attention to detail is second to none and I am in awe of her knowledge, wisdom and rigorous fact and language checking. I'm truly grateful, Sue. And Rose Fox has worked on several of my books now and I so appreciate her wonderful contributions, her kindness, patience, professionalism and endless wisdom. If any errors have slipped through, they are down to me and me alone.

Thanks also to the rest of the Boldwood team. Amanda Ridout is an absolute inspiration, and I'm hugely indebted to Nia Beynon, Claire Fenby, Sue Lamprell and all the other wonderful publishing people who work so creatively and brilliantly on behalf of the authors and their books. I'd also like to acknowledge the Boldwood authors, many of whom I'm lucky enough to count as friends now. You're such a lovely, generous group and it's a pleasure getting to know you.

I remain indebted to my wonderful agent, Marianne Gunn O'Connor, to Pat Lynch and Vicki Satlow; the best team ever.

Thank you to those lovely authors, bloggers, readers, writers, journalists, librarians, book sellers, teachers and others who support and promote books and reading on social media. Every single day, I feel proud to be part of this incredible, talented and creative community.

I must also say thank you to Sicily and to the people of Sicily, who were the inspiration for this novel. Kevin and I first visited the Valle del Belice area that was devastated by the 1968 earthquake about ten years ago. It had a profound effect on me and I have wanted to write about it ever since. The locations and events in this book are a combination of real, and fictional, but I would urge anyone who is interested in this incredible and beautiful island, to visit this area, which remains off the beaten, tourist track. I'm always worried about not doing justice to a place I love in my writing. Sicily, I hope I haven't let you down.

BOOK CLUB QUESTIONS

What is the eponymous secret of the Villa Alba?

1. The story is told through the perspectives of Irene, in the 1960s, and April, in the 2000s. Which storyline felt more real, to you? Why do you think that is?

2. Did you like Irene, as a character? Why/why not?

3. What about Enzo? Is he a good husband? A good father?

4. The story of Irene and Jack is driven by their characters, but also by events beyond their control. Which aspect do you feel is more important to their story?

5. What are your impressions of Maddalena? Did they change as the book progressed?

6. The action is centred around a part of Sicily that's relatively unknown beyond the island itself. Did the descriptions of the countryside and towns sound appealing, or not? Was this a good location for this story?

7. Why did Irene marry Enzo? Should she have done so? Do you have sympathy with her decision?

8. Donatella is very keen for Irene and Enzo to have a family. How do you feel about the way she tries to manipulate Irene?

9. What do you think about the popularity of the kind of 'true crime'

television shows that Milo Conti's programme epitomises? Is populist journalism a good thing, or not?

10. Sam compares the Villa Alba to Hotel California, referencing the line that once you're there, you can never leave. What are the different factors trapping Giuseppa, Sam, Daria and Enzo in the villa?

11. Will Maddalena and Irene be able to have a healthy relationship going forward? Why/why not? What about April and Luca? Do you think they will have a Happy Ever After ending?

MORE FROM LOUISE DOUGLAS

We hope you enjoyed reading *The Secret of Villa Alba*. If you did, please leave a review.

If you'd like to gift a copy, this book is also available as an ebook, large print, paperback, digital audio download and audiobook CD.

Sign up to Louise Douglas' mailing list for news, competitions and updates on future books.

http://bit.ly/LouiseDouglasNewsletter

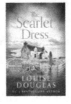

ABOUT THE AUTHOR

Louise Douglas is an RNA award winner and the bestselling author of several brilliantly reviewed novels. These include the number one bestseller *The Lost Notebook*, and the *The Secrets Between Us* which was a Richard and Judy Book Club pick. She lives in the West Country.

Follow Louise on social media:

facebook.com/Louise-Douglas-Author-340228039335215
twitter.com/louisedouglas3
bookbub.com/authors/louise-douglas

Boldwood

Boldwood Books is an award-winning fiction publishing company seeking out the best stories from around the world.

Find out more at www.boldwoodbooks.com

Join our reader community for brilliant books, competitions and offers!

Follow us
@BoldwoodBooks
@BookandTonic

Sign up to our weekly deals newsletter

https://bit.ly/BoldwoodBNewsletter